ALSO BY RUSSELL ROWLAND

In Open Spaces

The Watershed Years

West of 98: Living and Writing the New American West

WWW.RUSSELLROWLAND.COM

HIGH AND INSIDE

HIGH AND INSIDE

Russell Rowland

BP Bangtail
Press

Published in the United States by

Bangtail Press
P. O. Box 11262
Bozeman, MT 59719
www.bangtailpress.com

Cover photo and interior photos: Dejan Stanisavljevic/Shutterstock

To my dad, who broke the chain.

"Liquor took him through all
the hells of Dante."
Willa Cather

"Every song is a comeback."
Wilco

Chapter One

Rumor has it that Pete Hurley, the former Red Sox
reliever who put one of the most promising Yankee
prospects in years out of commission a few years
ago, is moving to Montana. So the East Coast may
be safe at last.

Theyankeeyipper.com
Blog entry for September 14, 2009

Six months after Dave lost her leg, I approach Bozeman, where the mountains rise— up into the dusk like blue gods. My mind is fuzzy from the long drive and a day alone with my thoughts. For the last four-hundred-mile stretch of my trip from Massachusetts, I've tried to focus on good thoughts, replaying some of my best moments as a pitcher for the Red Sox.

But lately, each time I review these memories, they always end with the same scenes, as if some divine editor has snuck into the film room and spliced the memories I've been trying to forget into the loop.

I turn onto Elm Street, park, and stretch my legs in front of my sister Danielle's white clapboard house. It's early fall, cool enough for a jacket, and a light breeze ruffles my hair and blows a flock of leaves across the lawn. Dave gives chase, hopping after them with a crippled determination. The grass is just about to turn. The leaves swirl around Dave like a swarm of flies. She bites the air, missing a leaf, then barks, biting again, her teeth coming together with a crisp clack.

"Where's Charlie?" This is the first question out of Danielle's mouth after we greet and hug. Danielle is about a foot shorter than

I am, and she steps away, holding my upper arms. She wears her usual weekend attire—jeans and one of her husband's sweatshirts, a flow of thick blue cotton that is massive on her. Her long black hair gathers at the back in a sort of hybrid—somewhere between a bun and a pony tail. When she smiles, the freckles scattered along her cheeks fall away from each other where a few slight wrinkles have formed.

"He didn't come," I answer.

She tilts her head.

"He changed his mind."

Danielle's husband Barry appears, his girth considerably wider than when I saw him last, and I'm amazed to think that it has taken six months to return to Montana. Although I hatched the plan about a year ago of moving here to build a house with my own two hands, there have been several detours, along with a few barriers.

Part of the delay was waiting for Dave to heal up. Six months ago, I came to Bozeman to scout out some plots of land, and on a walk through the snow with Dave one morning, she raced out into the street and got hit by a car.

But the delay was mostly because of me—thinking, debating, changing my mind, changing it back again, then wrapping up business so I could finally make the move. Part of me did not want to leave Amherst. But the damage I had done there ultimately pushed me westward.

Barry wraps my hand in a warm handshake. "Good to see you again, Pete. Is Charlie coming in, or is he going to sleep in the truck?" Barry laughs at his joke, an endearing habit of his. Endearing because it is combined with a twinkle in his eye that says "I know this joke isn't one bit funny, but I just love to laugh."

Danielle steps to Barry's side, slipping a hand in the crook of his elbow. "Charlie's not with him."

"I thought he was." Barry fixes a steady blue eye on me, unwavering, waiting for an explanation. He is still grinning, and the dimple on the left side of his mouth burrows into his cheek.

"Well, he decided not to come." I bend down and scratch Dave's skewed ear, then pick up my bag, hoping to prompt the conversation forward.

"Why?" Barry asks.

"I don't think Pete wants to talk about it," Danielle says.

"Oh, sorry." Barry laughs, and I smile. "Takes me a while."

"It's all right."

"So how was the drive?" Danielle motions with her head for me to follow.

"Fine...long."

"Ah, and here's Dave," Barry says as Dave rushes past him, hopping ahead of Danielle and Barry's two boys. Barry pats her head, studying her shoulder. The two boys kneel closer, observing their father's inspection. My older nephew Stevie peers at Dave's shoulder with a frown, his frosty blue eyes intent. He has lighter, curlier hair than his brother Gus, whose eyes and hair are a matching chocolate brown. Gus is distracted, looking at Dave, then up at me, then back down at Dave. His lower lip pokes out with concentration.

"Looks like she's healed up real nice," Barry says, reaching for the spot where her leg once started. But Dave nips at his hand.

"Sorry, sweetheart." Barry scratches her ear, and she licks his hand.

"Can you play catch with us, Uncle Pete?" Stevie asks.

"I'd love to, bud...how about we do it tomorrow...I've had a long day." I haven't had the heart to tell these youngsters that I haven't played catch with anyone since my career ended. That I can't even throw any more. I've become a belly itcher.

Stevie's shoulders slump. "All right."

Inside, we settle into the living room while the boys play with Dave in the yard. And I get the look from Danielle and Barry. The look that I've become so accustomed to seeing from friends and family alike. It's the look that says, "We're not going to ask what we really want to ask, but it's all we can think about."

"So how's it going, Pete?" Barry asks.

And I can't say what I want to say, either, which is, "I'm so tired of people worrying about me." So instead, I say, "I'm good. Glad to be here."

"Yeah?" Barry nods. "Have you closed the deal on your land yet?"

"Tomorrow. I have an appointment tomorrow afternoon."

Danielle props her elbows on her knees. "Then what?"

I shrug. "Then I get a little trailer and move in until the house is done."

"How's Simone doing?" Barry asks.

"Barry!" Danielle's head swivels toward Barry.

"What?"

"It's okay," I say. "She's doing all right...I think."

"Well, that's great." Barry's enthusiasm suggests that I have just announced that Simone, who is Charlie's sister, has won a Pulitzer Prize.

Simone is another big reason I'm here. Just as I was about to get over the incident that ended my baseball career, a drunken accident left this young girl paralyzed, and I was in the news yet again.

Charlie has been my best friend since sixth grade, when we moved across the street from his family. Actually, he ended up being more like a brother. Four years after we moved into that house, my father's girlfriend woke up next to Dad's corpse one morning and stormed into my bedroom screaming. I never saw her again. She didn't even come to the funeral.

Meanwhile, I wandered to Charlie's house with a five-quart pot containing my toothbrush and some clean underwear. Days later, I was surprised to learn that I was a millionaire, at least on paper. My father had apparently been a brilliant investor and had quietly acquired real estate all over Amherst. But my share of the money wouldn't be available until I was eighteen, so the Watsons insisted I live with them until that time. Danielle invited me to move to Bozeman where she had just moved for college, but I was already developing a reputation as an athlete, so I wanted to finish my high school career at the same school, with the same team.

"Did you eat?" Danielle asks.

"I did. I stopped in Billings."

"Well, are you still hungry?"

"No, no...I'm fine. I hope you guys didn't wait."

"No, we ate," Danielle responds. "We didn't expect you until late."

"Yeah, I made pretty good time. These highways are so clear out here. I never even saw a patrol car."

"Well, you're probably tired, huh, Pete?" Barry stands and slaps his palms against his thighs. "Driving always makes *me* tired."

"You're right. I am pretty tired." Everyone stands and stretches as if we haven't stood for days, and as we go our separate ways, I can feel the relief throughout the house.

THE NEXT MORNING, I watch my sister's family and their daily routine with a sense of familiarity. Because we lost our mother when she was six and I was four, Danielle became the mother in our home, and she still maintains that same authority. The constant motion makes me dizzy especially knowing that any urge I have to help would only disrupt the flow. Gus and Stevie scamper around the house between breakfast, bedrooms, and stolen moments with video games. They pass in blurs of bright colors and sound, occasionally dropping a question about something I know nothing about.

"Get *down* here!" Danielle shouts, and I laugh when the boys *and* Barry come running down the stairs as if they're at boot camp. As the boys fly out the door, Danielle stands in the kitchen for a moment. Barry starts out the door, but it's clear that there's some interruption to their routine. He looks confused.

"You coming?" he asks.

"I'll be right out."

But Barry just stands there, as if the disruption is too significant to comprehend. Then comes the moment of recognition. "Ah... okay." And he leaves.

Danielle approaches with her face toward the floor, which is unlike her. "Are you going to be okay?" she asks.

"Of course...why wouldn't I be?"

Danielle looks at me sideways. "Pete, are you going to tell me you don't remember what happened last time?"

"Last time I was here, you mean?"

Danielle hmms.

"You mean with Dave?"

She tilts her head forward. "No, after."

"I don't."

Danielle stares me down.

"I really don't."

"Well, let me just ask you a favor then."

"All right...anything."

"Please try not to drink too much while you're here."

I feel myself blinking. "Okay," I say. It's not the first time someone has asked me this, but it's the first time it's come from Danielle, and I have admit it hurts. "Okay."

BEFORE MY APPOINTMENT with the realtor, I wander the streets of Bozeman, making my way over to Main Street. People out raking their leaves wave or say hello, their smiles ready, trusting. I always forget this about Montana, the old stereotype about people being so friendly.

I study these houses, reminded of old sitcoms like "My Three Sons." These neighborhoods have always made me uncomfortable, because they remind me how out of place I feel in the world. Despite my money, and my success in baseball, the trappings never have appealed to me. I used to drive right through block parties, ignoring the dirty looks. And part of it was because the way these people talk to each other, the way they seem so at ease in the world, has always felt completely foreign to me. From as far back as I can remember, I felt as if I've been dropped into this world from somewhere else. Danielle and I used to call these people "Christmas Light People," because they devoted so much of their time to creating an image by dressing up their houses. I never put up Christmas lights.

JUST AFTER FIVE, Danielle and the kids enter the house with the same burst of energy they had that morning, as if they've been running at the same speed all day.

"Hey, Uncle Pete!" the boys both shout as they race upstairs to the television room.

"Are you cooking?" Danielle drops her purse on the table and hangs up her jacket.

"Yeah, I'm making some pasta."

"How was your day?"

"It was good. I closed the deal on my land. Found a nice coffee shop downtown. It was nice to have some time to get a feel for this place."

"It's a good town, Pete. You're going to like it."

I stir the noodles. "I hope so. You know, I don't know what you were talking about this morning."

"Yeah, I figured." Danielle sinks into a chair at the table. "Listen, Pete…I know you've had a hard year. I understand that. But we've got two little boys in this house. We can't have them seeing you stumbling around drunk. It scares them."

I hold out my hands. "Do I look drunk?"

Danielle sighs sadly. "I just want to make sure you understand. Last time you were here...well, we were worried."

I focus on the pasta, stirring, staring at the noodles floating around and through each other and themselves. "I wish you'd tell me what I did."

"It doesn't matter, Pete...it wasn't any one thing. It was just not the kind of behavior kids should have to see. You were drunk most of the time after Dave's accident, and a couple of times they had to listen to you getting sick. It really scared them."

"Okay." I turn to her. "I'm sorry. I really had no idea."

"I know that, too. I probably should have said something sooner."

Barry's truck pulls into the drive.

"I'm going to go make sure the boys get cleaned up for dinner... is it just about ready?" Danielle asks.

"Just about there." I whisk the marinara sauce and check the noodles for consistency.

Barry enters just as Danielle starts up the stairs.

"Hey," Barry says. "How was your day?"

"It was good." I resist the urge to say, "until a few minutes ago." "I closed on my land."

"That's great." Barry hangs up his coat, then ducks into the fridge, where he pulls out a carton of milk and drinks from the carton, and I imagine he's listening for footsteps so he doesn't get caught. "I'll take you out for a beer later to celebrate."

Ignoring a guilty tug, I smile to myself at the competing forces here. "Sounds good."

But it doesn't escape my notice that Barry waits until we're almost finished eating before he mentions this idea to my sister.

"Wonderful," Danielle says, and she seems sincere. "You haven't had a chance to get out for a while, honey."

Barry pats her shoulder. "You see why I married this woman?"

THE BAR THAT BARRY chooses is a sports bar. It is, in fact, called "The Sportsman." The walls are covered with flat screen TVs showing various baseball games, although most of them are tuned into the Colorado Rockies, the closest team to Montana.

We settle into a corner booth with draughts and a bowl of peanuts.

"So what happened with Charlie?" He takes a healthy swig from his beer. "If you'd rather not talk about it, I understand."

"There's not much to say, Barry. He's having a hard time forgiving me. They all are." I'm talking about the Watsons, of course. Back in Amherst, Massachusetts, Simone Watson is lying paralyzed from the waist down because of my foolishness. My drinking.

"It must be hard..." Barry stares into his glass. "But it *was* an accident."

"It was an accident. But that doesn't make it any less painful. I don't blame them."

And that's about all there is to say. It's all I've been able to say about the whole incident ever since it happened. I know I should talk about it. I know there are probably feelings buried deep inside me that I should be exploring. But this goes against everything I know. It's not the kind of thing I've ever learned. I'm glad I'm in a bar. "I'm going to get some whiskey...you want a shot?"

"Yeah, I'll take one," Barry says.

I motion for the barmaid, who is a cute little blonde. She's been paying particular attention to an older guy at the end of the bar. He's a bit heavy, with a thick nose, and thin slabs of grey hair slicked along each side of his head. But his clothes indicate wealth. A silk western shirt and an impressive silver belt buckle. When she brings our drinks, I notice a wedding ring.

"Thanks, Barry," she says when he pays.

"You know her?" I ask when she's gone.

Barry nods. "Sure...Barb. Barb Weaver."

"Is she married to that guy?" I point.

"Yep. That's Clint. Why?"

"Just curious...seems like an odd match."

"It *is* an odd match."

I'm just about to ask him more when I realize that Clint is almost on top of us. I wonder whether he overheard us.

But he reaches to shake Barry's hand. "Hey Barry. How's it going? Can I buy you boys a drink?"

"Hey, Clint. You don't have to buy us a thing. You can join us for free."

Clint chuckles, then groans a bit, easing his heavy frame into the booth. He is a massive person.

"This is my brother-in-law, Pete." Barry holds his palm toward me.

Clint says hello, and I can tell from the way he looks at me that he knows who I am. I've seen this look too many times, usually from Yankee fans. But I know my manners. I ask him a couple of friendly questions, which he ignores. Barry makes several blatant attempts to include me in the conversation. But Clint bats them away with complete disinterest.

This is the dark side of fame, the side most people don't want to hear about. It's the infamy that comes from making a mistake that cost someone a bet, or let someone's team down. The ugliness you see from people who've never even met you is sometimes startling, and confusing. And of course, it's gotten even worse with the increased technology. Twenty-four hours of ESPN and blogs and Twitter—people shouting out their invectives about people they'll never meet has become a plague.

Some famous people handle it better than others, I know. My dad used to tell me I'm too sensitive. "If you're going to be an athlete, you can't let that stuff get to you." I knew he was right, but how do you change something like that? It doesn't seem to occur to people that having everything we're supposed to want in life doesn't guarantee a thing. That it's still possible to have an emptiness inside you no matter how much shit you have surrounding you.

"Pete moved here to build a house just outside of town," Barry finally says.

This finally piques Clint's interest just enough for him to say, "Oh yeah?" His eyes settle on me briefly, then dart back over to Barry.

I glare at Clint, trying not to take his attitude personally.

"Pete?" Barry says.

I blink. "Yeah?"

"I was just asking when you think you might be starting on your house."

"Depends."

"You ever built a house before?" Clint asks, one side of his mouth rising into a smirk.

"No, I haven't."

He snorts, turning his head to one side.

My back is up. "I thought about starting with my second house, but I couldn't quite figure out how to pull that off."

He studies me with a serious scrutiny that lasts way too long. "You ever filled someone's cavity?"

I just shake my head, not as in "no" but as in "Jesus, what a stupid question."

"It's the same principle. You can't just waltz into a dentist's office and start drillin'."

Now I'm pissed. I take a quick glance at Barry, and he looks worried.

"I'm sorry, but did I miss the part where I asked for your opinion?"

Clint looks pleased that he's gotten to me. "I'm just sick of people like you and your rich California friends coming up here and thinking you're going to turn this place into your own little private playground."

"I don't even *know* anyone from California."

"Guys, maybe it's time to change the subject." Barry leans forward between us. "In fact, it's actually starting to get kind of late...maybe we should head out, Pete."

"Why don't you go back to where you came from? We don't need people like you around here," Clint says.

"Fuck you," I say.

I see what's coming, but my reflexes aren't what they used to be, especially when I'm "impaired." Before I have a chance to respond, a white light flashes right through my head, an explosion so bright and powerful that I have the momentary thought that I'm dying. But it's only a punch in the head. Unfortunately, it's quickly punctuated by another. And a third. After the third, I'm out cold. Or so I'm told.

SINCE THE ACCIDENT with Simone, I've found that I'd rather fight than spend the night with a woman. I'm much more comfortable with a punch in the jaw than I am with a tender touch. My win-loss record is about even in these fights, but I prefer losing.

The next morning, my head aches. My eye is purple, raw. My

jaw feels as though it has been jarred loose from its anchor. It makes me happy.

It's Saturday. I hear the kids in the family room, watching cartoons. That also makes me happy. I wasn't sure kids still watched cartoons. Danielle and Barry talk in low tones in the kitchen.

I pull on some jeans and a Red Sox sweatshirt, then weave down the hall.

"Morning," I say, and it hurts.

"My god, look at you," Danielle says.

"Sight for sore eyes?" I say.

She doesn't respond.

"You okay?" Barry asks.

"A little tender."

"You took some shots."

I look Barry over. "Looks like you didn't do much to defend me."

"Sorry," he says sheepishly, his dimple appearing.

"No, don't apologize. That guy's big."

"Well, like I said, I also know him."

"That's right. I forgot that part." I pour myself a cup of coffee and sit across from Barry. "You didn't help *him*, did you? Get a couple of pops in?"

Barry chuckles.

"You guys think this is pretty funny, huh?" Danielle's eyes burn a hole in me. "You think those boys'll be proud of their Uncle Pete, showing off his new tattoos? Did you forget your promise that quickly?"

I look at Barry, who lowers his eyes.

"I didn't start it," I protest.

Danielle glares, and I won't, can't, look at her. She leaves the room.

"Shit." After thinking for a moment, I say, "I better go talk to her."

"Before you do that...I need to tell you something else, Pete."

"All right."

"You should know...that guy that you got into it with last night...Clint?"

"Yeah?"

"You know he's a construction engineer, right?"

"I got that from the conversation, yeah."

"Well, there's a little more to it than that, and it could be nothing, but I just thought you should know."

"All right, Barry. What is it?"

"Clint is the president of the local chapter of ASCE." Barry looks at me, anticipating my response.

"Barry, you honestly think I know what that is?"

He clears his throat. "Sorry. It's The American Society of Construction Engineers. Which means he knows all the engineers in town...including the inspectors. He's got a lot of pull, Pete."

"Ah..."

Barry nods. "Yeah."

We both sit silently for a moment, and I ponder the conspicuous beginning I've made in my new home town. "I guess I'm going to have to do some damage control."

Barry nods.

I stand. "I better start now."

I KNOCK ON DANIELLE's bedroom door. "Can I come in?"

"All right," I hear.

I open the door, where Danielle hunches over her sewing machine. The needle bobs angrily through a solid blue fabric.

I sit on the bed. "What are you making?"

After a pause, she says, "I forget."

I can't help myself. I laugh. She surprises me by laughing too. And then we are both silent, with the machine whirring away, stitching up a minute or two.

I flop onto my back, resting my bicep across my aching forehead. "I'm sorry." My voice sounds tired, weary of apologies.

She sews. I close my eyes.

"You know what really pisses me off about you?" she says.

"What?"

But she doesn't answer right away. I grasp my aching forehead.

"You think you're punishing yourself so privately," Danielle finally says.

The sewing machine revs up. I cover my eyes with my hand. "No I don't. I don't think that at all." I'm lying. Actually, it has never occurred to me that my suffering is anything but private.

She stops, swiveling in her chair to look at me. "Then you

realize how much you hurt everyone else by not taking better care of yourself?"

"I realize it," I say. I move my hand from my eyes. "I just don't know what to do about it." This is perhaps the only true thing I've said during the conversation. Maybe for months.

Danielle turns back to her work. "Well, just so you know...if it were anyone else—if you weren't my brother—I wouldn't put up with it."

I don't respond. What can I say?

"What happened to you, Pete? We used to take such good care of each other."

I shake my head. "I really don't know."

Chapter Two

Pete Hurley has become the Robert Downey, Jr. of Major League Baseball. You want him in your movie, but you don't want him at the cast party.

Tony Kornheiser
Pardon the Interruption
September 24, 2005

M y best game for the Boston Red Sox came during the 2005 season, in Fenway Park. The scheduled starter came down with a sore elbow during warm-ups, and Terry Francona pulled me aside twenty minutes before the national anthem. For seven years before that, I'd been a steady presence in the bullpen, with occasional spot starts. Even in those starts, I was merely consistent. I had an average fastball, a good curve, but the pitch I was known for was my change-up.

That night I fell into a rhythm. The best part: we were playing the Yankees. Bernie Williams got a leadoff double in the fourth, but his teammates left him stranded on second. In the seventh, with two outs, Posada hit a long liner that probably would have been a home run in any other park. But the Green Monster knocked it down, holding him to a single. Those were the only two hits I gave up in that game. Johnny Damon, still a Red Sock, tracked down a fly to dead center at the warning track, and Kevin Millar dove to spear a drive down the first base line that would have been a sure double.

The only blip in early innings was when I hit Jeter in the third.

There were a few shouts from the Yankee dugout. A couple innings later, Andy Pettitte hit Varitek right in the back, and the umpire issued a warning to both teams.

Varitek called a masterful game, and it seemed that wherever he positioned his mitt, whether it was on the outside black or down at the knees, the ball popped within an inch or two of the target. My curve spun like a gyroscope, and my change-up had the batters swinging way before the ball arrived.

When I strolled out to the mound for the ninth inning, the crowd gave me a standing ovation. I'd never experienced anything like it. For that moment, I felt completely adored. Maybe for the only time in my life.

Unfortunately, the second batter of that inning was the one I became famous for. On a two-two count, I decided to give my fastball a little extra, and the pitch got away from me. The ball sailed high and inside, and the crack of ball against bone lifted my balls right up into my throat. The crowd, still standing, moaned as the player crumpled. I hit him square in the eye socket. He never played again. And neither did I.

It takes two full recovery days before I'm presentable enough to shop for a trailer. During each of these two days, I drive out to my land, lying in the grass, body aching, picturing where I'll build my house. Dave and I limp around Bozeman, often joined by Barry. He introduces us to a dog park, and Dave is in doggy heaven, hopping after her four-legged companions, who take no notice of her handicap.

It's a nice park, clean and well-stocked with cottonwood and pine trees. I would have considered it a huge park as a boy, before I saw Central Park, or the Boston Common.

I toss the Frisbee, and many owners remark on how well Dave catches it, considering her condition. Their compliments bother me, and I realize it's because I have this notion that she'll feel like an outsider if people draw attention to her.

Both days that we're there, a man brings his young, handicapped son to the park. The boy is probably ten years old. He looks as if he has no muscles at all. His skin hugs his bones, but it's also loose, like a shirtsleeve. Both days, the boy has brought a bright yellow whiffle ball, which he loves to throw. He throws the plastic ball from the time he arrives until the minute his father takes his hand to leave.

He throws with a long, awkward arc of his thin arm. When his arm flops forward, the ball goes straight up in the air, landing close to the boy's feet, sometimes even behind him. But each time he throws, he looks forward, expecting the ball to land out where a healthy boy would throw. Nobody approaches the father and says that his son throws well considering his condition, even though the boy's determination and optimism seem even more remarkable than Dave's.

SIX DAYS AFTER my arrival, still stiff and sore from my introduction to Clint Weaver, I buy a house trailer that I park on my property—a twenty-footer. It's smaller than I'd hoped, but it's good quality and in excellent shape, stocked with solid furniture, and reasonably priced.

It's been too long since I was excited about something. But I'm ready to start on the plan that's been percolating for the past year— the plan to build a house with my own two hands. And although fall might seem like an odd time to start, with Montana winters putting a four to six-month halt to construction, this is also part of the plan. Because I have no idea how to build a house. I need time to learn. To study. I plan to construct the foundation, then lose myself in education during the winter months. When spring arrives, I'll be ready to create. The framework. The walls. The roof. And the innards. The heart, arteries, and veins.

BARRY FLIPS HIS WRIST, flinging the Frisbee thirty feet in a slowly leaning line drive. Dave hobbles after it, running with remarkable, cockeyed speed. She jumps, but the Frisbee bounces off her nose. Undaunted, she nudges it, lifting one side just enough to hook a tooth under the lip. She jerks her head, flipping the Frisbee into the air and catching it between her jaws. She trots back, as pleased as if she had caught it in mid-air.

"So when should I get the front-end loader?" I ask.

Barry bends to grab the Frisbee, which Dave is not quite ready to give up. "Backhoe," Barry says. "You can't dig a hole with a front-end loader. You need a backhoe." Dave and Barry engage in a Frisbee tug of war. Dave stares directly at Barry, challenging him, her front foot set, all her weight leaning back into her haunches. She growls.

"Exactly. Just testing you."

"Well, it's not quite that simple, Pete. You can't just go out there and dig a hole in the middle of your property." Dave finally relinquishes the disk and ducks her head, ready to run.

"Why not? It's my land."

Barry tosses the Frisbee, but he overestimates Dave's range, and it lands twenty feet past her. This just makes her happier. She gets to run. So she fetches it, trotting back with tongue flopping to one side of the Frisbee.

Barry sports a patient smile, his dimple sinking into his left cheek. "You've got to get the place surveyed, so you know where the corners will be, and so everything conforms to code." The mention of codes brings Clint Weaver to mind, and I hesitate to ask the next logical question. "All right...who do I have to talk to about all that?"

Barry sighs, bending to wrestle the Frisbee from Dave. "We could actually do the surveying. I can bring a gun home from work. We could do it this weekend."

"A gun?"

"That's what we call it. A transit."

"Oh...that thing on the tripod? That telescope looking deal?"

Barry nods. "I thought you dabbled in real estate back home."

"Hey, you know I inherited that property. I never learned anything about construction. You sure that's a good time for you?"

"I'll make sure—check with the boss." Barry winks. "I don't think she has anything important planned this weekend. Besides, it'll only take a couple hours."

Dave trots back again, but this time she veers away from Barry and drops the Frisbee at my feet.

Barry sighs. "She's a one-man woman, Dave is."

"Pretty much. She'll flirt with you, but when it comes right down to it, I'm the one."

A squeal rings out from across the park, and we look over to see the young handicapped boy running in his awkward, muscle-less lope toward the whiffle ball, which has landed twenty feet away. He laughs hysterically, and his father beams. A few people applaud. I have found a hero.

BACK AT THE HOUSE, we enter to the smell of frying hamburgers. "Back so soon?" Danielle says. It's a bit of a dig. Our walks to the park have gotten longer, and I'm beginning to wonder whether Barry savors this time away from home. For the first time that I can remember, I have noticed some tension around their house. Sharp looks and heavy sighs. An occasional snide comment. The other night, I heard Danielle whisper to herself, "My god, would you please just shut up," while Barry was telling the kids a story.

Now, tonight, Barry doesn't respond. "Smells good," he says.

Danielle flips a patty. "You got a phone call."

"Who was it?" Barry asks.

"Not you."

"Me?" I ask.

Danielle nods.

"From who?" I feel a bit anxious, thinking mostly of negative possibilities.

"Charlie."

"Ah." This is one of them.

Danielle nods again, scooting the hamburgers around the skillet.

"What did he say?"

"Not much, really."

"Yeah?"

She shakes her head, but I can always tell when Danielle is lying, because she drops her eyes.

"Does he want me to call him?"

She continues shaking her head.

"He must have said something."

Danielle stops shaking her head.

I sink into a chair.

Danielle spreads a paper towel over a platter, folds it, then scoops the patties on top. "He asked me not to say anything," she says. "He wants to talk to you himself."

"Well if he calls again, ask him if he wants me to call him."

Danielle sets her spatula on the stove. She looks up, at the ceiling, and sighs, puffing her cheeks as the air escapes. "God, I hate holding things in," she says.

"I know. We're not much alike there, are we?"

Danielle pulls her mouth to one side. "He said that Simone wants to see you." She turns her head, looking away.

"Wow." Barry studies me. "Wow."

Chapter Three

People often make the mistake of looking for a piece of land they can afford, without much thought about how that location will impact their lives. For instance, a lot of people dream of a house in the country, or a cabin in the mountains. But, living miles from nowhere, or tucked away in the trees, is challenging in ways that many people don't anticipate. Choosing where your house will be located requires knowing yourself. It requires a lot of thought and reflection.

Your House, Your Self
Chapter 1
"Location, Location, Location"

My land. What a wonderful phrase. These words feel good in my mouth—like soft, warm, homemade caramel. My. Land.

My land is lush. It's green, thick with grass, brush, and a stand of sturdy pine. It smells of fresh, moist soil. The Bridger Mountains are not close, but they are extremely present, their rocky peaks angular across the horizon. When I stand in the middle of my land, I'm amazed how much I feel the mountains. Without them, my land would be more vulnerable, and less beautiful. The mountains provide a visual image of something—what to expect, maybe. Hopes. Dreams. In open spaces, there is too much unknown.

"Dave!" I call out, realizing that she has wandered off. Looking to the stand of pine trees, I assume that she has followed her instincts to explore. I enter the woods, and the temperature drops ten degrees. The rich pine smell fills my nose. I call out again, but hear nothing, see nothing.

Fifty feet into the trees, I encounter a barbed wire fence. There are several "No Trespassing" signs posted. So I traverse the length of the fence, calling Dave's name, scanning what little is visible. I'm not panicked. Dave is a dog, after all. She's resourceful, an adventurer. Even if she hears me, she may not be interested in being found just yet.

I'm mostly thinking about this revelation that Simone wants to see me. The last time I saw anyone from her family other than Charlie, it ended badly. It was just days after the accident, days after I left their daughter paralyzed. And the message I got that day was clear. So why would things suddenly change?

After seeing no sign of Dave, I cross the fence and push deeper into the trees. The floor of the woods is soft, dark, moist soil, mostly free of living plants, but covered with a thick blanket of pine needles. The smells are rich, earthy and wonderful. I can feel the air, as cool and soothing as a liquid. Squirrels scamper from view, and a deer elegantly pokes her hooves into the wheat grass in the distance.

I become so absorbed in the atmosphere that I forget my purpose. After roaming for fifteen minutes, I crouch to study a rotting tree stump that is crawling with life. Then I stand, take two steps forward, and come face to face with a rifle barrel.

"Damn." This quiet exclamation takes all the breath I have.

The face at the opposite end glares at me, steady and serious. The eyes do not appear wild, or angry—just steady, challenging. "Who are you?" A woman's voice—as the picture comes more into focus, I realize that a big felt cowboy hat and hair pulled into a ponytail have disguised her sex.

I take a deep breath. "Have you seen a dog?" A pause. "A three-legged dog?"

Her brow furrows, and she frowns. "You serious?"

"My dog wandered off. She's only got three legs."

"Is that why she wandered off?"

I smile, although it doesn't seem like a very good idea. She does not smile. "Could be. But I don't think so. That was just offered as information—a way of identifying..."

"Who are you?"

I hold out my hand, offering to shake, reaching as far as the gun will allow. "Pete. I just bought the next lot over."

"Pete what?"

I'm annoyed with this oily appendage in my face. It seems

extreme. Maybe even illegal. "Do you mind?" I tilt my head toward the gun. "I've never had a gun pointed at me. I don't like it much."

Although her eyes soften a bit, her brow lowers until it nearly hides her eyes. She appears to be young, fresh-faced, with apple cheeks and a full mouth. Like a teenage boy without the peach fuzz. "Maybe there's a good reason for it," she says.

"Yeah, I suppose there could be. But I'm your new neighbor, not just some random homeless person. I'm sorry I climbed over the fence, but I wanted to find my dog."

"Where are you from? You have an accent." Slowly, she tilts the gun and allows the barrel to slide through her hands. The stock comes to rest on the ground next to her foot. But she looks nervous, tense, ready to pull it back into position at the slightest hint of danger. And it's at this point that I recognize that the expression in her eyes is not threatening, angry, or crazy, but simply afraid.

"Back east," I answer. "Massachusetts."

"Why'd you move to Montana?"

"To build a house."

Now the scene is odd. It's like party conversation, but with a twist.

"So you come here often?" I ask in my best lounge lizard cool.

This prompts a very slight grin.

"What's *your* name?" I ask.

"Annie," she answers with a glint. "Annie Oakley."

"Ahhh...congratulations on the resurrection thing."

She doesn't laugh, but the smile becomes a little wider. Very little. Her face reddens. Seconds pass, and it's apparent she has nothing left to say.

"So you haven't seen my dog?"

She shakes her head. "Three legs, huh?"

I turn, heading toward my property, first backwards, then a little to one side, always with an eye on Ms. Oakley to assure her I'm not going to make any sudden moves. I'm in a cowboy movie, striding with the senseless confidence that my bravado will trump any danger. I'm John Wayne.

"Let me know if you see her," I say.

"What's her name?"

"Dave."

Another slight smile, but she won't give me any more than that.

"Okay. Dave the three-legged girl dog. Got it."

"I'd invite you over for lunch sometime, Annie, but I think it would be hard to eat and hold a gun at the same time."

I've nearly lost sight of her.

"My name's Leslie," she calls out. "Leslie Monday."

"Ah. So you use an alias." I wave. "Good strategy."

I weave my way through the trees, calling Dave's name as I go, and after climbing back into my land and nearly emerging from the forest, I hear the uneven rhythm of three legs padding over the soft bed. I'm happy to see the brindle coat winding between the pines.

"Where you been, girl?" I crouch and Dave's tongue bathes my cheeks. "Did you get a good look around?" Dave smiles, breathing hard, and leads me out of the trees, as if she can't wait to show me something. We break from the trees into the open, where my land spreads out before us.

"What do you think, Dave?"

She looks at me, barks once, and trots forward, her torso rocking like a hobby horse. I would say that she's never been so happy except that I don't remember her ever being anything other than happy.

"Are we home?"

The Watsons presented Dave on my twenty-eighth birthday, just a year after my baseball career ended.

"We thought you could use some company," Charlie told me, but I knew what he really meant, and I gave him a look.

"Hey, I'm just trying to help," he said.

I wondered how much he'd told the others. My transition from pro athlete to regular guy was still in its infancy, and it wasn't pretty. I felt like a seventh grader again, awkward around people, constantly obsessed with whether they were talking about me. Wondering how much of the press they'd seen. It was damn embarrassing. And one of the most embarrassing aspects of it was a budding case of impotence. I had told Charlie about this one night when I was really drunk.

"A dog, Charlie? Seriously?"

"When was the last time you left the house?" he asked.

"I leave the house every day!"

"Yeah? To do what?"

The hesitation was profound.

"See?" Charlie pointed at Dave. "Now you don't have an excuse. She has needs."

Chapter Four

ESPN reported today that Juan Estrada is in danger of losing his eye. The chances of him ever playing baseball again are slim. Meanwhile the Red Sox are reporting that Pete Hurley, the best Yankee enemy in years, is on the injured reserve list for "psychological reasons." I could have told them he needed help years ago if they'd only asked!

Theyankeeyipper.com
Blog entry for September 26, 2005

During my first night in my new home, I discover what will prove to be one of the greatest challenges of living a few miles out of town. It's so damn quiet. And of course this is exactly why I decided to do this, to escape the noise. The constant chatter of television, and the internet. In town, sounds drift outside my windows even in the quietest moments. But here, long stretches pass in complete silence. Like a lot of people, I've always had romantic notions of this kind of life...peace and quiet in the country, alone, with no distractions. The part that you don't count on is the fact that you're stuck with your own head, where everything gets magnified in ways that you can't possibly control.

It doesn't help that my trailer is so small. The walk from my "living room" to the kitchen is three steps. Another ten feet and I'm in my bedroom. It's an Airstream, so it's nicer than your average trailer, but it's still a tin can when it comes right down to it. I'm still trapped in a space that is twenty feet long and about ten feet wide.

The first night, I eat some spaghetti, and after feeding Dave, I stretch out with a beer. But the trailer is claustrophobic, especially with Dave lying at my feet. I take her out and hook her up to the 50-foot chain I bought to give her some exercise. Before I get to the door, she's already chewing on the rope leading from her collar to the chain.

Inside, I'm still restless, my legs jumpy. I regret my decision to sell my luxuries—my television, iPod, computer. I crave some noise to distract my thoughts from where they're going.

After trying to delve into *Your House, Your Self*, a book that Barry gave me about building your own house, I surrender. And like the proverbial moth, I head for The Sportsman. Part of it is the simple need for a drink, and the fact that I don't know any other bars. But I have also been concerned about the fact that Clint could make trouble for me. I am entertaining this vague notion of apologizing.

THE BAR IS ABOUT half-full, and I settle into a corner booth. Clint's wife is the only barmaid, although I don't see him. But I'm not surprised when I don't get served right away. When she finally meanders over to my table, she doesn't look me in the face. "You've got some nerve," she mutters. "I could get you kicked out, you know."

I bite my tongue, thinking that I didn't even throw a punch. "Listen, I thought maybe Clint and I could sit down and talk. We didn't get off on the best foot."

She acts bored, in a practiced way, like someone who's probably not used to having the upper hand and thinks this is what it looks like. "What can I get you?" she finally asks.

I order a whiskey and a beer.

"A ditch?" she asks.

"A what?"

"You want water in your whiskey?"

"Yeah. A little."

"That's a ditch." You moron, her look adds.

"Okay," I say, and she leaves with no further comment. Maybe she'll come around when she's had some time to think about it, I decide. Best to remain friendly, at least. New in town and all.

The crowd is young—students, mostly, I suspect. Montana State University provides nearly a fourth of Bozeman's population. Lots of baggy jeans, hoodies, sullen looks.

Barb returns and sets my drink on the table. I hold out a ten-dollar bill.

"It's covered," she says with annoyance.

"What?" For a moment, I think this must be her way of acknowledging my effort to smooth things over, but she tilts her head toward the bar.

She indicates a row of stools along the bar. Two young women look over at me, and one of them waves and smiles. Since my Red Sox team won the World Series, this is not an unusual occurrence. But only in New England. I'm surprised to have it happen in Bozeman, Montana.

I wave a thank you, and the same woman waves back. The two converse, and it's obvious that the one who waved, who has dark, curly hair, is trying to talk the other into coming over to my table. The blonde finally relents. I experience a familiar dread, assuming they recognize me, wondering whether they're Yankee or Red Sox fans. But as they approach my table, I recognize the blonde. Annie Oakley, aka Leslie Monday. I point my finger at her like a pistol. "That's far enough," I say.

She responds with that one-sided smile. Her hair is down, hat free, and it falls straight, halfway down her back. Her cheeks still shine red—if anything, they are even redder in the warm bar. The other woman laughs freely, showing an impressive set of teeth. I offer them a seat.

"I'm Arlene," the dark-haired one says.

"My sister," Leslie offers.

"Really?"

I study Arlene, looking for similarities. There are none. Her hair is almost black, in a cascade of tight curls. Her complexion is olive, her face narrow, with high cheekbones. Leslie's face is an almost perfect oval. Arlene's nose slides into a slight ski slope, whereas Leslie's turns up like a kid's. Arlene's eyes shine light, a combination of green and yellow. Leslie's are brown.

"You're sisters?"

Arlene laughs, but Leslie responds with a serious nod, as if she's prepared to provide documentation.

"She looks just like our Dad," Arlene says. "And I'm my mother."

I glance from Arlene to Leslie. "Who's older?"

They both point to Leslie.

Looking at Leslie, I say, "Let me guess. You're twenty-five?"

She frowns and closes her eyes, looking disgusted.

"I'm twenty-five," Arlene says. "She's twenty-nine."

"Most women like it when you underestimate their age," I say.

"Leslie is not most women," Arlene says.

"Yeah, I found that out."

Arlene laughs again, clutching my arm. "She was just telling me about that. You must have wondered what you've gotten yourself into. Deliverance!!!!" Arlene pretends to play a banjo, and I start laughing.

But Leslie doesn't crack a smile. Her sullen expression takes the air out of our levity.

"You two live together?" I ask.

Arlene nods, but Leslie is still staring off into space, as if she would pay good money for an excuse to leave. And in that strange way that we sometimes wonder why someone would dislike us, I find myself craving her approval. Arlene is easy, with her quick laugh, and her open manner. I turn my attention to the challenge.

"Are we boring you?" I ask.

Arlene scoots over, next to her sister. She throws an arm around her and smiles. "Leslie's a grump. I love her to death, but she's very grumpy."

One side of Leslie's mouth curls up. "You don't seem like someone who would move to Montana."

"I know. But I've always loved it here. And my sister lives here in Bozeman."

This makes no impression on Leslie, but Arlene lights up. "What's her name?"

"Danielle Alderson. Her husband's name is Barry."

Neither of the sisters knows them—no big surprise in a town of nearly forty thousand people.

"But why are you here?" Leslie persists. "Why did you leave?"

"Change," I answer, feigning confidence. "I needed a change."

Leslie shakes her head, smiling, turning to the side again.

"What?" I ask. "What does that mean?"

The music suddenly seems louder. She leans toward me, resting her elbows on the table. "You know what it means, when somebody says they need a change?"

I shake my head. "Well, I try to take people at their word, but maybe you can educate me."

"It means they're running from something."

"Really?" A hint of sarcasm sneaks into my voice. "Always? Every time?"

Leslie says yes, and although I find her complete assurance annoying, I also admire it in a way. It's hard not to admire someone who is so sure of themselves. There's also the small matter of her being right.

"What do you two do?" I ask.

Arlene answers. "Leslie is a lawyer," she announces with an endearing pride. "And I'm going to school and working at a restaurant." Arlene's jaw is slightly off-set. She touches the side of her chin from time to time, as if this constant pressure will eventually force the jaw into place. This is not her only tic, either. She adjusts her hair, and her shirt. She checks her top button. She plays with her rings.

"What are you studying?" I ask.

"I can't decide." She laughs. "I've changed my major about 400 times."

"What about you?" Leslie's eyes bore into me. "What do you do?"

"I'm building a house."

"So you're a carpenter?"

"Not at all."

"An architect," Arlene decides.

"No, not an architect, either. I just decided to build a house."

Arlene looks alarmed. "By yourself?"

I nod.

"What did you do before?" Leslie asks. "You can't just quit your job, buy land in Montana—especially around here—and build a house unless you've got something socked away."

"True." I turn to Arlene. "Is she always this direct?"

Arlene nods, smiling.

I'm thirsty. I down my ditch with one hearty swig. Then I guzzle half my beer. "All right, Leslie Monday. Because you're obviously not going to rest until you know every single thing about me, I'll give you the goods."

Leslie rolls her eyes, but Arlene collapses against her giggling.

"Here's the story. I made quite a lot of money when I was young, doing something most boys only dream of. Plus my dad was a very good businessman, and when he died, I inherited a small fortune.

So I took the money, started my own little drug cartel in Boston, and made a shitload of cash. Now I moved to Montana to get away from the law."

Arlene's eyes get wide but Leslie finally cracks a smile. "He's lying."

"You think so?"

"You've never sold drugs in your life."

I decide that Leslie is probably a very good lawyer. She reads people well. But the drug thing is the only part of my story that isn't true.

"Were you an athlete?" Leslie asks.

"Uh huh."

"Which sport?" Her eyes narrow.

"Baseball."

"What's your last name?" Leslie asks.

I tell her.

She turns to Arlene. "Pete Hurley."

And Arlene squeals. "You're the pitcher?"

I blush.

Leslie points at her sister. "She loves sports. I could care less."

"You were great in the World Series," Arlene says.

"Well, we had a good team."

"Red Sox...2004," Arlene informs Leslie.

"Are you the bloody sock guy?" Leslie asks.

Arlene hits her on the upper arm. "That's Schilling. Pete was the set-up guy. The Mechanik!"

"Very good," I say.

Leslie looks slightly impressed. She thinks for a moment. "You said you lost your dad. Was he alive then?" she asks.

I shake my head.

"Too bad he wasn't able to see you," Leslie says.

I make a little noise in my throat, blinking hard.

"What about your mother?" Arlene asks.

I shake my head. "Died when I was four."

"You lost both your parents?" Arlene asks. "How sad!"

Leslie turns to her. "So did we. You act like you've never heard such a thing."

"Oh shut up, grumpy," Arlene says.

"You lost both your parents?" I ask, not directing the question to either of them.

They both hum, confirming, and we sit for a long, thoughtful minute. And then another. At first, the silence makes sense, as a sort of tribute to our shared orphan-hood. Then it gets awkward—too long—to where the sadness starts seeping in. We fidget. Arlene touches her chin.

"Where's Barb?" Leslie asks, searching the room.

"Barb?" I ask.

"The barmaid."

"Ah." I clear my throat. "I think it's actually my fault that we're not getting better service."

"Why's that?" Leslie asked.

"Oh, I guess you could say I had a little meeting with Barb's husband the other night."

"That was you?" Arlene shakes her head. "Wow. I thought you looked familiar."

"You were here?" I ask.

Arlene makes a guilty face, stretching her mouth to the side.

"How could you not recognize someone after watching them get their face kicked in?" I ask.

"Well, I didn't get very close. I don't like fights."

"You don't strike me as a fighter," Leslie says.

"You don't know me as well as you think you do," I say, and Leslie gives me a skeptical eye.

Arlene catches Barb's attention and motions her over. Barb does not hurry.

"Did you find Dave?" Leslie asks.

Barb interrupts. "Another round?"

"Yes, on me this time," I say.

"Who's Dave?" Arlene asks.

Barb leaves, apparently insulted that we didn't pay closer attention to her.

"Dave's his dog," Leslie answers.

Arlene straightens. "Oh, what a great name!"

Leslie sports a half-smile. "That's not the best part," she says. "Dave is a girl, and she's only got three legs."

"A girl? You named a girl dog Dave?"

"Yeah."

"That's cruel," Arlene says, her mood swing remarkably smooth.

"She doesn't know the difference," I insist. "She likes her name."

"I love it," Leslie says. "It's like that Johnny Cash song…"

"Except that Sue gets the shit kicked out of him," I cite, holding up one finger. "Nobody has bullied Dave."

"What about people laughing when you tell them her name?" Arlene asks.

"She thinks they're happy," I answer. "Besides, they're not laughing at her."

"Well, I still don't like it," Arlene says. Leslie smiles.

Barb returns, and I take out my wallet.

"How's Clint doing?" Leslie asks Barb, and I have a sudden urge to make Leslie buy her own drink.

Barb glares at me. "He's fine."

I shake my head. "Hey, I tried to smooth things over. Besides, I got the worst of it."

"Yeah, well, that doesn't change the fact that you're an asshole." Barb slaps my change on the table, then turns on her heel.

"Damn!" Leslie exclaims. "What the hell did you say to him?"

"I really didn't say anything," I reply.

"I can't believe she said that," Arlene says.

"Well, she doesn't really know me, so she has no way of knowing whether I'm an asshole or not." I drain my beer, and stretch my arms out along the back of the booth.

"Neither do we," Leslie says, and her sly smile charms me.

Chapter Five

Pete Hurley's just doing what former athletes have always done when their careers are over. Leave the guy alone!

Woody Paige
Around the Horn
September 15, 2008

I'm drunk. Again. I could blame this on the Monday sisters. After all, they talked me out of leaving. Several times. Actually, I say "they," but Arlene was the one who convinced me to stay. Leslie made it clear that she didn't care one way or the other.

Anyway, I'm drunk—very drunk—and when I drink, I tend to lose blocks of time. I've been fading in and out, and of course I don't know for how long. But I do know that while I was gone, I missed two important things.

The first is that Arlene has scooted along the bench so that her hip is nestled against mine. And even in my drunken, half-forgetting state, I can see that Leslie is either jealous or pissed, or both.

The second thing I've missed is that Clint Weaver—the man who bounced my head around like a basketball—is back. He's in the same spot, perched on his stool at the end of the bar, like a big fat owl. He's staring at me, and that's how his eyes look—owly. I'm not sure which of these makes me more nervous. First of all, I don't want to sleep with Arlene. Even sitting close to her makes me nervous. Getting this close to a woman is too much of a painful reminder of my condition...my limp noodle. And as for Clint, I'm not afraid that he'll beat the hell out of me again. I'm more afraid of how much a part of me wants him to. I'm fighting an ugliness which is trying like hell to creep into my heart. The earlier spirit of forgiveness has been drowned in a current of whiskey and beer and resentment. All thoughts of avoiding the problems Clint might cause with my house are quickly fading.

"I think he's looking at us," Arlene says. "Do you want me to talk to him, Pete?"

And I realize we've been discussing him.

"What're you gonna say to him?" I ask Arlene.

And then, as if he was looking for the right time, or gesture, Clint leans off his stool, nearly toppling it, and starts toward us. His jaw is set. He's bigger than I remembered—maybe even bigger than I am—and my heart pumps a little faster.

"Shit," Arlene mutters.

"Lemme handle this," I announce.

Leslie stands. "I don't think that's such a good idea." She meets Clint halfway across the floor. I make an attempt to follow her, but Arlene's fingernails dig into my upper arm.

Leslie and Clint's exchange appears to be cordial. He doesn't seem the least bit annoyed with her intervention. His hands dangle loosely at his sides, and he listens with a calm, attentive expression, nodding from time to time. Meanwhile, Barb materializes at his elbow, also listening intently. And although I'm annoyed at being held back, I'm impressed with the respect Leslie commands.

Now I'm looking at them from an angle. Clint has tilted to one side, as has Leslie, and Barb.

"Come on, sit up." I feel a hard shove to my shoulder, and realize I'm the one who has tipped over, onto Arlene. "You're too drunk to fight."

"Never too drunk to fight," I drawl. "Might be too drunk to win, but never too drunk to fight." I try standing again, and it is then that Clint starts toward us, with Leslie at his side, and Barb slightly behind. Arlene keeps a tight hold on me, and I can't stand. In fact, I nearly tumble back onto her.

Clint approaches, and just as I expect the white explosion of a fist to the head, he places his drink on the table and slips into the opposite side of the booth. Leslie slides in next to him, and it appears we're about to have a peace negotiation.

"How you doing, Clint?" Arlene asks.

"All right, Arlene." Friendly as all hell. Barb stands at the table, just as any barmaid would, as if she's waiting to take our order.

"Bring us another, sweetheart," Clint says. "On me."

"You got it." Barb snaps her gum, then makes a drum majorette turn.

"So you feeling any better?" Clint asks, and I'm slow to zero in on his face, although I assume he's talking to me.

When he finally does come into focus, and I see his eyes are on me, I nod. "Yeah, definitely feeling better than the last time you saw me. And you?"

Clint smiles. He's got a nice smile, and for a moment, I understand what Barb might see in him. "Can't complain." He takes a deep breath, sniffing in through his nose. His chin tips up, and he stretches his arms out, resting them along the top of the booth. "So I hear you tried to make peace earlier on..." He leaves the sentence hanging, ending with a rise in his voice. Now he waits, looking at me with those round, owly eyes.

"I did bring it up, yeah. Your wife didn't seem all that interested."

Clint brings his arms down, casually, and leans forward, resting his elbows on either side of his drink. He locks his fingers together. "Yeah, well, maybe we're a little bit picky around here, but we don't really appreciate obnoxious strangers." He smiles, but it's not a kind smile.

I nod, and as drunk as I am, I manage to hold my tongue.

"Why would you decide to move here?" Clint asks. "Of all the choices you have in the world?"

"He's building a house," Arlene announces.

My nudge to her ribs is intended to be subtle, but my drunken state impedes my depth perception. She jumps and gives me a look.

Clint smiles. "Still planning on building that house, huh?"

"Sure am."

Clint shakes his head and I really don't like the way he's shaking his head. And despite all the reasons that I know I should do otherwise, part of me wants to say something. The presence of the Monday sisters keeps me silent. But because I'm drunk, I can't prevent myself from giving him the look. With my eyes, I tell him that I'm ready to meet his challenge. That I'm not afraid of him. I stare him down, just like I used to stare down batters. I tell him with my eyes that if the Monday sisters weren't sitting there, I'd be on him like a cat in a moving car. I'm too drunk to tell if he's responding. So I intensify my message.

"What's your problem?" Clint suddenly asks.

"Clint!" Arlene scolds. "He didn't say a word!"

"He doesn't have to...I can see it in his face."

Barb brings the drinks, setting them one by one in front of us.

The next instant, I make a decision I probably wouldn't have made if I was sober. The look on Clint's face is so unbearably smug that I decide I need to knock it across the room. I lunge, an effort to throw a punch that I would no doubt find humorous if I could see myself. And of course, the table prevents me from even being able to reach him.

Just as Barb is about to set my drink in front of me, she splashes it in my face. And then the explosion comes. My vision goes completely white for a fraction of a second, and then black. My nights in Bozeman are coming to a predictable end.

I'M REALLY NOT happy about the pain this time. I wake up to a throbbing in my face. It feels as if my cheek fills the entire left side of the room. I can't see anything to my left, and I realize it's not just my cheek. My left eye is swollen shut.

I'm in a room I've never seen before. It's a room that doesn't appear to have been used for awhile. The dresser is bare on top, except for a dark wooden box. Most of the family photographs on the wall are ancient, black and white, or sepia. There is an alarm clock—the old-fashioned kind with a big bell on top. Two photos across from me catch my attention—studio poses with airbrushed, pastel colors. Arlene and Leslie's graduation pictures.

I creep from beneath the covers and pull on my jeans and shirt. My movements must have drawn someone's attention, because a soft knock sounds on the bedroom door.

"Yeah?" I say.

The door opens slowly, and the head that peeks in is dark-haired.

"Good morning," I say.

Arlene wears a white bathrobe—terry cloth with a pink flannel bunny sewn on the pocket.

"Morning, Mr. Tyson," Arlene says.

I palm my forehead. "You must be talking about the Buster Douglas version," I say.

She laughs. "You look terrible. I can't believe what a jerk that guy is...Clint. I never have liked him."

"Yeah? What's his deal anyway?"

Arlene shakes her head. "Well, it's kind of a long story."

I squint. "Yeah? Tell me. I got all day."

"Well..." Arlene settles into an overstuffed chair by the door. She carefully sets her cup of coffee on a table. "Do you want some coffee?" she asks, holding the cup toward me.

The mug is thick white ceramic, shaped like a nuclear cooling tower. Coffee always tastes better to me in these mugs.

"Is there enough?" I settle back onto the bed. "Where's Leslie?"

"She's in court. She does most of her work here, but she had a case today. I'll be right back." As she walks away, I see that she has a big fluffy bunny tail attached to the butt of her robe.

She returns with a matching mug for me, and I take a big gulp. "Your sister has a court case and she was out drinking last night?"

Arlene shrugs. "She's good at what she does. She was prepared."

I take another sip. The coffee's perfect, and although it burns my tongue, I'm happy to have some moisture in my mouth.

"No work today?" I ask.

"Dinner shift."

"Classes?"

She smiles.

"You're playing hooky?"

She looks down.

"Just for me?"

She slaps my arm. "Don't flatter yourself. I'm not exactly in top condition myself, you know."

"So Barb and Clint..." I prompt her.

"Ah, yes. Well, Barb's friends were really upset when she married Clint. He's successful, and important..." Arlene makes quotation marks with her fingers. "But he's not a very nice guy when he's drinking. I guess he's been on the wagon for a couple of weeks now."

"Really? Good thing for me. Imagine if he was drunk."

"Yeah. Well, anyway...Barb's lost a lot of friends because of Clint. You're just the latest person he's tangled with."

I sip from my coffee and nod. "Very unfortunate."

"Why's that?"

"Well, because of who he is—his position."

"What do you mean?"

"Let's change the subject; there must be more interesting things we can talk about."

But neither of us comes up with anything.

"I'm sorry I imposed on you," I say.

Arlene pats my arm. "It's no trouble. You were in bad shape. We were actually worried about you being alone."

"Well thank you for that."

"Your eye looks really painful," she says.

"It hurts...pretty bad, actually."

"You want some ice?" she asks.

"That's probably a good idea."

Arlene gives me a serious look. "Pete, how much do you remember about last night?"

"Not much," I admit.

She nods. "Okay." And I don't want to think about why she asked.

It was just after junior college, when I got my first minor league contract, that I went through my Harley phase. One luxury of not worrying about money was the freedom to pursue unconventional hobbies without giving a damn about the consequences. For reasons I can't explain, I have always been diligent about my investments, even during the most irresponsible periods of my life. So at twenty, despite others' concerns about injury, I bought a Harley-Davidson and filled my closet with black leather, Levi's, and t-shirts. Although it wasn't my intention, it ended up contributing to my image as a player. I was the bad boy...the guy brought in to scare people a little. They dubbed me "The Mechanik," after a really bad Dolph Lundgren movie.

On a sunny spring day, I drove my new bike to the Watsons, the receipt crumpled in my back pocket. I pulled into the driveway and revved the engine a few times for effect before shutting her down and striding in my best Marlon Brando (early, of course) to the front door.

But Mr. and Mrs. Watson showed little enthusiasm for my purchase. They said all the right things, but their voices were thick with concern. To my disappointment, they were the only ones home that day. It wasn't until the next evening that I got a chance to show my new toy to Charlie.

When Charlie saw my bike, he shook his head, but he was smiling. He circled the machine, dressed in his khakis and boat shoes, hands on hips. The Harley gleamed. The tank and front shield were blood red, with black borders. The saddle was black, and the intestinal tangle of flawless chrome circled around and through the black and red.

"That is a piece of metal, isn't it?" he finally said. "Look at the detail! It's fucking art."

I crossed my arms. "It's not bad."

"Not bad. You asshole. You're proud as hell, and you can't even show it. It's art. It's fucking Michelangelo in metal."

About then, Simone came running outside, her skinny legs flying out to the sides. She was ten, and still quite a tomboy. Her hair flipped out from the back of her head in a long braid. She squealed, which surprised me. I hadn't thought about Simone much during my college years. Whenever Charlie and I came back to Amherst, we were out raising hell. And if we happened to run across Simone, she either ignored us or we ignored her. I didn't really know her.

"I want a ride," she screeched.

"You do?"

Her head bobbed.

I looked to Charlie, whose face showed a pale doubt. "You better ask Mom and Dad," he said, knowing full well what answer she'd get.

So did Simone. "Come on, Charlie. I want a ride!" Without even waiting for an answer, she turned to me. "Come on, Pete. Just a short one. Please please please please please."

"Charlie's right. You need to ask." I tipped my head toward the house.

Simone's shoulders fell, and she marched into the house, hands balled into tight fists. Charlie and I exchanged guilty smiles.

But Simone bounded out of the house seconds later, her braid nearly straight out from her head, a big smile on her face.

"They said okay!"

"They did?" Charlie looked toward the house, searching for a face at the window.

I was also skeptical.

"They said we have to just go around the block." This alleviated some of my skepticism. "But we could go around the block a bunch of times."

"You'll get dizzy," I teased. "You'll fall off."

Mr. Watson came out onto the stoop, shielding his eyes.

"You sure this is all right?" I asked.

"Pe-ete," Simone scolded. "You don't believe me?"

"Just wanna make sure."

Mr. Watson waved. "Just be careful. Shouldn't she have a helmet?"

"I'll take it slow. We'll be okay just going around the block."

I climbed onto the bike, and Charlie lifted Simone up behind me, where she perched. I felt her fingers grip the back of my t-shirt, like a cat. I smiled at Charlie.

"You're going to need a better hold than that." I reached back for Simone's arms. "Put your arms around me. Hang on tight."

She put her arms around my waist, but they hung like a necklace. She was wearing a tank top. "You gonna be warm enough?" I asked.

"Yeah. Come on…let's go." She bounced on the seat.

"All right." I cranked the starter, coming down hard with my foot, and the unmistakable Harley rattle started. Simone's arms tightened. I warmed the engine for half a minute, then rolled out of the driveway, taking a wide, slow turn for Mr. Watson's benefit. We eased to the end of the block, where I took another wide turn. This street was four lanes, and just happened to be empty, and after I yelled again to hang on, I kicked it into a higher gear and let it out for a few blocks.

Simone screamed, but through a delightful laughter. I broke my promise, driving for a good half mile before doubling back. I figured I could convince them that we were winding around the side streets. I slowed to a crawl, then passed in front of the house. Simone waved, and Charlie and Mr. Watson waved back, looking unconcerned, even amused.

When we turned onto the big road again, Simone shouted, "Faster!"

I gunned it, and the air whipped our clothes into a frantic flapping of cotton. I hadn't thought to buy goggles, so I had to squint. The asphalt blurred, and the houses rushed by in a colorful smear. I turned my head just enough to ask Simone how she was doing, and in that instant I learned the lesson that most bikers do—that you absolutely can*not* take your eyes off the road.

A car pulled out from a side street, and I barely caught it from the corner of my eye. Twenty yards away, a face turned, and the eyes grew. The mouth opened in a silent scream, and brakes squealed. Hands spread into fans to cover the face. I never even knew whether it was a man or a woman.

Simone shrieked into my ear. I veered. My right knee clipped the headlight just enough to tear off a chunk of skin. It didn't even rip my jeans. Although we missed the car, I was pissed. So I kept going, not trusting what I'd do if I stopped.

I took the next right, slowing, and tried to breathe. I was about to cry, not from pain but from complete terror. Simone was silent, but I felt her fingernails digging into my stomach. My knee ached. I circled slowly until I was fairly calm. Then I stopped.

"You all right?" My voice shook. I tried to climb off the bike, but Simone would not let go. Her arms trembled. I twisted on the saddle so I could put my arms around her. And we held each other, shivering, while Simone cried.

"I'm okay," she whispered.

"You sure?"

"Yeah. I'm fine."

"We can't say anything, you know."

"I know." She nodded.

But it didn't matter. When we got back to the house, despite our best efforts, our pasty color and saucer eyes gave us away. I climbed off the bike and lifted Simone to the ground. Charlie and his dad strode, then rushed across the lawn. Simone wobbled when I set her down. Her face was pale as bread dough. Charlie stopped when he saw her. So did her father. Neither spoke.

"Well, that was fun," I said. And I felt the blood trickle down my shin.

Chapter Six

We used to talk about Pete Hurley and his ERA.
Now all we talk about are his DUIs.

Michael Wilbon
Pardon the Interruption
November 2, 2008

"Christ." Danielle turns away, stomping through the house. It's the reaction I expected. I've tried to stay away until my face heals, but I've already made excuses for three previous invitations. A week after the fight, my left eye is still like an eggplant, the color spreading down that side of my face, nearly to my ear. It looks as if a cashew is lodged beneath the skin on the bridge of my nose. And my eyeball has no white at all. Red as a cherry. My face is like a bowl of produce.

Barry looks up from the baseball game on TV. "Oh oh." This time, he's not amused either. "You volunteered for sparring duty again."

I settle into the couch. My head feels heavy, as if it might topple from my neck with a sudden motion. "I didn't go looking for it," I explain. "I ran into your friend Clint."

"Did you go back to The Sportsman?"

I drop my eyes.

"And you're trying to tell me you weren't looking for it? What the hell were you doing there?"

"I had this crazy notion about smoothing things over."

Barry shakes his head, showing more concern. "God, I had no

idea Clint could be so violent."

I raise my brow. "I would not describe Clint Weaver as laid back." I touch my cheek.

Barry looks back toward the kitchen. "So Danielle's not too happy, I guess."

"Not surprising."

As if on cue, Danielle appears, flying into the room like a ghost. She flings a bundle of letters into my lap, then flies out.

"Thanks," I call to her.

No answer.

I pull the rubber band from around the letters and start thumbing through them. Most are business-related. Although I sold most of my holdings to finance this dream, I still own three buildings in Massachusetts, so there are brokers, accountants, and lawyers to contend with. But my flipping stops abruptly at a particular letter. The handwriting is Charlie's. I try to remember whether I've ever received a letter from Charlie, and I'm sure I haven't. Strange, after a twenty-year friendship. I stare at the envelope as if I might glean some sense of what the letter says from its folds.

"Love letter?" Barry asks.

"Not likely."

"Who's it from?"

"Charlie."

Barry's brows rise to the middle of his forehead. "Hm."

I slip a thumb under the flap, tearing the envelope open. I unfold a piece of canary writing paper. The corner is torn at an angle. The writing is scrawled.

Pete—

> *I hear you don't have a phone, so I thought I'd drop you a note. Danielle probably told you I called a couple of weeks ago. Not much to report. Simone's therapy is going well. Mom's also doing well, but Dad's having some health problems. Nothing serious, so far. I just thought I should let you know that I miss you. The main reason I'm writing is to let you know that Simone really wants to see you. She thinks it would really help her recovery.*

*I promised her I'd pass the message along. Hope your
house is coming along.*

                                        Love, Charlie

I allow the letter to fall into my lap. I'm reminded again of
Danielle's assertion that I'm not punishing myself alone. These are
people I love as much as my family.

"You okay?" Barry asks.

"I'll be fine," I answer, but I'm really not sure I believe it. Ever
since Danielle told me that Simone wanted to see me, I've been
trying to forget.

"SO YOU'RE READY for the backhoe?" Barry scoops mashed
potatoes onto his plate, then a generous ladle of gravy. We spent
the previous Saturday, before the second fight with Clint, surveying
my lot, driving lathe into the soft ground. When we finished, the
lot was aflutter with orange strips of plastic tied around the tops
of lathe. Although I didn't understand half of what we were doing,
the work was intoxicating, just as I hoped this whole adventure
would be.

After studying the plat, Barry suggested that I alter the location
of the house, rotating it ninety degrees so that the main room gets
its full complement of sunlight. Charlie helped design the house,
which is actually just big enough to qualify as a house. It's a cabin,
with one cavernous room, and a loft for the bedroom. A bathroom.
A small kitchen. It's all I need. More importantly, it's exactly what
I've always dreamed of. The night after we finished the surveying, I
decided to pitch my little pup tent right where the bedroom would
be. I hauled out my mummy bag and crawled inside, finally letting
Dave in after she cried for a solid hour. And we slept under the
stars, me waking up shivering several times during the cold autumn
night. Dave slept like a dog, of course.

"Yeah, I guess so. I guess I'll need some guidance."

Barry nods. "No problem. It's not as hard as it looks."

I will soon find out otherwise.

Although Danielle has spoken to me, her disappointment in my
condition shows on her face throughout the meal. Gus and Stevie
stare at my black eye. The meal is awkward, silent, with Barry
making the biggest effort to fill the void.

"How's school?" I ask the boys.

They each give a short report of new teachers and classmates—talking quickly, as if overcome by a fear that speaking for too long, or too loudly, might somehow cause further injury.

"What did Charlie say?" Danielle asks.

"Not a lot." The words hang up in my throat. It takes an effort to clear it. "His dad's sick, I guess. He didn't say what it was, though."

"Cancer," Danielle says, matter-of-factly.

"What?" I stop before taking a bite of chicken.

"His dad has cancer. Charlie didn't say it was cancer?"

I shake my head. "Damn, he wasn't even sick when I left."

"It's been bothering him for several months. He just didn't get it checked until recently," Danielle says.

"So you talked to Charlie again?"

She nods.

"He said he didn't think it was serious," I mention.

Danielle sighs. "Well, it's cancer. I'm sure they're not taking it lightly. But it sounds like he's doing pretty well."

"What kind?" Barry asks.

"Prostate," she says.

"Oh, well that's good." Barry lightens. "As far as cancer goes, anyway."

"That's true," Danielle says.

As they talk, I sink slowly inside myself, thinking back to the day my dad died, when Mr. Watson sat me down, looked me in the eye, and told me that I was welcome to stay with them for as long as I wanted.

Chapter Seven

In our efforts to make a home on this earth, we push metal into it, we gouge parts of it from itself. We hollow out a place for ourselves, and line it with a shield for protection. When you decide where you want to build your house, look at this place. Study it. Take pictures of what it looks like before you mold it into your vision. Remember that there was something there before. Remember that buying a piece of land does not mean that you own it.

Your House, Your Self
Chapter 2
"Possession is Ninety Percent"

Digging a hole might seem like a simple task. It probably should be. It probably is for many people. But for me it has proven to be a huge challenge. My experience with machinery has been limited to putting gas in my car. Even that is sometimes overwhelming, especially when they have those springy rubber sleeves around the nozzle. I operate the backhoe as if I'm wrestling with Godzilla. And the machine makes moves similar to that monster—the Japanese version, of course.

I won't let Barry do the job. He offered, and he probably could have finished the hole in a day. But part of the deal is that I have to do this myself, even if it takes longer, and even if the hole ends up with rougher edges. I sent Barry home because watching me was killing him. I'm now almost through the second day.

Dave hops around the perimeter, peering into the hole with a fearless curiosity, barking, as if she might find a new leg, or a juicy bone. I climb down and hook her to her chain to prevent her from falling in, or from running under the machine just as I dump a load of dirt.

When I approach the machine again, I hear a vehicle. A black

Dodge pickup pulls into my drive. The man who climbs from the driver's seat is not familiar. He's a small guy, wearing a straw cowboy hat and worn Wrangler jeans. His face is ruddy, his nose small and beaky, with big wire-rimmed glasses perched on the knob.

"You Pete Hurley?"

"Yeah. What can I do for you?"

"Name's Burt Mackie. How you doin'?"

"I'm good...kind of busy."

"Well, I won't take too much of your time. I'm a city inspector. Building inspector. I heard you were getting started on a project out here, and I just thought I'd stop by and introduce myself, and see if you had any questions."

My shoulders gather up around my neck. "Well, that's thoughtful of you," I say. "But I don't have any questions."

Mackie starts to wander across my property, which brings out my territorial instincts. I follow him, even crossing his path a couple of times to try and discourage him from going any farther. Mackie plants his hands on his hips and circles the hole.

"So you're building a house, are you?"

"That's right." I find myself wishing I knew the law better, wondering whether he has any right to snoop around before I've even finished digging a hole. "A cabin, really. It's only about 1500 square feet."

Mackie squats, looking down into the hole.

"And you submitted your specs before you started digging this?"

"My specs?"

"You didn't submit your specs?"

"I didn't know."

"Well, you probably need to shut her down then until you get that taken care of."

"You're kiddin'."

"No I'm not. I'm serious as hell."

I turn and shake my head. "All right, Mr. Mackie. Do you have any forms or anything with you? What exactly is it I'm supposed to submit?"

Mackie pats his chest, as if he might just happen to have the forms in his shirt. "Damn, you know, I didn't think to bring those suckers. You'll have to come down to the office, or I can get them mailed to you."

"I'll come down," I offer, suspicious of his ability to hang onto my address from here to the pickup.

"All right. You know where it is?"

I shake my head.

Mackie pulls a card from his pocket and hands it to me. "I'll let you get cleaned up," he says. "I guess you've probably had a long day."

"I appreciate that," I say, my jaw tight. "Thanks for coming by."

Mackie shakes my hand, and when I look him in the eye, he averts his gaze. His glasses magnify his eyes, which are already round.

AFTER MACKIE LEAVES, I wait a few minutes to resume my work, steaming. I'm almost done with the hole, and I'm not about to let this little pipsqueak prevent me from finishing the job. Mackie sat in his truck for several minutes before leaving, as if he knew I wasn't going to quit. I went inside the trailer.

But now, back on the machine, I pull a lever, and the hydraulics scream. The mechanical arm reaches skyward, and I swivel it to one side, pulling the tractor forward a few yards. The art of using both foot pedals and the hydraulic levers simultaneously short-circuits my brain. My legs cramp.

The bucket falls, planting its wicked teeth into the ground, then burrowing with the strength only machinery possesses, down into the solid earth. The front wheels rise six inches. I pull the bucket toward me and up, scooping the dirt in an inward arch. Soil falls from each side of the bucket like a thin, brown waterfall. A pro would swivel the machine to one side at the same time that they're pulling the bucket toward them. This is how Barry showed me. But I have to do these steps one at a time.

After a full second day, nearly ten hours, I finish. I'm still pissed about the inspector but relieved that he didn't come back. The hole actually resembles a rectangle. The depth is nearly even throughout, and I didn't bust through any pipes, or hit a power line. I'm still alive. I crawl down, and now it is my body that moves like Godzilla, my muscles are so stiff. Dave leaps up to give me a kiss and the effort of holding her from my face is more than my sore muscles can muster. I fall on my ass, and Dave gets her kiss.

"Hello." A voice startles me, and the first thought is Mackie, of course. But I turn, and it is Leslie that stands a few yards away, her fists in her jean pockets, a slight smirk on her face.

"How long have you been here?" I ask.

"Four hours."

I chuckle.

"Really." A smile. She studies the hole. "I wondered what the ruckus was, so I wandered over. You operate that thing like you have a score to settle."

I hide the fact that this wounds my male pride. "It's my first time. Besides, I'm mechanically challenged."

She nods. "I don't suppose drug dealers have much use for heavy machinery."

It takes me a second to realize what she's talking about...the conversation in the bar. I roll onto my knees, stiffly unbending to my feet. "Just Uzis."

Leslie looks down, kicking a rock as I stretch my arms to the side. "This must be Dave." She bends to scratch behind Dave's ear. Dave loves this spot, and lets her know with a big smile. And Leslie learns the hard way, as many have, that scratching Dave's ear has an immediate effect. Dave's rear leg starts kicking, and she goes down.

Leslie panics. "Oh dear." She lifts Dave to her tripod, then resumes scratching, this time bracing her. "I'm sorry, Dave."

"She's used to it."

Dave pants.

"So is she what you expected?" I ask.

"I pictured you with a taller woman. Maybe a bit more sophisticated."

"She's deceiving. She's very interested in art, actually."

"Oils?"

"Woods. Easier to chew. And they taste better."

Leslie almost laughs. I wonder what it takes. She surveys the property.

"I've cooked some dinner," she says. "And there's plenty. I might even have some leftovers for Dave to gnaw on." She swivels on one leg, not looking at me. "If you're interested."

"No need to ask twice. I just need to clean up."

She appears surprised by my eager reply, but she recovers. "Oh, absolutely," she agrees. "I won't let you in the house like that." She's being sarcastic, and I can see she's very good at it. "Half hour?"

"It won't take me that long. I can be there in fifteen minutes, if that's not too soon."

"You already know what you're going to wear?"

"Oh, you want me to wear clothes? Okay, twenty minutes."

And at last, she laughs. But only slightly.

WHEN DAVE AND I arrive at the Monday house, I'm relieved to find that Arlene is working. I look forward to a quiet evening with Leslie, who doesn't seem the least bit interested in me.

She leads me to the kitchen. "I did some experimenting," she explains, opening the oven. "Since I half-expected to be eating alone, I thought it would be safe. But we can be guinea pigs."

I bend to try and catch a glimpse. "So what are we subjecting ourselves to?"

She flips a potholder into the middle of the table, then slips her hands into oven mitts and carries a clear glass dish, setting it carefully on the potholder. "It doesn't have a name," she says. "I made it up. But it's basically pork with a sort of Cajun tomato sauce, and some green peppers."

"Mmm." I rub my hands together. Leslie then outdoes herself, pulling one last treat from the oven—homemade garlic mashed potatoes—a favorite of mine since I can remember. My father loved them, and made them until Danielle couldn't stand to be in the same room with a potato. But I never tired of them.

I heap my plate, and Leslie can barely conceal her grin. "Hungry?"

"I dream in mashed potatoes."

"Hm. Interesting. Black and white dreams, without the black."

"What would Freud say?"

She adopts an intellectual pose, resting one finger against her chin, staring skyward. "That you only see one side of things?"

I smile, sprinkling salt and pepper. "Speaking of which, how's the world of law?"

Leslie spoons a much smaller helping of potatoes onto her plate. "It's better than washing dishes."

I manage to speak without a mouthful of food. "I know some dishwashers that would take exception to that."

"I guess all jobs have their pluses and minuses."

"And what are your pluses?"

Leslie lightly peppers her potatoes. "I love the law. Especially when I can use it in constructive ways."

"And what do you see as constructive?"

I don't mean to put her on the defensive, but she seems to think so. She takes a deep breath, chews a healthy bite of pork, which is tender and rich with juices, and swallows. "I mostly represent women. Women who've been abused, or are going through difficult divorces."

"Ah." I have the irrational feeling that I'm the enemy. I think of the rifle in my face. "So you do a lot of pro bono work?"

She tips her head back and forth, which I take as a yes.

"Do you think your work has made you more suspicious of men?"

"Absolutely."

"That's very frank."

"Well, we are formed by what we see and experience, are we not?"

"Absolutely."

"And frankness is a quality I've been burdened with."

"Burdened? I wouldn't call it a burden."

The smile returns, and I even detect a bit of color in the already pink cheeks. "And what would you call it, Mr. Hurley?"

I swallow a delicious mouthful of mashed potatoes, and I can tell she used a lot of butter. "A gift?"

She looks up at the ceiling. "I'll have to think about that. Never thought of it that way."

We eat silently, and I curb my tendency to inhale my food. I've always been a fast eater...my father used to put a timer on the table and challenge me to stretch out my meal until the bell rang. It never did.

I scan the house, which I'm certain is the house where the Mondays grew up. It has that feel—the feel of being lived in for a very long time. Faded pictures. Furniture that appears to have been resting in the same spot for decades. Rooted. Although everything is clean and orderly, it doesn't look as if they've bought anything new in years. When I breathe in the air here, it feels old, rich with lingering emotions.

"Your eye seems to be recovering," Leslie finally says.

"I'll probably heal up just in time for the next fight."

Leslie shows no reaction, as if she didn't hear. She eats deliberately, with the kind of decorum I've noticed among my more refined friends. The term "well brought up" comes to mind.

"How much do you remember about that night?" Leslie asks.

"Most of it—until I got punched out." I reconsider. "Well, maybe not most. Maybe less than most."

There is a long pause, during which we each chew a mouthful of food, then another.

"Why?" I ask.

"Just wondered. It seemed like you were pretty far gone. For awhile, you acted like a completely different person."

"I was drunk."

"Yes. I'm well aware of that."

"Don't you act differently when you're drunk?"

She shakes her head. "Well, I don't drink much. But no, not really. Not like that."

"What do you mean?"

"Nasty different. Cruel, even."

I am about to take a bite of pork, but I hesitate, studying her face. She doesn't look at me. Her eyes are on her food, but not in a way to suggest that she's avoiding me.

"Cruel?"

She looks up. "Yeah."

"Are you sure your work hasn't affected your attitude more than you think?" I mean this as a joke, but it comes out more bitterly than intended.

Leslie's eyes narrow, and her wry smile returns. "I knew what cruelty looked like before I became a lawyer."

"Well, I'm sorry if I did anything to offend you." I turn my attention back to pork. I'm dying to know what I did, but I don't want to ask. Another long silence passes, during which we finish most of our meal.

The silence finally gets to me. "Well, since we're being frank, do you mind if I ask you something?"

"Please do." It is a challenge more than an invitation.

"What happened to your parents?"

"They died."

I stab a piece of pork. "I know that much, but..."

"They were murdered."

I stop bringing my fork to my mouth. Leslie starts stacking dirty dishes, and it's as if the light has shifted in the room, as if the sun moved from the west window to the east. And I know that my opinion of Leslie Monday has been altered. I understand the rifle, and the hesitation to allow that wonderful, full mouth to curl into a smile. The cynical glint in her eye. The air feels suddenly warmer.

"I'm sorry."

She doesn't say anything, rising from her chair and carrying the dishes into the kitchen.

Now I feel horrible—I feel bad in the way a person does when they come face to face with the worst of human nature. I know this part of life exists, but it's not something I like to look at directly if I can avoid it. And as usual, when I do come up against it, I am lacking in the way of words. These aren't my specialty anyway— words. The moments when they seem to be needed most remind me of this. Instead, my body feels restless, like I should get up and throw something.

The water is running, and I decide to help with the dishes. I gather the strays and tiptoe into the kitchen, easing up to Leslie's side and setting the dishes on the counter. I scrape the food from the plates into the trash can, then grab a towel and start drying.

Dave lays in the corner, chomping on a cold hamburger, a full dish of water next to her.

"How long have you lived here?" The question feels weak, inadequate. But at least I've broken the silence.

"We grew up here," Leslie confirms. "Dad farmed this place. We used to have a little over four thousand acres."

"Really?" I rub the dishtowel in circles around a plate. "You must've owned my land then."

Leslie nods. "Arlene and I sold the farm in sections after they died. I lived off that to get through school."

"When did it happen?"

I expect this question to cause a moment of uncomfortable silence, but Leslie doesn't hesitate, as if she could tell me the exact number of days. "Eight years ago."

"You were twenty-one?"

She nods. "And you? When did you lose your father?"

"I was sixteen."

"And you were four when your mother died?"

"Yes."

She shakes her head. "Damn."

"There are times I feel lucky, in a twisted sort of way."

"Why?"

"When I hear people complaining about meeting their parents' expectations, or dealing with sick, incapacitated parents..." I pause. "It's sad. But you have to look for the positive, right?"

"That *is* twisted," Leslie says, the smile turning up one side of her mouth.

We finish the dishes, and Leslie makes coffee. Then we settle into opposing chairs in the living room, where we sit cross-legged, staring at anything but each other. Dave limps into the room, licking her chops. She lies at my feet, resting her chin on my boot.

After several sips of coffee, Leslie turns to me. "I have to ask you something."

"Shoot."

She rests her finger on her lower lip, staring through narrowed eyes. The hesitation seems uncomfortable for her.

"Did you sleep with my sister the other night?"

I laugh, an airy laugh, through my nose, and turn my head to one side.

"It's not funny."

"I think it is. You saw what kind of shape I was in."

"People have performed in worse condition."

"I find that very hard to imagine."

"I guess that means no, then."

"Of course it does. I slept in your parents' bed."

Leslie nods, a single nod. "Of course."

For a moment, I consider telling her about my budding impotence. "Why do you ask?"

"Well, I hate to bring it up, but Arlene is a very vulnerable woman. She's fragile."

"Who isn't?"

"I don't appreciate you ridiculing this situation."

I sigh, letting my chin fall to my chest. "I'm sorry. I didn't mean to ridicule. I was serious. I don't know many people who aren't vulnerable. Some hide it better, maybe."

"Of course there's some truth to that. I just want to make sure you don't play with my sister's emotions, if you know what I mean."

"Well, I wasn't planning on it, first of all...but it seems to me that Arlene is old enough to take care of herself."

"Under normal circumstances, I would agree with you." She frowns. "Maybe you ought to go."

This surprises me, coming as abruptly as it does. I don't respond, wondering whether she needs a moment to allow this feeling to pass. But she shows little indication of changing her mind.

"All right." I feel as if I should apologize for something, but I'm not sure what. So I stretch my aching legs, tipping Dave's head from my boot, and stand. Dave also rises and stretches, yawning. "Thanks a lot for a truly wonderful meal."

Leslie walks in measured steps toward the door. "Turned out pretty good, huh?"

"Sure did." I follow, and somehow, in the way that uncomfortable exchanges sometimes inspire, I feel closer to her. I've seen a slight crack in the rocky façade. I watch her walk—a smooth, rhythmic rotation. This is a mistake. She is wearing Levi's, which I love. By the time we reach the door, I want to kiss her. Or at least give her a hug.

But Leslie swings the door open, and her look does nothing to invite such a gesture. "See you soon," she says, without smiling.

I am both bothered and relieved to say goodbye and head out into the night, feeling the pain in my legs, along with the beginnings of an erection, the first I've had in months. Dave limps along beside me. It is a cloudy night. Moonless. Starless. And here we are. Two three-legged cripples, hobbling in absolute darkness.

Chapter Eight

The foundation is the most overlooked component of a house. It is also the most vital. If you use an inferior quality of concrete, or don't accurately measure the balance between cement and water, you risk having your foundation slowly disintegrate beneath you. If your house does not have a good foundation, not only is the place where you live out of balance, but so is your life.

Your House, Your Self
Chapter 3
"Building Support"

I had no idea that pouring a foundation would be such a complicated job. It's not as simple as dumping a bunch of concrete into a hole. I guess that's how I pictured it, if I ever thought about it at all. Instead, you have to build a framework. You have to create a structure within the hole—a series of walls that will mold the concrete in the shape required. It's like building a crude house within the hole.

So I've begun this job, forging ahead with a clumsy determination. I've learned many important things from this experience. First, it doesn't matter whether you buy the best gloves on the market—if your hands aren't used to swinging a hammer or pumping a saw, you *will* get blisters. I was out of commission for two days because of blisters. I would be the laughing-stock of a construction crew, taking time off for blisters.

Barry helps me on weekends, and has even come out a couple of evenings after supper. And as much as I value his strong back, I am even more grateful for his knowledge. His tips make each small task easier, saving time. After a week of countless mistakes, I'm happy to listen to his advice.

So it's been nine days since I started the pre-foundation. Seven days' hard labor, and two of convalescence. I've seen nothing of either Monday sister in these nine days. Nor have I ventured back to The Sportsman for another meeting with Clint. However, I did follow the instructions of Burt Mackie and visit the county courthouse. I asked for the forms for pre-specs, and the guy behind the counter looked at me as if I'd just ordered a cheeseburger. My sense of duty prompted me to explain exactly what I needed.

"I'm building a foundation, and I was told I need to submit forms for pre-specs. I haven't started pouring the foundation yet."

"Who told you that?"

"Burt Mackie."

The guy frowned. "Burt told you that?"

By then, I figured out what was going on, and I told him I was sorry to take up his time. But I asked Barry about it later, to make sure.

"Pre-specs?" Barry said. "I have no idea what the hell he's talking about."

I explained Burt Mackie's visit, and Barry made that hm sound that said, Ah, I understand. "Okay, well, Burt is a friend of..."

"Clint Weaver," I finished. "That's what I figured. So if I go ahead with this foundation, nobody's going to haul me to jail?"

"Not without breaking the law themselves."

So I PROCEED. I'm also getting used to the quiet out here. I live on a gravel road, about fifteen miles from Bozeman city limits. The trees shield me from almost any view of civilization, which was a huge factor in my choice of this particular tract. Through the branches, I can occasionally see the flickering of downtown. One of those lights belongs to The Sportsman.

I talk to Dave. I even read some evenings, wading through the pop psychology of Your House, Your Self to get to the good stuff, the useful information. Sometimes I haul a chair outside and sit in my hole, staring up at the massive Montana sky, with poor Dave hopping around the edge barking, wanting to join the fun. I lifted her down into the hole once, but after a brief trot around the perimeter, she wanted no part of being trapped.

On the ninth night, I'm on my way to Danielle and Barry's for a dinner date. It's Barry's birthday, and I'm happy not to have to prepare another solitary meal. I even shopped for a present—a new reel for Barry's fly rod. It's a nice one, according to the salesman. I wouldn't know the difference. But it looks fancy, with its graphite sheen and pearly handle.

Dave sits on the passenger side, staring out the window. She leans against the door, a trick she's learned after falling over one too many times on the curves. An inch of her tongue hangs dripping from between her teeth. Her dark eyes are half-closed but watchful.

It's beginning to feel like winter. Almost dark, although it's not yet six o'clock. The windshield threatens to mist over. It's a beautiful night, with all the stars out—even the shyest show their faces. The moon is half-full, a jack-o-lantern eye turned on its side. The heater hums on low.

Behind me, at a stoplight, another guy sits waiting with his dog next to him. They look like a couple that's been fighting. The guy keeps looking over at the dog, but the dog is ignoring him. He finally reaches over and scratches the dog's neck. At first, the dog continues to ignore him. But after he leans over and buries his nose in the dog's neck, the dog finally turns and licks his ear. It makes me laugh.

"Hungry?" I ask Dave.

She turns her head, smiling. She knows this word, and the promise of food that comes with it.

"I bet Danielle has some good stuff for you tonight. Not your basic Alpo."

Dave's tongue drops a couple of inches, with a slight waggle. A dollop of warm saliva falls to the seat. She slurps a couple of times.

"I bet the kids might even go out and play some Frisbee with you."

Dave's ears perk. Frisbee is another familiar word. Food and fun. What could be better? I envy Dave's state of mind. Especially when my body aches as it does now.

"Don't ever try to build your own house, Dave."

She looks away, back outside, as if this is the most absurd idea she's ever heard.

BARRY ANSWERS THE door, smiling like a kid. He's wearing a funny hat, a wool dome with a brown leather bill. The body of the hat

looks like a sheep—a big mound of wooly, off-white fluff. I bust
out laughing. Dave just stares. "What the hell is that?"

"Danielle found this in some used clothing store." Barry rests
his hand on the hat.

"It's beautiful."

"Don't you love it? I'm going to wear this thing every single
day." Barry grabs my hand, shaking it.

"Happy birthday." I hand him my gift, still in its shopping bag.
"Sorry it's not wrapped. My only option for wrapping paper was
an old sleeping bag."

"Ah, bullshit. You didn't have to get me nothing, much less wrap
it."

In the kitchen, the kids help set the table, chattering, bouncing
at the knees. Danielle bustles from counter to table to fridge. They
all wear green pointed party hats, covered with cartoon sheep. Gus
hands me one. Stevie grabs another and crouches, easing it onto
Dave's head. She sits with a look of paralyzed humiliation, but
only for a moment. With her single front leg, Dave can't reach up
and swipe something from her head without first lying down. So
she lowers herself to the floor, and reaches up with that single paw,
pushing the hat down her nose. Stevie tries to put it back on.

I start putting my own hat on, but the elastic breaks. "Why
don't you give me that one, Stevie," I tell him. "Mine broke."

"This one's for Dave," he insists.

"I don't think she wants it, buddy," Barry says as Dave paws her
head again.

"Aw, Dad." Stevie tries one last time, but she hasn't changed
her mind. Finally, Stevie, pouting, hands the hat over to me. It's
crumpled, but I don it proudly.

"What's on the menu?" I ask.

"The same thing we always have for Barry's birthday," Danielle
announces. "Ever since we got married."

"Some of us are happy with the simple life," Barry says without
the least hint of apology.

"What is it?" I ask.

"Beans and weenies!" Gus announces.

"Damn, Barry. Most people would go a little more upscale on
their big day."

Barry is still wearing the sheep on his head, as well as a grin.

"I'd rather have fun."

"Wait til you see the cake." Danielle and the boys bust out laughing, and the way they look at each other shows that if they had their way, they'd bring the cake out right then.

I'D SAY THAT the beans and weenies are the best I've ever tasted except that I've never noticed any variation in this delicacy. There are many jokes, as this is Barry's fortieth birthday. Barry shares his favorite birthday story, about Oliver Wendell Holmes' ninetieth birthday. Holmes' family threw a party, and when someone asked him how he felt about being ninety, he answered, "Well, I'd rather be sixty again." When the friend asked why, Holmes shouted, "Because I'm ninety!"

"I'm amazed I made it this far," Barry says.

"Oh stop it," Danielle says, but she's obviously more amused than annoyed.

"So what's your secret, Mr. Alderson?" I thrust my fist toward Barry's mouth, as if I'm holding a microphone.

Barry clears his throat, then dips his chin into his neck, leaning toward the mike, trying to look important. But he has a face that's impossible to take seriously. It's too round, too much like a kid's. The dimple burrows deep into his left cheek. Before he even speaks, the rest of us are laughing.

"The key to a long, happy life is...beans and weenies..." He holds up one finger. "Once a week, I bathe in beans and weenies. And at night—a bean and weenie facial." Barry touches his fingertips to his cheeks. "Before bed, bean and weenie incense while I meditate."

After dinner, we clear the table. While Barry makes a pot of coffee, the kids pile his presents in the middle of the table, staring at them as if they are their own. Even knowing what's inside each package doesn't curb their excitement. My brown paper bag looks like an uninvited guest in the midst of the colorful pile.

Danielle ducks into the pantry, where we hear the sound of a wooden match being struck, the ignition of flame. Gus bounces in his seat. And Danielle emerges, cradling a cake like none I've ever seen before. It is cut in the shape of something, but it's impossible to make out at first glance. It looks like a big lump of coconut. It's round, like an upside-down bowl.

Danielle kicks off the birthday song, but the kids are laughing too hard to sing. So Danielle and I warble through the song as she sets the cake in front of Barry. And it's then that I notice an addition to the cake, a sliver off to the side that is covered with chocolate frosting. I suddenly realize, looking at Barry, then at the cake, that the cake is a replica of the hideous sheep cap. It hits Barry at the same moment, and he cracks up, throwing his head back.

"Oh man, that's the ugliest thing I've ever seen," Barry shouts.

"Isn't it?" Danielle says.

"It's too ugly to eat," I add.

"No it's not," Barry argues. "No such thing as a cake that's too ugly to eat." He grabs the serving knife Danielle has provided and slices a huge piece, dropping it onto a plate. And he stuffs a bite into his mouth. "Mmmmmmm. Orange."

We pass the cake around, each cutting our own piece. The cake is delicious, complimented perfectly with coconut frosting and vanilla ice cream. And a cup of coffee completes the unorthodox birthday meal. I feel good. Happy. I can't remember the last time I've laughed this much.

We've just about finished our dessert when the phone rings. Danielle answers, and straightens up. After a brief reply, she covers the receiver.

"It's for you, Pete."

"Who is it?"

She pauses, looking down. "I don't know."

"Why don't you just tell him?" Barry asks.

"You should take it in the other room," Danielle answers.

My immediate thought is Charlie, and I don't want to talk to him. I almost tell Danielle this, but I don't want to ask her to lie. So I slink to the living room—thinking, thinking, but unable to think of what I want to say.

"Hello?"

"Hi Pete."

The voice is immediately familiar, and my heart falls to my heels.

"Simone?"

"Hi Pete."

"How are you?"

"I'm okay...things are tough."

"Are you all right?"

She doesn't answer right away, and I can hear sniffles. "I'm good, Pete. But I have to tell you something. My dad's cancer has metastasized. He's not going to be around much longer."

I bury my thumb and forefinger into my eyes. "Shit. What next?"

"I'm really sorry to have to tell you, but I didn't want you to hear it from someone else."

"I appreciate that."

Her breath comes more quickly. "Pete, do you think there's any chance of you coming back to see him?"

I close my eyes. "What would that be like for you?"

"That doesn't matter now...this is bigger than what happened to me."

"You're right. You're absolutely right. Do you think your father would be willing to see me?"

"Of course he would. Mom might be a different story, but you can't worry about what other people think right now...do what you think is right, okay?"

I choke back some unidentifiable feeling. "How long does he have?" But the line goes dead.

Chapter Nine

I hate to admit it, but the Red Sox wouldn't be the same team without Pete Hurley as their set-up man. He might be a jerk, but if you need someone to come into the game and baffle hitters for two innings, The Mechanik is your guy. I think I know how Red Sox fans must feel about Mariano Rivera. I hate this fucker.

Theyankeeyipper.com
Blog entry for June 15, 2004

Being in the middle of a major league baseball game is an experience that's hard to describe. You'd think that having thousands of people watching your every move would create a sense of self-consciousness that would make it difficult to concentrate. But it's just the opposite. Once I threw the first few pitches, I felt as if I had stepped into my own tiny creation. Although I could hear and see the crowd, the sense that really came alive was smell. The aromas of fresh grass, wet dirt, hot dogs, and leather would fill my nose and put a mute on all of my other senses. Each time I struck someone out, and the crowd either cheered or booed, the energy from those thousands of people swirled around me and became part of who I was. When I got into a rhythm, the batters became insignificant. Even the most feared hitters in the game didn't intimidate me. Holding that ball in my hand felt like the most natural thing in the world. The whole experience was like a spiritual IV. I sometimes got lost and couldn't step back into the real world after the game was over. It is the closest I've ever come to feeling like I have complete control.

For years, drinking prolonged this feeling. The crowd followed us to the bar, where we could continue to play the heroes. The fans paid for the privilege of being part of the story.

But it wasn't long before the alcohol worked against me. It's not unusual for a relief pitcher to be called on to work nearly every game, and there were many times that my previous night's activities interfered with my concentration. My body didn't recover as quickly. I started to lose the desire. I started to question whether it mattered. I watched some of these arrogant assholes who spent the whole game practicing their game face for the moment when the camera pointed in their direction. And I knew, as all the players did, that they didn't give a shit whether our team won or not. But the last two years with the Red Sox, we had almost no one like that on our team, and my love for the game was reenergized. We rode the hope that we might deliver the first World Series title that Boston had seen since 1912. When we won, I felt as if I would be happy from that point forward. I honestly believed that nothing could diminish that feeling of joy.

But every pitcher eventually learns that the feeling of control is an illusion, and in the time it takes a fastball to go from the pitcher's mound to home plate, I was proven wrong.

JUST AFTER MY baseball career ended, I went to visit the Watsons after not having seen them for months. I arrived with apprehension. It had been a rough few months, with my pitch to Juan Estrada's head played over and over on ESPN. It just so happened that the issue of trying to hit batters intentionally, especially in the head, had become a hot topic. The talking heads were all calling for new rules. Even though nobody was sure whether I threw at Juan Estrada on purpose, I became the poster boy for this movement. People recognized me on the street more than ever before.

I could no longer pitch. When I tried throwing, it was as if the tendons to my arm had torn loose. I never knew where the ball was going. I made Rick Ankiel look like Greg Maddux. Nobody would even get in the batter's box in practice. I tried a sports psychologist, a hypnotist, an acupuncturist. After two months, I told them I was done. I retired. If it hadn't been for that single pitch, my departure from baseball would have gone completely unnoticed. But it ended up being front page news, at least in the sports section. And there it was again, every day, it seemed—the replay. ESPN seemed to blare from every television in every bar I visited, and I spent a lot of time in bars.

SIMONE ANSWERED THE door, and it was the first moment that I saw her as something other than a kid. She was eighteen, and she welcomed me into the house with a gracious but cool handshake.

"Good to see you, stranger."

I dipped my head. "Hopefully, I won't be such a stranger now that I'm not..." I paused, not knowing quite how to describe what I'd just been through.

"Overwhelmed?" Simone suggested.

I smiled, unable to hide my pleasure at her assessment.

"Well, come in." She turned and started toward the family room. "Everyone's anxious to see you."

I was immediately struck by her manner. It didn't fit her age. She didn't giggle or act bored. She almost seemed too mature. She didn't seem to have any of the expected teenage insecurities. I was twenty-eight, but she acted more mature than I felt.

"What are your summer plans?" I asked.

She was very definite in her answer. "I'm going to do a lot of reading." We arrived in the living room, where Mr. and Mrs. Watson rose. "And I'll be concentrating on my lessons."

"Lessons?"

"Hello, Pete." Mr. and Mrs. Watson converged, with Mr. Watson taking my hand in a firm shake. "Good to see you. You're looking great...just great." Mr. Watson was a stocky man who battled his weight with a regimen of workouts and nutrition that was both impressive and baffling to me when I was young. He was an expert on diet long before it was fashionable. His success with the fight was always in direct proportion to how well his business was doing, to the point that it was a family joke.

"Business is good?" I asked, clapping his firm belly.

Mrs. Watson reached up and took my face in both hands, pulling me toward her so she could plant a kiss on my cheek. I wrapped an arm around her. She was a tiny woman, with piercing green eyes and a poise that always made me stand up straighter without thinking. Mrs. Watson's strong presence came from an unwavering conviction that she was always right. Her focus was often the glue that held the Watson family together, but her inflexibility could also be incredibly destructive. Once you got on her bad side, that was where you stayed. Even facts would not sway her opinion.

"It's good to be here." I surveyed the room. "You've done some remodeling."

"Yes." Mr. Watson planted his hands on his hips. He looked around as if he had to remind himself what they'd done. He settled into his easy chair. "How are you holding up?"

"I'm doing all right. Keeping busy."

"Good, good. That's the best thing. You can always find reasons to feel bad if you sit around too much, right?"

Simone rolled her eyes.

"What can I get you, Pete?" Mrs. Watson asked. "Coffee? Soda?"

After a half hour of small talk, I realized that I had been stealing glances at Simone since I walked in the house. But it wasn't her beauty that drew my eyes. It was this uncanny poise. She looked me square in the eye without a hint of flirtation or challenge. It was a look of complete, adult, serene curiosity. I was both impressed and unnerved.

"You said something about lessons."

"Yes. Violin," Simone answered.

"I didn't know you played the violin."

"I just started a few years ago."

"She's quite good for only playing so long," Mrs. Watson added.

I was hesitant to ask her to play, knowing how adolescents generally feel about being put on display.

"Would you like to hear what I'm working on?" She tilted her head to one side.

"Absolutely."

Simone disappeared into her room, and emerged with a well-worn black violin case. She carefully lifted the instrument from the case and prepared her bow. And then she played, and it was beautiful. Even an untrained ear like my own could tell that she was gifted. She played part of a Brahms concerto, and became completely absorbed in the music. Every movement of her body contributed to making the instrument sing. She swayed, and her long hair swayed with her. Her eyelids drifted shut, and her knees bent slightly, as if she was holding a morsel of effort in check. Her knees straightened just as the piece climaxed, and when her mouth formed a private smile, my face got flushed. A rush went through me. And I had the feeling that Simone would never need anyone the way that most of us need people.

I sit in my trailer, reading *Your House, Your Self.* Dave lies at my feet, dozing, her chin resting on my boot. A spot of saliva gathers on the toe. And I'm absorbed, gathering facts about pouring a concrete foundation, and embedding rebars and bolts in the concrete to anchor the frame. I'm fascinated by how much goes on under the surface of a building. It's not even accurate to say that I've taken this stuff for granted because I never knew it was there.

I've nearly finished the wooden frame. But it has been frigid for the past few days. I haven't been able to bear the sting of slamming a hammer against a nail. So I've been reading as much as I can remember reading. But it's still not enough to keep me distracted.

I realize that my greatest enemy right now is time alone, by myself, in a silent room. I have a desperate compulsion to escape the silence. Because it makes me too sad, being alone. Any silent moment that isn't active, and my mind sprints toward the sound and tenor of Simone's voice in the last phone call.

BEFORE I LEFT Amherst, I found it odd how many of my friends suggested ways to cure my sadness—quick fixes. Therapy. Medication. A new girlfriend. Exercise. Diets. Even grief retreats. Not a single person suggested that I get used to it. It didn't seem to occur to anyone that I might need to be sad for awhile. That it might make sense. That there are no short cuts through grief.

People became uncomfortable around me. I felt it from the time Dad died, and even more so after "the pitch." After Simone's accident, the discomfort became almost solid, as if I could wrap my arms around it and squeeze. It eventually made my decision to leave easy. I could tell that being around me had become a chore. I don't know whether my friends became afraid of my sadness, or of the fact that I became comfortable with it. I understood that people would be concerned that this sadness had taken up permanent residence in my heart. That I might become one of these people who are permanently wounded.

But I didn't want that, which is exactly why I came here.

Dave's eyes open, and she lifts her head. She approves.

Chapter Ten

*Budget is a concern whether you're shopping for
the best deal on applesauce or planning a trip to
Europe. But the quality of your tools and materials
affects your ability to do your job well. It can also
affect your attitude. A broken saw blade can ruin
not only a piece of plywood, but your whole day. If
you have the money to build a house, chances are
you have the money to build a quality house. Don't
cut corners if you can afford good quality. Think
long-term.*

Your House, Your Self
Chapter 4
"It's Not Immaterial"

Again it's best that I work and keep busy. I force myself outside
despite the icy cold. During these fall days, with their preview
of winter, Dave also prefers the warmth of the tiny trailer.

Outside, when my wooden-handled hammer hits the nail
squarely, it doesn't hurt. However, when I miss completely and the
hammer thunks against wood, the sting travels like a bullet through
my fingers, up my forearm, tickling my elbow like a bang on the
funny bone. But it is when the hammer head bounces slightly off
center that my arm goes numb. I have to stop and work my fingers
to get the blood flowing.

This cold front is supposed to pass before the weekend, and I
remind myself today is Thursday. Maybe I can pour concrete on
Saturday or Sunday.

I drive a nail—several clean blows, then a half-miss. My arm
tingles. My fingers loosen on the handle. Two more clean blows,
and the nail is buried. I look around at this odd framework of

plywood and two-by-fours, which really is like a small house. A sunken, roofless structure.

"Hello."

I jump. The silence of this place, except for the pounding of my hammer, is something I take for granted. I don't expect sounds, especially voices.

Burt Mackie is standing so close to the hole that the toe of one boot peeks over the edge.

"How you doin'?" he asks.

"All right...a bit chilly, but all right." I make no effort to crawl out of the hole. "What can I do for you?"

Burt takes a deep, important breath and strides around the edge of the hole for a few minutes. "Well, I just came by to see what you're up to."

I nod, tasting blood, worrying about the condition of the tip of my tongue.

"I understand you never did submit those specs we talked about."

"Yeah...you heard the whole story, did you?"

Burt frowns. "The whole story?"

"Never mind."

Burt clears his throat.

"I went by the offices...did they tell you that?"

Burt looks down at his feet. "Yeah, they said you gave them a pretty hard time down there. Not a very good way to get things done around here." He looks up, taking off his sunglasses. "You might want to rethink your strategy there."

"I'll take that under advisement."

Burt strides toward me. He stops just above me, standing over me like a kid pretending he's a gunfighter. I can almost picture one of those plastic holsters wrapped around his waist. "You need to shut this thing down until you get those specs submitted...or we're going to have to fine you."

"Really."

Burt just stares at me.

"Well, if that's the way it is, then that's the way it is," I say. "I'll go down there tomorrow. I'm about to shut down for the day anyway."

"Yeah, like now," Burt says.

I glare at him, and a part of me wants to hop out of this hole and bury a shoulder right in his chest. "Thanks for stopping by," I say instead. "I'm sure I'll see you again."

But Burt is not about to leave. He stands there for a few more minutes. I make all the right moves to show that I'm closing up shop for the day...gathering my tools, arranging things, throwing the debris into a pile. Finally, Burt seems satisfied that his work is done.

He walks toward his truck, saying, "See you soon" over his shoulder.

As soon as he has driven off, I pick up a big rock and throw it in his direction. This makes me feel better for a second or two. Then I start back to work. And not five minutes into it, I'm surprised yet again by a voice. This time I fall over.

Arlene stands at the edge of the hole, her hands buried deep in her pockets. I realize that this may be one of the few things the Monday sisters have in common—the way they stand. One hip slightly cocked. Her black hair is stuffed under a thick, striped wool stocking cap. Several shades of blue. She wears a brown suede coat, with fleece lining. Despite her dark complexion, her cheeks show spots of red.

"Sorry to scare you." She rubs her chin.

I roll to my knees, then stand and brush myself off. "You and your sister are good at that...guess I was distracted."

"That's good." Arlene smiles. "You must be enjoying this."

"I don't think 'enjoy' is the right word. But it's satisfying."

"I bet it is."

"How about some coffee?"

"No, no. Don't let me interrupt. I just haven't seen you for awhile."

I climb the makeshift ladder I've built to get in and out of my hole. "I'm ready to knock off for the day anyhow. It's too damn cold."

"Okay."

I crawl out stiffly, and Arlene follows me to the trailer, where I have to hold Dave back, despite her cries.

"Not enough room, girl," I tell Dave, rubbing her ears.

"Ohhhh...poor Dave." Arlene stoops and hugs Dave's neck.

"She'll be all right." I try to camouflage my guilt. I close the door, gesturing toward the sofa. "Have a seat."

Arlene sits, not sinking completely into the sofa, but propping herself on the front edge of the cushion. I take off my gloves and run some water in the sink, holding a finger under the flow until it's warm. I grab a bar of soap and scrub.

"So how's it going?" Arlene asks. "Are you going to pour your foundation soon?"

"Should be ready in a day or two." I dry my hands, then check my pot of coffee from lunch, making sure it's still hot. "How's school?"

Arlene has taken off her cap. She shakes out her hair, and starts adjusting it with her fingers—fluffing, pushing, pulling. She touches her chin. "I've been missing a lot of classes. I get so tired sometimes, from work and everything."

I nod as I take a seat in the only other comfortable chair. "I suppose it's hard, working and going to school."

"It is hard. I've actually been a little sick lately, too," Arlene says. I fill the first mug. "Yeah? The flu?"

"Actually, Pete, do you have tea? I don't really want any coffee."

"Oh, sure. It's just your basic Lipton, though."

"That's fine."

"More coffee for me."

Arlene smiles as I fill my teapot. "Actually, it's not the flu," she says.

"No?"

"Mm mm." Arlene shakes her head, touching her chin. "It's more like...um...nausea...in the morning."

"Hm. That's no fun." I settle in with my coffee. And a silence passes, during which Arlene shifts a few times. And finally, in one of those moments of passing from fairly blissful ignorance into instant understanding, I turn to Arlene.

"Nausea? In the morning?"

Arlene nods.

"Are you...?"

She looks shocked. "Oh no. I'm not pregnant. Jeez, no." She laughs nervously. "It did sound like that, didn't it?"

"Well, it did, yeah."

"Not, it's just a bug. A stomach virus or something."

"That's good...well, not good, but better than the alternative."

Arlene nods, then clears her throat. "Pete, do you mind if I ask you something?"

"Sure. Not at all."

Now she looks around my little trailer, as if she might wish she hadn't brought it up. "Just something I've been wondering about."

"Yeah, sure, Arlene. What is it?"

"Do you have a girlfriend?" She tilts her head shyly.

I clear my throat. "No. Hell no."

Arlene laughs. "Wow, are women that distasteful?"

I feel my face getting flushed. "I'm sorry; it's not that. I just... well, it's a long story."

"Do you remember kissing me the other night?" Arlene smiles.

"You mean the night I stayed at your house?"

Arlene nods hopefully.

"Jeez, Arlene, I don't remember much at all about that night. I'm sorry. I kissed you?"

She waves her hand. "I shouldn't have brought it up. I just thought..."

"Listen..." I take a deep breath, trying to think of how I can explain everything, but it's so much—years of explanation. "I moved here to try and clear my head about a lot of things, including that kind of stuff."

"You mean dating? Women?"

"Yeah."

Arlene takes a good hard look at me. Suddenly she's completely free of any nervous tics, any signs of insecurity or anxiety. "What happened to you, Pete?"

The tea kettle sings, and I pop back up and prepare her cup.

"Oh, you know...the usual. Boy meets girl. Boy paralyzes girl."

Arlene looks shocked for a moment, then gazes at the floor. She apparently decides I'm joking. "Well, I don't even know if you're interested..." She looks up. "I can't tell. But if you ever want to just have some dinner, or see a movie."

I hand Arlene her cup. She looks at me intently, and it's such a sweet, compassionate expression that I know I owe her more of an explanation.

"Arlene, I think you're just about as nice as a woman can be." I cradle my cup of coffee and sit. "It's just that I've been through some kind of private hell the past few years, and it's got me so messed up inside that I haven't even been able to think about dating."

Arlene nods. "I understand." She sets down her tea. "You know, you'd probably be surprised at how many people have been through similar stuff." She stands. "If you ever want to talk about it, you just let me know, okay?"

"You're taking off?"

She nods. "Yeah, I think it's best."

"Sorry I'm not better company." I stand as well.

"It's not you, Pete. It's that big old toxic pond you're dragging around behind you." She smiles and touches my cheek, a touch so kind and gentle that it makes my whole body start to tremble.

Thankfully, Arlene has already turned away, so she doesn't see this. "See you later, Pete."

Chapter Eleven

If a man's house is his castle, then it is also his winter chalet, his Swiss château, his split-level ranch, and his run-down shack. It all depends on his state of mind.

Your House, Your Self
Chapter 5
"The Life Inside"

Tonight, my house is a dungeon. My padded cell. My trailer feels like a cracker box, and a restless energy builds, boiling up until I feel as if I'm swelling out toward the walls. It's just a few hours since Burt made his second visit, and a half hour since Arlene touched my cheek. And I'm still shaken by that touch.

I jump in my truck, instructing Dave to make sure no one steals the trailer or fills the hole.

Despite many voices screaming at me to rethink my strategy, I pull up to the scene of my worst moments in my new home town and I climb from the cab with a blind, murky resolve.

Inside, Clint is on his usual stool—the big, fat owl sitting round-eyed and staring at me like I'm the mouse that he's ready to swoop down on and clutch in his talons. He has the dull, tired look of a man who doesn't even pretend to care about people any more.

Part of me feels like walking up to Clint and popping him right in the fucking nose. I stew on the visit from Burt Mackie, and Clint pounding on me, and feel as if I would be perfectly justified. It's why I'm here, of course. To confront the demon.

Instead, I take a deep breath and adopt a well-practiced businessman persona, one that took me years to perfect.

I sit down right next to Clint. "How's your drink? You ready for another?" I remember Arlene's assessment that Clint was on the wagon, and I study the liquid in his glass. It could be anything.

Clint gives me a bored look, and doesn't answer.

I order a ditch, and point to Clint's drink. The bartender nods.

"What are you doing here?" Clint asks.

"Oh, you know...just came by for the company."

Clint snorts.

"Listen, Clint. I don't want trouble. Not today, not in this bar, not in this town."

"So?"

"So what's it going to take to put an end to this little feud we seem to be starting?"

"What the fuck are you talking about?"

I laugh through my nose. "Well, where should I start? My battered body? Burt Mackie?"

"I guess they grow 'em paranoid back east, don't they?"

"Yeah." I nod with a forced, teeth-clenched smile, and I swallow the inclination to give him the reaction he's looking for. I think about how many times in the past couple of years I have looked for this kind of fight, just hoping to feel something. "So tell me, Clint...what advice would you have for someone in my position, someone who's learning the construction business, someone new in town."

"Well, I'd start by telling him he should try not to piss off the wrong people."

"That's damn good advice, Clint."

Clint sighs, and his eyes lock on mine, somehow giving the impression that he's looking down at me. "Why are you such a smartass? When it's the last thing in the world you should be. You know what kind of problems I can cause for you?"

"I don't know why, Clint. I really don't."

"I'm trying to think of a good reason for even listening to what you have to say, Hurley."

"Well, you've got a point there, don't you? I obviously need you more than you need me."

He looks annoyed again, and I have to wonder whether he's offended that I would state the obvious, or if he thinks I'm just being a smartass again. The longer I sit here, the more I realize that I have almost no leverage in this situation. I drain my ditch, which brings a warmth, first to my throat, then to my stomach, and finally to my head. I signal for another.

"Let me make you a deal," I say, not even sure yet what I'm about to propose.

Clint looks off in the other direction.

"You don't give me any grief on my house. I'll stay out of this place. I'll never come back."

Clint turns to the front, still not looking at me, and raises one brow. "You call that a deal?"

"Come on. Work with me here. You got a better idea?"

Clint shakes his head. "Man, you're desperate, aren't you?"

"Desperate? Hell no. I don't have to stay here. I could move somewhere else tomorrow if I wanted. I'm just trying to make life a little easier for both of us."

Clint plants a dull gaze on me. "I can't think of one good reason..." he says.

I listen, anticipating the end of this thought. But it soon becomes clear that this was the end.

"For what?"

"For talking to you."

"How about common courtesy?"

"You're one to talk about that."

"What the fuck is that supposed to mean?"

Clint just sits, drinking.

"All right," I say. "Let's just say I still have a lot to learn. I'm willing to accept that. But what's the point of throwing oil on the fire? Can't we..."

"Shut up, Hurley. Jesus, you're full of shit."

"*I'm* full of shit?"

Clint raises his brow, smiling. "Your friends haven't told you that?"

I shake my head, partly out of disbelief. "No, I guess they decided to keep me in the dark on that one."

"Well, they're not very good friends then."

"Or maybe they just know me better than you do."

"Or maybe you just don't have any friends."

"And you do?" I feel ridiculous about resorting to such juvenile banter.

"I got more friends right now...today...than you've had in your life."

"Yeah, and I'm sure not a single one of them is just sucking up to you because it's to their benefit."

"That's right."

"They all love you for your charming personality."

"At least I have one."

I almost feel like saying, "Same to you, but more of it," and the thought brings a smile to my face. Clint's expression draws an immediate shadow.

"That's funny?"

I shake my head, a tired motion that nearly takes all the energy I have. "Nothing about you is funny to me."

Just about the time that I feel the tension growing, about the time that Clint's eyes get narrow, and his body tenses, I decide to step back.

"Listen, Clint...I don't know what I did to invite this kind of attitude from you, but I'm sorry. Honestly. I moved here to get away from this kind of bullshit."

"Yeah?" Now he's got that smirk on his face, as if he knows he's got me backed into a corner.

"If there's anything I can do to make things right, just let me know. I'm just trying to mind my own business here." I hold my hands out as if he's pointing a gun at me. I take another step back.

"You really are a paranoid son-of-a-bitch, aren't you, Hurley?"

"Whatever you say."

But I can see the wheels turning. Maybe Clint isn't used to having someone tell him the truth straight out.

"You just think about it," I finally say, and I turn to leave.

"I got a question for you, Hurley!" Clint calls out. I stop and look at him.

"Did you hit that guy on purpose?" he asks.

I turn. "What do *you* think?"

Chapter Twelve

*I don't care what anyone else says. I don't care what
the investigation reveals; that was not an accident.*

Tony Kornheiser
Pardon the Interruption
September 28, 2005

M ost of America didn't learn the story of Juan Estrada's life until
after my fastball ended his baseball career. But once the story
emerged, it became part of the lore. Juan was one of the thousands
of young ballplayers who had made their way to America from
the depths of poverty in the Dominican Republic, with dreams of
playing the great game, achieving fame and fortune, and becoming
a national hero like my old teammates Pedro Martinez and David
Ortiz.

He was a second baseman, and an excellent fielder, making
acrobatic plays that brought comparisons to Roberto Alomar. He
also showed promise at the plate, a gap-to-gap hitter with speed
who led the minors in doubles and triples each of the five years he
played there, waiting for his chance to hit The Show.

His chance came the year before our encounter, when they
had the end-of-year call-ups. Juan didn't play all that much, with
Robinson Cano showing even more promise at the plate. But Juan
hit .289, and stole nine bases before the year ended. People started
to notice. There was talk that if he kept it up, the Yankees might be
able to use him as trade bait for another good pitcher.

The next year, he was called up in the middle of the season when
Cano got injured. Estrada had an immediate impact with his flashy
infield play and his incredible speed. He became a fan favorite.

When my fastball crushed the bone around his eye, reporters focused on the story of the young Latin phenom and the tired white veteran reliever, and the contrast created a wonderful storyline—it had everything—race, class—boy from the depths of poverty versus the trust-fund kid, and of course, the decades-long rivalry between the Red Sox versus Yankees. It was the kind of story that wouldn't have garnered much attention, but the call for a new rule, before someone got killed, kept the story very much alive. Especially when the sportswriters jumped on the bandwagon of turning this incident into a campaign to change the rule about throwing at a batter intentionally. ESPN couldn't get enough.

I HAVE TO PUT OFF pouring the foundation until Barry is available to help. I'm looking forward to some time alone with him. But he's been busy with work.

So the next Saturday morning, I do a little housecleaning. And although the job only takes an hour—one of the things I love about my new home—I notice more than ever a missing element. I have gone without music, and at times like this I miss it. So I make a run to Bozeman, to an electronics shop I've noticed in my travels. I take Dave, planning to stop by Danielle's afterward.

Big Head Electronics is a tight little place, obviously a Bozeman institution, crowded with dial- and knob-covered black and silver boxes. The saleswoman is young, with deliberately bad hair, and holes in her jeans, and hardware attached to various parts of her face. I'm skeptical about her qualifications, but she knows her stuff. When I tell her what I'm looking for, she makes a quick, decisive recommendation. After a brief listen, I approve of her choice, and she even tells me where I can buy CDs around the corner. I'm so impressed with her professionalism that when I leave, I shake her hand, feeling guilty about my initial judgment.

I proceed to the music store, where I choose quickly, buying several classical discs, Wilco's latest, some Radiohead, a couple of Buffalo Tom CDs, and for mellow occasions, Bill Evans. Next to the counter, I notice a stack of newspapers, and on the front page, down in the left hand corner, is a picture of me. I pick up the paper, and see that next to my picture is a picture of Clint Weaver. The headline reads, "Weaver Tangles with Troubled Former Red Sox Pitcher."

"Christ," I mutter, tossing the paper back on the stack without reading the article. This has become the adjective most associated with my name. Troubled. I can't begin to guess how many times I've heard this in the past few years.

Throwing the CDs in the front seat, I acknowledge Dave with a wave. She answers with a hearty bark, and we're off. The rain smears the features of my new town, and the clouds hang low and dark. At Danielle and Barry's, I lead Dave to the backyard where several of her toys are gathered. She snatches a Tupperware bowl that she will chew and fling until its shape is yet again altered. Simplicity. Dave is the queen.

No one answers the bell, which puzzles me considering both vehicles are in the driveway. I try the door, which is unlocked. I shout a hello. When there's no answer, I make my way through the living room. Finally, I hear slow, heavy footsteps on the stairs. Standing at the bottom of the double stairs, I watch Barry's stockinged feet round the bend.

"Did I wake you up?" I ask, but when I see Barry's face, I sense that I've interrupted something more than a nap. Barry's expression is unsettling, considering his usual cheerfulness.

"What's wrong?"

Before Barry can answer, Danielle descends behind him, her footsteps quicker, more purposeful. But she wears much the same expression.

I feel a panic. "Where are the kids?"

"At the neighbors'." There is no inflection in Barry's voice.

"We need to talk." Danielle pushes past Barry, who shows no offense at her aggressiveness.

"We do?"

"Yes," Danielle answers. "I don't know why you're here, but it happens to be good timing." She pushes past me, into the kitchen. "I'll make some coffee."

Barry finally reaches the bottom of the stairs, looking as if he'd rather be on an Arctic expedition. Neither he nor Danielle has looked at me.

I follow Barry to the kitchen, where we slump into chairs while Danielle makes coffee. The Bozeman paper sits on the table, my picture staring back at me. None of us speak for many long minutes while the coffee brews. As Danielle pours the coffee, I hear the toilet flush upstairs, then footsteps above us, and down the stairs.

"Somebody's here?"

Danielle sets steaming mugs in front of us and sits, and before either of them answer, Leslie appears, her expression equally grave.

"Is Arlene okay?" I ask.

Barry can't suppress a deep sigh.

"She's fine," Leslie answers.

I look around at three sets of eyes that are diverted from mine. "So what's going on?"

Barry shakes his head, eyes still down.

I study their expressions, waiting for clues. Barry has a look of dread. Leslie's full lips roll inside her mouth. Her eyes are narrow, focused. Danielle appears more concerned than anything. She clears her throat, and her eyes lift, almost visibly moving closer together. She starts to speak, but hesitates.

"We're...we're worried," she finally says.

"About what?"

"About you, of course." Leslie speaks with her usual authority, pointing at the newspaper.

"I'm sorry, but I don't understand why you're even here," I say to Leslie.

"Because I care about you," she answers without a moment's hesitation. "Jesus, you act like we don't have any reason to be concerned."

"You don't."

Leslie gives me a puzzled look.

"What?" I ask. "What does that mean?"

Danielle takes a step toward me. "Pete, considering what you've been through the last few years, it's easy to understand that you might be..." She falters, pursing her lips.

"Might be what?" I ask, and now I'm starting to feel some anger seep in. I'm annoyed that they seem to think I'm so fragile that they have to speak to me carefully, as if a simple phrase might break me in half. "I want to know what you think I am."

"You seem a bit lost, Pete," Leslie says, and for once I don't find her self-assurance admirable.

"How would you know this?" I ask. "I don't want to be rude, but I really don't understand why you're here. Did you come here to talk about me?"

"Yes."

I'm disarmed—again—by her frankness. For some reason, I expect something different.

"And if you were worried about me, why would you talk to these guys instead of me?"

"Hold on, Pete." Barry's voice slides like a canoe into the waves of anger. The water slows to a ripple, but does not settle completely. Leslie and I stare each other down. Her cheeks shine red.

"Just calm down," Barry adds.

I turn to Barry, and see an expression I've never seen from him. It is direct and firm. His chin is low. He peers through his eyebrows. And this look does calm me. I feel my shoulders drop a few inches.

"You need to hear us out," Barry says. "Just sit down and listen for a sec."

I remember few times in my life when my mind has been so completely blank that it stands still. But looking at Barry now, his expression so grave, it feels as if his eyes have acted as a vacuum, sucking all thoughts from my head. My face must tell a similar story, as blank as a freshly-painted wall. I have no thought of defending myself. I have no questions. No answers. I feel a mental, physical, and emotional exhaustion.

Barry hasn't averted his gaze, but his voice softens. "Pete, we don't want you to think we're being critical."

"No, that's right," Danielle jumps in nervously. "Barry's absolutely right, Pete."

"Let me finish, sweetheart...please." Barry's direct, serious gaze now quiets Danielle just as it did me. I've never seen this before, either. He turns back to me, and I see his mind working. "This is the most important thing, Pete. We want you to know that we're not judging you. But we also want you to know that..." And the words are lost. He keeps the steady look, but his mouth clamps shut, in apparent frustration at trying to arrange the thoughts in his head.

But Danielle can't contain herself. "We're concerned...that's mainly what it is. We care about you, and we're concerned."

"Yes," Barry confirms. "But it's not that simple."

"Yes it is," Danielle says. "It is too that simple."

Barry rolls his eyes.

Danielle turns to me. "It is that simple."

"If I could interrupt, I think Barry has a point." Leslie steps forward.

"Oh?" Danielle turns to Leslie as if she forgot she was there.

"Yeah." Leslie nods. "I don't want to interfere, but besides being concerned, aren't we also frustrated...maybe even angry?"

Danielle's eyes jump to mine, then back to Leslie.

"That's right," Barry says. "That's what I was trying to get to."

"Yes, well, I suppose..." Danielle says.

I listen, and a part of my brain is telling me, "Hey, they're talking about you. They're saying these things right to your face. Say something, for Christ's sake."

But there is another, calmer voice that listens to the conversation with detached wonder and amusement. A childlike attentiveness. Because they are talking about me as if I am a child. Like parents sometimes talk about their children as if they're not standing right in front of them.

I don't care whether their anger is justified. But how has my behavior made them this angry, this concerned?

"Pete...have you ever thought about your drinking?" Leslie asks.

"Now let's not get into that," Barry says emphatically. "This isn't..."

"Why not?" Leslie replies.

"My drinking?"

"That's not what we're here to talk about," Barry says.

"But it's a huge part of it," Leslie says.

"What does my drinking have to do with anything?"

"It has everything to do with it," Leslie says.

"Now wait a sec." Danielle steps in. "Don't exaggerate."

"I don't think I am," Leslie offers.

"Well, I do," Barry replies.

"You don't think his drinking has led to these other problems?" Leslie points at the newspaper again.

"What problems?" I can't believe what I'm hearing. "I'm just trying to build a house. These other things just happened. They aren't problems. These are things that just happened...things that happen to everyone."

"Everyone?" Leslie points at me. "That's the problem."

"What?" My curiosity gives way to a slow but steadily rising indignation.

"Responsibility," Leslie answers.

"Wait a sec." Barry jumps in. "A minute ago you said it was his drinking, and now..."

"But that's really it." Danielle's palm strikes the table. "Taking responsibility."

"Part of it," Leslie agrees.

"You know nothing about me," I tell Leslie. "And why is this any of your business?"

"You're my neighbor...and my friend," Leslie says. "That makes this my business."

This leaves me speechless for a moment. She considers me a friend?

Danielle walks behind me, resting her hands on my shoulder. I start to feel some resignation.

Barry twists in his chair, facing me. "The point is, you came out here to get your life in order, to sort through things...right?" But before I can respond. "Instead, you're created more problems. And whether your drinking is the cause or not, you need to figure out a way to address these things. That's the point." He turns to Danielle, then Leslie. "Isn't it? Have I summed it up to your satisfaction?"

"Don't be sarcastic, Barry," Danielle scolds.

"Well, Christ..." Barry's head jerks with the force of this exclamation. "We've spent more time arguing with each other than we have telling Pete here what we..."

"I'm sorry," Leslie interjects. "I'm mostly to blame for that, I think."

"Well hell," Barry says. "I don't know if we have to blame anybody."

The sentence fades, and then no one seems to have anything to say. Heads drop, and it gives me a moment to reflect, and to realize how cornered I feel.

The silence is a long one. And for those sluggish, silent minutes, I experience the unsettling sensation that everything in my life has happened at once. That there's been no chronology to it. The indifference of before is replaced by the extreme opposite. All the joys and disappointments have just happened, and I feel the effect of it all. I'm riding in the hearse, with my mother's casket behind me, trying to get my father to tell me where we're going. I hear my father's girlfriend screaming after she wakes up next to his cold corpse. I watch a fastball sail from the tips of my fingers toward the skull of Juan Estrada. And I see Charlie, shaking me awake from a roaring drunk, telling me that Simone is hurt, and that I'm responsible. All of it has just happened.

"So what is it that you're suggesting?"

And there's another long silence.

Finally, Leslie looks at me from across the table. "You really don't know?"

"I don't."

"What do you think you should do?" she asks.

"I don't have a clue...I still don't see this the way you do, obviously."

"So what's the problem?" Leslie asks.

"There isn't a problem. It's like I said before...these things happened. It's just timing. It's not as if I came out here looking for ways to create more problems for myself."

Leslie persisted. "But don't you see—you were drinking when all these things happened."

"I was in a bar," I argue. "I was in a goddamn bar. Of course I was drinking. Drinking is the only thing that gives me any relief from all this stuff!"

"I don't understand what's happening," Barry says.

"What is happening?" Danielle echoes.

"I don't know, but this is ridiculous." It's all I can do to stay in the room. I want to storm out.

"Denial is what's happening." Leslie is so certain in this statement that I feel an urge to beat her down with words. My anger frightens me.

"Denial is not what's happening," I say.

"You're fooling yourselves. Maybe I should leave," Leslie says.

"Wait a sec," Danielle says. "We need to discuss this. Nobody should be storming out of here."

"What's there to discuss?" I ask. "This woman has decided to barge into our lives and pass her judgments about me, and about you..." I point to Danielle. "She's telling me that I don't know how to deal with my problems, even though I've managed pretty well for the past thirty-two years; she's telling you that you're in denial. You guys have never even mentioned any of this stuff, and all of a sudden, because the savior here..."

"I'm trying to help." Leslie's voice rises. "I thought we were all trying to help."

"You have strange notions about helping."

"I'm sorry," Leslie says. "But I think you're letting your feelings for Pete get in the way, and it's very frustrating."

"You don't know me." I start toward her. "Stop acting like you know me. You don't."

Barry steps between us again, putting a hand on my chest.

"I know enough," Leslie insists.

"How can you know enough to make these wild accusations?"

"Because I've seen too many men like you."

"That's enough," Danielle says. "That's uncalled for."

"How can you pretend to know so much about me?"

"I'm not pretending."

"Okay." Barry eases me toward the corner of the kitchen. Leslie follows him.

"I still think I should leave," Leslie says.

"No, I'll leave," I offer. "I'm the one who wasn't invited." I start for the door.

"Pete," Barry says, and Danielle simultaneously calls "Wait!"

But I slam the door, rushing out into a light rain. I bunch my jacket around my ears, dodging puddles on my dash to the truck. I waste no time, not even checking to see whether any of them are following. I drive, reckless, sliding around corners, so angry my face feels feverish. Despite the cool damp air, sweat gathers inside my shirt, running down my torso.

And I drive, thinking of the chilling assurance in Leslie's face, and of how much I would have liked to crack that expression, with the right words, or a slap. I've never hit a woman in my life, but for the first time, I can comprehend the feeling that fuels that kind of anger. I drive, and I'm lucky I don't slide off the slick road. I know I'm driving too fast. The wipers beat across the windshield, brushing the misty rain to the sides.

And I'm nearly home before I realize I have to turn back. I've forgotten Dave.

Chapter Thirteen

*Even if you're living alone, make sure and design
your house to provide space for two people to get
some time away from each other. This may be one
of the leading causes of divorce.*

Your House, Your Self
Chapter 10
"All You Need is Loft"

I slam the door of my pickup, rushing to Danielle and Barry's
back yard. I want to retrieve Dave quickly, without facing my
sister or her husband. I imagine that they're still angry, and I don't
want a fight. I definitely don't want to see Leslie again.

But Dave is gone. The yard is empty.

I pound on the back door. But I don't wait for an answer. I burst
in, shouting before it's even open. "Where the hell is Dave?"

Danielle and Barry sit at the table, looking stunned, tired, as
if they've just returned from a long vacation. There's no sign of
Leslie.

"Where's Dave?" I repeat.

They don't respond, looking at me as if I'm speaking Japanese.

"What do you mean?" Danielle asks.

"Dave's gone."

"Gone?" Barry stands.

I pace. I pace. I pace. "Shit. She's got her. She left? Leslie?"

Barry nods. "Right after you did. She probably just noticed that
you forgot Dave. She's probably returning her."

"I've got to go." I head for the door.

"I'll go with you," Barry offers.

"Yes," Danielle says. "Take Barry."

"What, do you think I'm going to do something stupid?"

They drop their heads, but Danielle quickly recovers. "No, but it would be good to have him along, just so you..."

"...don't do something stupid," I finish. I pace. "You're probably right."

"I'll throw on some clothes." Barry climbs the stairs.

"It's starting to rain, honey," Danielle shouts.

"Okay," he answers from the stairs.

Danielle and I are quiet for a moment.

"Don't worry, Pete. I can't believe you have a thing to worry about."

"I'm sorry, but that's the most useless piece of advice I can imagine right now."

Danielle studies me from the side of her eyes, with apprehension. She's careful about what she says, cautious in her movements, which bothers me. I have never felt like a big person. I don't know whether other big men experience this, but I'm so used to seeing the world from up high that I'm not aware of my size. I usually feel inconspicuous, although at six feet five, I know I'm not. When I see group pictures, I'm always surprised how much I tower over people. So it's always disconcerting when someone is afraid of me.

"You want to come, too?" I ask. I'm still pacing. I ball my hands into fists, shoving them in my pockets, pulling them out, working my fingers. I clench my neck, trying to massage the knot from my muscles.

"No, no," Danielle says. "The four of us together would be a very bad idea right now."

Barry finally lumbers down, buttoning his flannel shirt. He pulls a rain jacket and a purple wool baseball cap from the coat closet.

"All right." He gives me a look of work to be done.

"Be careful," Danielle says, and Barry's answer overlaps, anticipating the question. "We will."

THE DRIVEWAY TO the Monday house is long, winding—a gravel path to a cluster of buildings tucked behind a shelter belt—a wall of cottonwood and poplar trees strategically planted to block the bitter winds whipping in from the eastern plains.

The buildings tell a story, a story I already know in part. The huge barn, the silo, and the complex maze of chutes and corrals suggest a busy past—a time when hundreds of livestock lumbered across the lush pastures surrounding this place, livestock bearing the Monday brand, which now only serves as a symbol in fading white paint on the side of the barn. A flying M.

The house also indicates that the Mondays were good ranchers. It's not particularly large, but it's solid, well-designed, not something that was thrown together without thought. It was built to last, a place where a couple who loved this ranch expected to spend the rest of their lives.

But the house is the only thing that's not in a state of disrepair. And even it needs a coat of paint. One side of the corral has collapsed. A quarter of the shingles have fallen from the roof of the barn. The silo is badly rusted.

We slide to a stop in the gravel driveway, and my eagerness to find Dave is muted by the sadness of this old ranch, especially knowing what I do about the Mondays. I remember that I've been meaning to find out more about the murders.

Barry's hand grips my forearm.

"Are you okay?"

I jerk my arm away. "Jesus, everyone's treating me like a bottle of nitro." I climb from the cab.

"I just don't want you getting into any more trouble," Barry says. "I know you're pissed, but there's probably an explanation."

"Let's go." I stride toward the house, and Barry rushes to catch up, then pulls slightly ahead. He gets to the door first and knocks. I ring the doorbell, and Barry smiles.

He adopts a bumpkin look, sticking his front teeth out. "You city folks sure are smart, figuring out these newfangled gadgets."

And despite everything, despite the anger coursing through me, Barry manages once again to make me laugh. It's in the midst of this chuckle that the door opens, and Leslie appears. Her boyish face shows no surprise, but when she sees my expression, she frowns.

My smile fades. "Where's Dave?"

She tilts her head, and her eyes go skyward, as if trying to remember.

"This is not amusing," I say.

Her eyes drop, boring into me. "Oh? Someone seemed to think so just a minute ago."

Barry moves between us again, although there's a screen door. "Is it possible for you two to act civil just long enough to get through this conversation?"

There's a long pause, and Leslie and I pin matching glares on each other, like pre-bout boxers, itching to get back to our corners, where we can shed our robes and start bobbing, weaving, punching the air, waiting for the bell.

"Look, we know you have her," Barry says. "Now let's just settle this so we can get on with things."

"I have a condition." Leslie doesn't avert her eyes.

I keep mine locked as well, trying to convey how much I despise her at the moment. "You what?"

"I have one condition."

I turn my back to the door, take a deep breath, and swing my head around until I'm looking at her again. "Bullshit. You want to risk your legal license just to make some ridiculous point? This is *illegal!*"

"I'm not worried about that right now."

I throw my arms in the air. "What did someone do to you?"

"Why is it so hard to imagine that I might actually be this angry at *you*?"

"Stop!" Barry shouts, with a ferocity that shocks us both into silence. "For Christ's sake." He takes a deep breath, trying to blow the color from his face. "Are you two sure you weren't married in a previous life? Good God, for the sake of decency, please try to talk to each other with a little respect."

Neither of us speaks. I know I can't. She has my dog. Leslie appears to share this attitude. Her expression hasn't softened. There may be no possibility of the rational discourse Barry has requested. The patter of rain beats against our coats and our baseball caps.

"Tell her to give me my dog."

Barry nods, then turns to Leslie, staring at her, transferring the message telepathically. Leslie frowns as if she's trying to decipher his thought patterns. She lifts her chin into a proud, unyielding point.

"He has to meet my condition."

"You're kidding," I mutter. "You've got to be kidding me."

"What's the condition?" Barry asks.

"Go for one month without a drink," Leslie says. "You promise to go thirty days without a drop of booze, I'll give you your dog back."

"Are you joking? You think I'm going to wait a month for my dog? You think I'd make that kind of..."

"You don't have to wait a month. I'll give her to you now. You just have to promise."

I reconsider, puzzled. It's a ridiculous request. "All right." I nod. "You've got yourself a deal."

Leslie looks satisfied, in her understated way. She disappears, and I wonder whether I've overestimated her intelligence.

"What's she thinking?" I ask Barry.

He drops his eyes.

"There's no way in hell..."

Barry shakes his head. "You got me."

When Dave appears, she's in a state of joy I've only seen a few times, where her tail wags so furiously that she keeps losing her balance. Her front paw hops from side to side, trying to keep up with her shifting torso. Her tongue hangs nearly to the floor, and she barks—two crisp, loud exclamations.

I gather her into my arms, and turn to leave. I don't thank Leslie. I don't repeat my promise. I want to give her every indication that I hope to never see her again.

"See you," Barry says behind me.

There's no answer, and I feel the hot glare searing a hole in my back as I walk away. I press my face into Dave's precious brindle coat.

Chapter Fourteen

*The poetry that is baseball was interrupted by an
ugly exclamation point this week. For years, the
league has danced around the issue of the payback
pitch, and it will continue to be a black eye on the
sport, until either someone gets killed or those in
power finally step in and alter the rhythm of the
game.*

Roger Angell
The New Yorker
September 20, 2005

In the months following the pitch that just about killed Juan
Estrada, the Red Sox did everything they could to revive my
career. The psychologist pumped me full of positive affirmations
and suggestions for getting past the flashbacks that were starting to
find their way into my dreams. He referred me to a PTSD specialist,
but I had a hard time putting what happened to me in the same
category as a rape victim, or a war veteran. I couldn't take her
seriously.

But the main person who tried to help was the Red Sox pitching
coach, a man that I had never gotten along with very well to begin
with. His approach to this situation didn't change that. He was old
school, and thought the psychologist was a waste of time. "You
just gotta pitch your way through it," he told me time after time.
"It's all in your head."

I considered pointing out to him that if it was in my head, the
psychologist might actually make sense, but I knew this was a
waste of time.

ESPN followed the story as if it was of national importance.
There were many who believed that I hit Estrada on purpose
because Pettitte had hit Varitek earlier in the game. I knew better.

But I think my arm rebelled against every effort to save me. Every time I planted my toe on that rubber, completed my windup, and went into my throwing motion, the baseball would spin off my fingers like a child's top. I never knew where it was going. My efforts made Wakefield's pitches look as straight as a baseline.

After six weeks, the Red Sox released me, which was such a relief that I drank myself into oblivion every night. The people in the bars in Boston funded my escape, and provided an occasional bed for the night. But it all felt empty. When I was playing, sleeping with women felt like an extension of the game, a way to prolong the glory, which also became empty in its own way. But now it felt like an offer of condolence. An act of pity. It wasn't long until my other performance became a problem. Even those little blue pills didn't help. Another problem that was in my head, which was getting very crowded.

MEANWHILE, SIMONE's accomplishments as a musician surprised no one. Mrs. Watson worried about her not having any friends because she was always practicing. But from the time she started playing violin, it was obvious that getting chosen for the cheerleading squad or catching the eye of the boy behind her in history class were not among Simone's concerns. She dreamed of playing with Yo Yo Ma. She spent her summers in music camps at Tanglewood and practiced without being reminded.

Simone applied to Juilliard, and to no other schools. And she was accepted, receiving a scholarship.

The summer after Simone's junior year at Juilliard, she came home for a month. It had been less than a year since the Red Sox released me, and I was still a mess, drinking pretty much every night. Simone returned on a Saturday, and I joined the Watsons for dinner. From the moment we sat down, I noticed a difference in her. She was nervous, talkative. Although she was much thinner, she barely ate. But what struck me most was an almost desperate need for assurance. After each statement she made, Simone would turn to one of us and raise a brow, as if waiting for a nod, or a verbal confirmation. This loss of confidence disturbed me. Considering that it was her first time away from home, and that she was living in New York, I had to wonder about drugs. Although I never did them myself, I'd been around them enough to know the signs.

Simone got up to use the restroom, and when I got up to do the same after I heard her come out of the bathroom, we met in the hallway.

"Pete, I'm so glad I have a chance to talk to you. What are you doing tomorrow night?" She grabbed my forearm, both hands wrapping around it like a vice.

"Hmm...I don't think I have anything going on. What's up?"

"I need your help with something. I'll buy you dinner if you give me a hand."

"Okay. What is it?"

"Just this thing," she said. "It won't take long."

"Sure," I agreed, despite the fact that something about the exchange made me uncomfortable.

THE NEXT EVENING, we went out for greasy hamburgers, but Simone realized she'd forgotten to bring any money when the time came to pay the bill. After I paid, she suggested we go for a walk in a nearby park. Simone was talkative, fueling my suspicions. But she talked mostly about Juilliard.

"It's frightening, Pete. Everyone is so fucking good." She had grown. She was now about five-eight, and willowy. Her hair hung straight, halfway down her back, chestnut, parted on one side. It swept across her head in a dramatic wave that she flipped from her face from time to time. As we rounded the park in the lingering dusk, she didn't simply walk. Her body evoked the emotion of whatever topic she was discussing—coiling, weaving, dancing. Just like the first time I saw her play the violin.

"Everyone at Juilliard was the best musician in their city, or even their state. So we all come in there expecting to blow everybody away, and nobody does, Pete. Except for maybe two people, we're all the same level, and it's fucking scary, because we know that only a few of us will make it, you know."

I walked with my hands pocketed, head down, comparing her experience to my first year in the minor leagues. It still amazes me sometimes that I made it to the majors, I was such a nervous wreck those first few years in pro ball. "What do you mean by make it?"

"Make a living, you know. Everyone wants to get the chance to play the big halls. We all come thinking this is where it's going to start...that we're going to be discovered and that it's just a matter of time before we're recording, or making guest appearances with the New York Philharmonic."

"There's this wall there, Pete...in one of the buildings, in the hallway...this wall with the pictures of all the famous alumni. All these incredible names, incredible musicians. You can always spot the new students because they'll stand in that hallway, gawking at these pictures. And they always look embarrassed, and try to act like they weren't staring. But we've all done it. We've all hoped for a few minutes alone in that hallway to stare at these heroes and dream about having our picture up there."

I smile to myself, thinking about my first game with the Red Sox, when I stared at one of those self-same walls, at pictures of Babe Ruth, Ted Williams, Carl Yastrzemski, Jim Rice and Carlton Fisk. "And why shouldn't you?"

"Because, Pete, that's just it..." She turned toward me, and made fists with both hands, shaking them at me as if she'd beat the realization into me if she had to. "There are something like fifty pictures on that wall. Maybe sixty. And each year, there's about two hundred new students. And the school has been there for more than a hundred years. That's one every other year, Pete. One prima donna every other year. It's fucking scary."

I laughed, which prompted a sudden turn from Simone. "It's not funny, Pete. It scares the hell out of me."

"I'm sorry. I'm not laughing at that. I've just never heard you swear so much. You used to be so refined."

Now she laughed. "Oh my God. You don't know me very well. You probably still see me as a kid."

We walked for a very long time, although it was mostly Simone that talked. She obviously needed to vent, so I kept my thoughts to myself. As the evening ended, and I dropped Simone off, she sat on the passenger side, her hand on the door handle.

"I've talked your ear off. I hardly asked you a single question."

"Yeah...well, next time will be my turn."

"Yes. I want to hear about you." She looked sideways at me, pushing her hair from her face with the back of her hand. "I've heard all the rumors about you, you know."

"What, you expect me to sit on my hands?"

"Yeah, right. A famous guy like you. You've probably got groupies hanging all over you wherever you go."

I felt myself blushing. "Don't believe everything you read." As I looked over at her, wondering whether we were leading up to something we probably shouldn't even consider, something occurred to me. "Hey, what was it you needed help with?"

Simone frowned.

"The reason you asked me to come with you tonight, remember?"

"Oh, yeah." She waved a hand. "It worked out."

"So we went out for no reason?"

She thought. "Yes."

And we both laughed. During the course of the evening, I had tried to ignore the overwhelming physical attraction I felt for this woman. But it had gotten stronger as the hours passed. And as it became more evident that she didn't want to go inside any more than I wanted her to, we reached a crucial moment.

"So what are you doing tomorrow night?" she asked.

I sighed. "Simone, we really shouldn't."

She leaned slightly toward me. "And why is that?"

"Oh come on. Your parents would be so pissed."

"You think so?"

"You know they would."

Simone looked down at her hands. "Do you want to kiss me, Pete?"

"No."

"Oh, you're such a liar."

"I am not. I'm not lying."

"Okay, why don't you want to kiss me?"

"Because you're hideous."

She slapped my arm.

"Really, Simone. I think you should probably go."

But she didn't. Instead, she reached over and touched my wrist. She unbuttoned my sleeve, and ran her fingertips along the inside of my forearm.

From that first touch, there was a chemical reaction, and what ensued was a combination of exhilaration and danger that I've never experienced before or since. I took Simone back to my place, and for the first time in a long time, I was a wreck about being alone with a woman. We raced to the bedroom, but once we got there, and started tearing off our clothes, I started to have a difficult time breathing.

Simone took my face in her hands. "Are you okay?"

"I'm kind of a mess."

"Maybe we should slow down."

I agreed and we lay on the bed and held each other for awhile.

"What's wrong?" Simone finally asked.

"My little guy has been rebelling lately." She rubbed the front of my jeans. "Damn teenagers."

"I know...they have a mind of their own."

While we lay quietly for awhile, kissing and touching all over, Simone rolled over and stretched her lithe body over mine, aligning our limbs, although her feet came to my mid-calf. The feel of her whole body against mine had a profound effect on me. I felt both captured and engulfed. And in a slow, deliberate manipulation, she brought me to life in a way that I hadn't experienced in months. Probably years.

For the next four weeks, Simone and I couldn't be apart for more than a few hours. There was nothing calm or comfortable about it. It was a hunger. Like junkies. Skin junkies. We couldn't get enough kissing, touching, tasting, licking, skin to skin. I just assumed that when she returned to New York, the affair would end.

But in the meantime, we crept around like two teenagers, agreeing that her family shouldn't know. I said nothing about the future, not even the immediate future. But just a few days before her departure, I lay on the bed, studying some financial reports.

"You're going to have to come and visit me." Simone had just climbed from the shower, the water glistening on her slender body. After all these weeks, I still couldn't stop looking at her.

I acted cool. "Yeah, I guess I will."

"Well, don't feel obligated." Simone swiveled into the bedroom, still naked, water glistening down the middle of her back.

"Don't start," I said. "You know I'm kidding."

But her movements were stiff, tight, and she didn't speak as she dressed.

"What's wrong?" I asked.

"Nothing." She pulled her pantyhose over her hips, rocking from foot to foot.

I tried focusing on the papers, but I retained nothing. "Are you worried about going back?"

"No." She twisted her black pleated skirt, straightened it, and fastened the hooks.

"Simone, come on. What is it?"

She put on her bra, then a white cotton blouse. She adjusted her clothes, pulling at her skirt, tugging her sleeves. And she sank to the bed, her back to me. "I don't want to go back."

I touched her shoulder, but when she stiffened, I pulled my hand away.

"I know I have to go back," she said, as if to herself. "I've worked too hard."

"That's right."

"But I don't want to."

I touched her shoulder again. This time she didn't resist. "You can handle it."

She looked down, studying her palms. She stared at them, and touched the calluses on the fingertips of her left hand. "I just don't know if it's what I want anymore."

Chapter Fifteen

The bedroom is usually associated with passion. But it is also the room where the average person spends more hours in a day than any other room in the house. So while your living room should reflect the image you want to present to the rest of the world, your bedroom should be a direct reflection of who you are. It should be a room you're anxious to see each night. It should provide the heartbeat of your house.

Your House, Your Self
Chapter 7
"A Heartbeat, It's a Love Beat!"

The first couple of weekends in New York were perfect. Simone and I stayed in a hotel near Lincoln Center, and we did the city the way it should be done, eating in great restaurants, attending Broadway plays, walking through Central Park.

Simone was still apprehensive about school, but feeling better now that classes had started. She was playing well. This improved her mood. These two weeks were the first time that there was a sense of something brewing. Something long-term.

The third weekend we decided on a break, so that she could practice, and I could get caught up on some business obligations. The following weekend we met in Boston. We hung out in Harvard Square, saw "Sweet Smell of Success" at the Brattle, and drank lattés.

It was the following weekend that the strain began. That Saturday night, we attended the Metropolitan Opera, and went to an Indian restaurant afterward. Simone was quiet, distant, even petulant. She picked at her daal, letting spoonfuls plop onto her plate. I tried carrying the conversation, hoping that my forced cheerfulness would convince her to tell me what was on her mind. When it didn't, I finally asked.

She sighed. "I don't know, Pete. I really don't."

"Did I do something?"

"No. Nothing at all. It has nothing to do with you."

"School?"

She pulled her mouth to one side. "School's about the same."

I chewed a bite of lamb, wiping the corner of my mouth. Our waiter, who was overly attentive, asked if everything was okay.

"Yes, fine," I answered impatiently. He bowed.

"Just start talking," I suggested. "It might trigger something."

Simone frowned. Her hair was back, held with a silver comb, which she plucked from its anchor. She pushed the heavy side from her eyes. "I don't feel like talking, Pete." She didn't look at me.

So we didn't. Outside the restaurant, a couple of Yankee fans recognized me and asked me what the hell I was doing in New York. I had become accustomed to this, but it always bothered Simone. When we got back to her place, while I wordlessly prepared for bed, Simone ducked into the bathroom and came out dressed in a flannel nightgown. She'd never worn anything to bed before.

She lay down with her back to me and tucked under the covers, and I got the message. It was a long night, where we both slept fitfully. I put my arm around her at one point, and she snuggled up against me. I got aroused, and she reached around and gently took me in her hand and stroked.

We made love and were finally able to sleep, but something was missing. She wasn't present. It was almost clinical.

We talked on the phone on Monday, but we didn't discuss anything meaningful. And then came this: "Pete, I don't think you should come down this weekend."

"Oh?"

"I think it would be better if I had some time to myself, to sort through some things."

"You haven't had enough time to yourself this week?"

"No, I haven't. I've been practicing a lot with my quartet. Almost every night. I told you that."

"That's the only reason?"

A heavy sigh. "Pete, come on. Don't get silly on me."

"Hey, I don't know what else to think. You're not giving me

anything to go on."

"I told you I can't figure it out."

"Well, are you unhappy with the way things are going?"

She didn't answer right away. "I don't know."

"Oh, come on."

"I really don't, Pete."

"So you think pulling away will help?"

"I don't know that either."

"Well, I don't think it will."

There was a long silence, and as seconds passed, I convinced myself that Simone was going to change her mind.

"So what do you say?"

"What about you? Are you so sure about all this?"

"Yes," I answered.

"Are you so sure about me?"

"Are you kidding? I haven't been able to spend more than two weeks with anyone for the past ten years."

Another silence. "That's nice."

"So I'm coming down."

"I don't think you should, Pete. I'm really sorry."

This time, I was the silent one.

"I really am sorry," she said again.

"So is there someone else?"

"Pete, dammit, would you knock it off with that. I wouldn't have time for anyone else even if I was interested."

"Well, let me come down and be there for you. That's my job, right?"

"No. I don't want things to be that way, where I'm leaning on you—on anybody."

I thought about this. "All right. That makes sense—honestly. So how about next weekend?"

"I don't know. Maybe I'll come up there. But I'm not sure."

"If that's the best you can do."

"Don't fucking guilt trip me, Pete."

"I'm sorry. I'm pissed. I want to see you."

"All right," she said after another pause. "Okay. Next weekend for sure."

Day five. The longest five days in memory. I sit in my trailer, my copy of *My House, My Self* lying open on my lap. I haven't read a word in the two hours I've been sitting here. Or maybe I have read a word or two, but I haven't retained a one of them. It's still raining, as it has for the past five days. Dave sleeps on the floor, her chin resting on my stockinged foot.

I hate Leslie Monday. The first thing I did after retrieving Dave was crack a beer. I drank it with what I thought was a defiant zeal. But a cloud of guilt has hung over me in the five days since, as if I've crumpled up some sacred pact and ground it under my heel. When I reach for a beer, I expect it to burn to the touch. Aside from that one beer, I haven't touched a drop in five days, and it's been torture.

Every time Dave looks at me, I feel as if she's expressing her disappointment. As if Leslie has somehow managed to inject her scrutiny into Dave's soul. I can't look her in the eye. If not for the rain, she'd be outside.

The phone rings. After two weeks without one, running to town to call Danielle or find a tool or to simply hear another voice, I surrendered and bought a cell phone. The first ring is a welcome interruption.

It's Danielle. "How's it going?"

I wonder whether Barry has told her about my agreement with Leslie. "Good. Tired of the rain, though. Getting a little bored."

"Well, that's exactly why I called. Come over for dinner tonight."

"Great."

This is Danielle's peace offering. We learned from Dad that forgiveness is always easier when you don't draw attention to it. A new baseball. An ice cream cone. A knuckled rub to the head. I never heard the words "I'm sorry" come from my father's lips.

On my way back to my chair, I'm under Dave's watchful eye again. Although her expression is drowsy, the scrutiny remains.

"I know." I hold out my hands, showing that they're empty. Her head drops to her paw.

I sink into my chair, and Dave's head returns to my foot. I pick up my book, and realize that it's open to the chapter on roofing. I've held it for two hours without noticing. I flip back to the chapter on foundations. And I'm able to start reading. And once I get past the Dr. Phil bullshit, I realize that the book describes the most basic things, such as how to mix concrete. How to smooth it once it's poured. The things I need to know.

The phone again. I swear. Dave lifts her head.

"Hello, Pete." At first, I think it's Leslie, and a twinge of anger rises in my chest. "This is Arlene."

"Oh, hello. How's it going?"

"I'm okay. You?"

"Fine," I answer with forced gusto. "How did you get my number?"

"Oh, I called your sister…I hope that's all right."

"Sure. What's up? Is something wrong?"

"No no, I was just wondering if I could come over for a while."

I NOTICE SOMETHING different the moment Arlene enters. She moves with a wide-eyed assurance, settling on the sofa. No sign of her tics. She doesn't touch her chin, or adjust anything.

"Something to drink? A beer?"

"Absolutely."

As I retrieve a beer for her and a Pepsi for myself, I watch from the corner of my eye to see whether she's spying on me. But Arlene picks up a magazine and studies the cover.

"All I have is cans…sorry." I hand her a Budweiser, along with a glass.

"That's okay. I like it in cans." And to prove the point, she sets the glass down, flips the tab, and takes a healthy swig.

"How's school?" I sit, opening my Pepsi. I can't take my eyes off the red, white and blue Bud can in her hand.

"All right."

"Good." I nod.

She pauses, glancing out the window for a moment. When her eyes turn back to me, it looks as though she's taken this time to rejuvenate her confidence. "I'm doing great." She says this so enthusiastically that I don't believe her.

I take a big swig of Pepsi. "So what's up?"

"Oh, nothing." She tips her beer. "I figured this rainy weather might be kind of boring since you can't work on your house."

"Well, thanks for thinking of me. I've been trying to keep myself occupied—mostly reading." I point to my book.

Arlene picks up *My House, My Self* and studies it. "This looks good, for what you're doing, anyway."

"It is good."

Arlene sets the book on the coffee table. "Have you thought more about what we talked about the other night?"

"Oh, I guess I've thought about it."

"So do you want to go into town—maybe catch a movie, or have a drink?"

I forget Danielle's invitation for a moment, and I hesitate, considering the offer. But there is a quiet but firm voice in my head telling me it's really not a good idea.

"My sister invited me for dinner, actually. But how about another time?"

Arlene sits up. "I have to work tomorrow night. But what about Thursday?"

"This is Tuesday?"

She laughs. "Yes. Must be nice, not having to keep track."

"Sounds good."

Arlene drinks from her beer. "That'll be fun."

I'm amazed how much more assured she seems. She holds my eyes, narrowing her lids, studying me, then burrowing into me with her eyes. She rests her chin in her palm. She's getting to me, and I have to look away.

"Listen, Arlene. I was serious about what I told you the other day."

"How serious?"

"I moved out here to get some things straightened out. And part of my agreement with myself was that I wouldn't get involved until I get my house built."

"Involved?"

"Yeah. You know what I mean. No sex. Nothing."

Arlene sighs with a sad resignation. She lowers her eyes for a moment. I notice what an unusual green they are—like fresh grapes. And I'm struck again by how many stark contrasts exist between her and Leslie. She looks up.

"I know what it's like to not want to talk about something," she says.

I shoot her a brief glance, just enough to acknowledge this statement. And despite my discomfort, I feel a stirring somewhere, a desire that I don't expect. Beneath all the pain and the guilt, the confusion and the fear, a small voice pipes in with a quiet suggestion. "Why don't you tell her what happened?"

"I'm sorry," I finally say. "I need to get ready...I need to leave soon."

Arlene, in her typical fashion, makes no effort to hide her disappointment. "Are you sure?"

"'fraid so."

After sitting in silence for another minute, Arlene stands, setting the half-finished beer on the coffee table. "Let's forget about Thursday," she says.

"I'm sorry," I say.

"Don't make more of it than it is," she says. "I'm a big girl."

Chapter Sixteen

*There is no longer a valid argument for not enacting
the Pete Hurley rule. It's time to protect these hitters
from permanent injury or death. It's long overdue.*

John Saunders
The Sports Reporters
October 30, 2006

Danielle greets me with a warm hug.

"I'm sorry I was so out of control the other day," I say.

She looks uncomfortable, but says, "Don't worry about it," before returning to the kitchen.

Barry emerges and grips my right hand, wrapping his arm around my shoulders. "How goes the race?" he asks.

"Ah, the rats are still ahead, but I'm picking up ground."

"Something to drink?"

"Soda?" I say.

"Pop?" Barry translates into Montana-ese, making for the kitchen. "One sody pop coming right up. Coke's all right?"

"Fine."

The scramble of kids' feet rumbles above us, in their upstairs bedroom, a squeal, and shouting. Then a resolution, and normal volume. I admire the simplicity of their conflicts—over and done within a matter of seconds.

Barry returns, proudly bearing two towering glasses of Coke, ice singing. I've never seen Barry drink a Coke. But after handing me mine, he sinks into the opposite chair and drinks with a sigh that suggests that it's the very essence of his life. Better than beans and weenies.

"So what you been up to?"

"Not enough. Sick of this rain."

Barry glances outside. "Ah...well, we can sure use it." It's the predictable response of a Montana native, whether the climate has any bearing on his profession or not. The inbred awareness, passed from generation to generation, that moisture is always good. The memory of every drought, and the fear of another, inspires an idolatrous worship of gray skies.

"How's work?" I ask.

"Busy." Barry nods. Again, this answer accentuates the positive. Not a burden, or a spell he hopes will end. "Very busy."

"Good."

"You guys hungry?" Danielle yells from the kitchen.

Barry jumps to his feet. "Oh yeah."

THE DINNER IS WONDERFUL—an obscene supply of ribs from a place nearby. The conversation remains safely rooted, avoiding anything that might provoke any unpleasantness. Until we're almost finished.

"I heard Clint's going to file a bunch of building code violations against you," Barry says.

"So much for making peace, huh?"

"Thought it would be better to hear it from me."

I nod. "You know any specifics?"

Barry shakes his head. "I'm sure they'll dig up something—probably a bunch of piddly shit."

"It's just a fucking hole, for Christ's sake."

Barry sighs. "Where there's a will..."

Danielle puts down her fork. "Did you decide whether you're going back to see Mr. Watson?"

I shake my head.

WHEN I LEAVE DANIELLE and Barry's, the rain has stopped—finally. The air is pure, the sky clear black—pockmarked with fierce little stars. The mention of the code violations has me discouraged. The thought of going back to my trailer is like being buried alive.

I'll go to a club, I decide. Not for a drink. Just for the atmosphere—some noise, the approximation of people, a reminder that I once had close friends.

I drive in the opposite direction along Main Street, west of town, where I find a tidy little bar, a dump—just the kind of place that will render me inconspicuous—The Kit Kat Klub.

At a corner table, I take in the tavernesque aroma—stale, musty cigarette beer air. It feels familiar and homey, and after ordering a soda with lime, drinking that in two gulps, listening to Patsy Cline's "Sweet Dreams" and Hank Williams warble "Your Cold, Cold Heart," I follow the natural progression and order a boilermaker. Then another. And a third. And on and on and on.

And as I sink into the melancholy of intoxication, feeling my muscles go limp and my mind molding into a jellied mass of convoluted memories—events and faces mash together in a plot I can't follow any more. I've lost my place in my own goddam story.

When I met Simone at Logan International, she barely responded to my embrace, kissing me quickly on the cheek. I chose to ignore the obvious signals.

"Tired?" I asked.

"A little."

"Hungry?"

"I could eat."

I handed her the helmet I'd bought her that summer.

She wore a maroon beret, and her hair was down, flowing out from under that colorful pool of fabric like an auburn splash. She frowned at the helmet. "You're on your bike?"

"I thought you liked my bike."

Her mouth pulled to one side. "It's not that I don't like it." She looked away. "I'm sorry. I'm just being a brat." She grabbed the helmet. "I don't want to mess up my hair."

I worked hard to convince myself that this was just a small irritation. We'd make our way past this, like strolling by a street evangelist.

When we climbed onto the bike, it was almost like the first time I gave Simone a ride, when she gripped my shirt like a cat. This time, she swung her leg over, but somehow managed to sit behind me without touching me. Once we were moving, she settled against me, but I felt the resistance in every muscle.

It was a cool evening, just enough that the wind numbed my

face. I took a sharp curve, and her arms gripped tighter. But she loosened her hold as we came out of the turn. I took each curve a little faster, until her body was plastered against mine like a blanket by the time we reached her favorite restaurant.

Simone climbed off, handed me her helmet without looking at me, replaced her beret, and marched into the restaurant.

We ate Italian. I had pasta primavera. Simone ate almost nothing, moving her gnocchi like chess pieces around her plate.

"So how's your quartet coming along?"

"About the same."

"You seem a lot happier about being back in New York."

She hummed.

"Well, you do. You didn't even want to go back. But now you're practicing almost every night. You seem to be enjoying it."

She agreed, but it appeared to be a mere concession. "I think I am a little more comfortable this year."

My efforts to nudge the conversation forward met the same disinterest—glances to the side, no inflection in her voice. She asked me nothing. I finally decided to enjoy my meal, and I did so in silence while she ignored both me and her gnocchi.

But after I was done, I put down my fork. "So what the hell is going on?" I asked in a hushed tone.

She gave me a weary look, then glanced away. "Let's go somewhere else."

"Why not here? Let's get this over with."

"Pete, don't start. Let's go to your place." She took her napkin from her lap, dropped it on top of her food, and left. A few other patrons glanced over discretely, then turned away. I paid the bill.

Simone was sitting on my bike, helmet in place.

"Well, that was pleasant," I said. "A nice quiet meal with the woman I love. Good food, good conversation."

I climbed on my bike, trying to avoid her. I heard a disgusted sigh from behind.

"What? You didn't have a nice time?" I asked over my shoulder. But I started the rattling Harley engine, intentionally drowning out her reply.

I had always been a cautious driver whenever I had a passenger. But that night, I pushed my driving abilities to their limits. I angled each curve until our knees nearly touched the pavement.

And I accelerated down the straightaways until the wind felt like ice against my face. Simone hit me, smacking her fist against my helmet after a particularly sharp turn. I sped up.

When we got to my place, Simone started pounding on my back. She was crying, yelling, calling me a bastard, a son of a bitch. I jumped off the bike, and it nearly toppled as she continued throwing punches.

"Stop it!" I shouted, trying to balance the bike while warding off her blows.

But she didn't stop. I managed to stabilize the bike, but not without being pummeled. I was glad I was wearing my helmet. I backed away, and Simone collapsed onto the saddle, burying her face in her hands.

I left her there. The energy from the ride was still coursing through me. Anger. Confusion. Fear. All intensified by a cold wind that had tightened the skin on my face. I sat, trying to calm myself, afraid of what would happen when, or if, Simone came inside. I'd reached the point where I hoped that she would simply disappear.

But Simone entered a few minutes later, closing the door as if she didn't want to wake me. When she realized I was right there, she stopped. She dropped the helmet on the couch. She faced me, and stood still for a moment, glaring. She took off her coat. Her eyes didn't leave me. They were red, and spectacularly sad, and there was moisture on her cheeks. She pouted, her lower lip dipping toward her chin.

She let her coat fall, still looking straight at me. I half-expected her to break into a Carole Lombard impersonation—telling me what a big lunk I am, and that I should just take a hike, for crying out loud.

Instead, she reached up with one hand and undid the top button of her blouse. Her eyes didn't move. Her hand dropped two inches to the next button, brushing the fabric lightly. She undid that one, then the next, and the next. Then she reached across her torso and undid the buttons on each sleeve. And she did that little move that is so sexy, pulling her arms behind her back and giving a small shrug. The blouse fell from her shoulders, sliding down her arms, down her back, splashing to the floor in a pool of white cotton.

She stood this way, looking at me, not smiling, not speaking. I became unbearably aroused, but I didn't know what to make of this act. Was it an invitation to our old passion, or a cruel extension of the past two weeks of torment? I didn't know whether to collapse at her feet, burying my face in her crotch or gather her in my arms and toss her out into the cold night air. But when she pulled her bra straps down to her elbows, I dove.

Looking back on this moment, I'm embarrassed at how quickly I was willing to forget the previous two weeks and push aside the lingering uncertainty of our relationship. Although part of me suspected that this was only a temporary delay, I surrendered without the least thought of not surrendering. I fell to my knees. I pressed my face against the seam of her black stretch pants. I lost my breath, and made no fight to get it back. I was willing to suffocate.

Simone's hands gripped the back of my head, clenching my hair. I licked, my tongue cramping as I ran it up and down the seam as hard and fast as I could. I tasted her. And she pulled me harder against the pelvic bone, her fingers gripping my hair and holding tight. She bucked, and climaxed, groaning, as if in complete agony. Her knees buckled. And as she pulled my skull against her, I heard a snap, and felt a sharp pain, and realized that my nose was bleeding. Blood ran down my lip, and I tasted it as it mingled with her juices. And still I did not stop. Didn't even think about it.

WHEN WE WOKE up the next morning, Simone rolled over toward me and laid a hand on my chest. "I'm sorry," she said.

"Me too...I shouldn't have driven like that."

"You really scared me."

I nodded.

She got out of bed and dressed.

We spent most of the day walking around Amherst, shopping, snacking. Simone took pictures. Although the mood was awkward, it was not an awful day. That afternoon, we sat under the big willow tree in Emily Dickinson's yard, talking about anything but what was on our minds. She was affectionate all day, touching, kissing me. My nose hurt like hell, and I fingered it now and then. There were purple smears under each eye, which made Simone smile when she saw them that morning. "Pain and pleasure," she said. "The essence of life."

"So..." I picked at the grass. "Did you get my card?"

"Yeah. I got it."

And too much silence followed. I wanted to say "And?" or "So?" I wanted to say something. No. What I really wanted was for her to say something. Anything. "You made a fool of yourself." Or "Nobody ever said such nice things about me." "I never want to see you again." "I'm totally in love with you."

Simone kept her head down. She chewed the inside of her lip, pulling her mouth far to one side. After watching her, searching for some sign that she might speak, I looked away. The little window of sky that was visible beneath the low-hanging willow branches had just started turning dark. The same blue as slightly worn Levi's.

Finally, she spoke. "I really don't know what to say. I feel cornered...I don't think I can give you what you expect."

"I don't expect anything."

Simone sighed and frowned. "Pete, I do love you." It was the first time she'd said this for two weeks, but it gave me no satisfaction. "But if I want to become as good as I should be, I need to devote everything to my music...for now. I just have to."

"All right."

"What do you mean, all right?"

"All right. What do you expect me to say?"

She looked up, with a baffled smile. "You're just giving up?"

"You're the one who gave up. You brought me back to life these last couple of months, Simone. You need to think about what that means. We've cultivated something, and it deserves some time."

Simone sighed, and dropped her head.

"You helped create this. You were there."

But as I tried to make this point, I could see from Simone's expression that whatever we had that summer was gone. Whether the music was to blame didn't matter. The feeling was gone, and Simone had passed over to a place I remembered and knew I would never revisit—that youthful deception that finding someone who loves you as much as you love them is easy. That it happens all the time.

"Things change," she said.

"All right. Let's go."

"What?"

"Come on. I'm taking you home."

"You don't want to talk?"

I stood. "What's left to talk about, Simone? You've made up your mind."

Simone considered this. Her face lost the ironic little smirk.

"All right." She rolled to her knees, then stood, and didn't hesitate. "Let's go." And as we walked toward my bike, from behind me. "I'm sorry."

I kept walking, but I could hear that she'd stopped. "Why are you acting this way?"

"Why didn't you tell me this two weeks ago? You had to put me through two weeks of bullshit first?"

"Pete, stop. Let's talk."

I ignored her and kept walking. I walked until I reached my bike, which I mounted. I pulled on my helmet. I started the bike and warmed the engine, not checking to see whether she was coming. But I felt her weight. Her arms circled me, a motion stiff and cold.

"Don't get crazy," she shouted.

And I didn't. I drove her home at normal speed, slowing on the corners.

I felt Simone's hands against my side, even through my leather jacket.

I pulled into the driveway, and Simone climbed from the bike and faced me. "I'm sorry," she said.

I drove to my favorite bar. And I drank. And I drank. And I drank.

It's morning...another morning after a night I don't remember. My eyes open very, very slowly, then the left one closes. Through the single winking eye, I see that the sun has indeed risen. I pull myself up by my elbow. My head pounds. My mouth has dried like an apricot. Dave is not on the bed next to me. I check the floor. She's not there either. I call her name, but there's no stirring from anywhere in the trailer. I must have been so drunk that I left her outside for the night. I sit up and pull the curtains aside. My land stretches out before me in a beautiful panorama of greens, browns, and blues. The rain has stopped. The clouds are gone. Dave is also gone.

Chapter Seventeen

If you look at a house as a body, then the plumbing is the veins, the wiring the nerve center. Bad plumbing can kill a house, rotting it slowly from the inside. If you don't know what's going on with your body, you call a doctor. If you don't know how to install plumbing or electrical wiring, you need to call someone who does know.

Your House, Your Self
Chapter 7
"The Body Electric"

When I realize that Dave is gone, I leap from my bed, pull on my clothes, down a massive glass of apple juice, and run to my truck.

The Monday house is not all that far from my own as the crow flies. But the road is a winding gravel snake. I'm all over the road, and off it, into the ditch and out again. My tires spit gravel in every direction, showering my pickup's underbelly. By the time I swing into the Monday driveway, my jaw is clenched so tightly that my teeth hurt.

I hit the ground stalking, arms bent at my sides. I pound on the front door. After several long minutes and repeated knocking, Arlene answers. She was obviously sleeping, and is surprised to see me. I study her, and decide she has no idea why I'm here.

"Morning, Pete." She blinks. I see that my expression scares her, and as always, this bothers me. "You're up early. What time is it?"

It takes everything I have to be civil. I concentrate on softening my gaze, taking a deep breath in through my nose. "Sorry to bother you, Arlene, but...um...is your sister here?"

Her jaw freezes, open an inch, for a silent moment. "Uh, yeah.

But I'm pretty sure she's still asleep." She pauses, clearly waiting for me to offer to come back later. Finally, she opens the door. "Come on in."

I'm tempted to stay outside, to walk around and burn up some angry energy. But I step inside, fists deep in my pockets.

Leslie appears some minutes later—rumpled, puffy-eyed. She is also surprised to see me. Arlene follows her, stops, and leans against the wall.

"Is something wrong?" Leslie asks.

"Where's Dave?"

"Dave?" Leslie gives a small shrug, then looks at Arlene, and Leslie is either a brilliant actress or she really doesn't know. "She's gone?"

"You don't know?"

"Why would I?"

I start to answer this question, but I stop myself, realizing that I was just about to reveal that I got drunk. "Where is she?"

"Honestly, Pete. I haven't a clue." Her expression is one of concern, with no hint of either guilt or triumph.

"Why would Leslie know where she is?" Arlene steps away from the wall, uncrossing her arms.

Her question is greeted with a brief silence, during which Leslie and I share an acknowledging glance.

"What's going on?" Arlene asks.

"I'm going to the cops," I announce. And I slam the door behind me.

Charlie woke me the morning after Simone dumped me. He barged into my bedroom, shaking me awake, both hands shoving hard against my shoulder.

I rubbed my eyes, then my temples, trying to massage my head from its alcoholic slumber. By the time my vision cleared up enough to get a good look at Charlie's face, I realized that something was wrong.

"What's up?" I asked.

Charlie just looked at me, his red-rimmed eyes boring into me with disbelief. "You're kidding. Please tell me you're kidding, because if you don't remember, I'm going to fucking kill you."

When he realized I wasn't kidding, his eyes narrowed and his lips tightened into a thin line, and I thought for a moment he really would kill me. He stood, backed away from the bed, and left. But on his way out, he spat two words at me. His voice cracked with emotion, but I understood. "Saint Vincent's."

"Christ." I rose to a sitting position. I inventoried my body, looking for bruises. But it was clean. No marks. No cuts. Nothing. I didn't know whether to feel relieved or guilty.

I called the hospital. The receptionist told me that Simone was in intensive care, which made my heart quicken. She wouldn't give me particulars. When I asked her to put me in touch with the family, she forwarded me to intensive care. But the nurse, after checking the waiting room, told me that the family wasn't available. I could tell by the tone of her voice what she really meant.

"Could you at least tell me what happened?"

"Ms. Watson has a spinal injury." A pause. "She has no movement from the waist down."

My breath caught. "How did it happen?"

The nurse cleared her throat. "Apparently it was a fall."

"A fall?"

"That's what I was told."

"How did she fall?"

"That's all I know, sir. I'm sorry."

"Yes. Of course. Thank you." I hung up, threw on my clothes, and barreled my way to the hospital.

"And what makes you think this woman has your dog?" The young county deputy can barely contain his smirk.

His attitude is about to push me over the edge. I'm already annoyed after a trip to the Bozeman police station, where I was informed that I'm not in their jurisdiction, that I needed to talk to the county.

"She's made threats," I explain.

"She threatened to take your dog?" He makes little effort to hide his skepticism.

I nod.

"And why did she do that, exactly?"

"It's a long story," I say. "Listen, I don't want to get into that. I just know it was her."

The deputy, who's been leaning on the counter, writing down the information, stands upright. His hair is brushed back, and it's stiff with spray, or goop. It looks soft, but I know that if you touched it, the texture would be like wood. He has a mustache that's barely better than Frida Kahlo's.

"Well," he says. "We'll take a trip out there and talk to her."

"Today?"

"Probably." I suspect this means no.

"Do you think you could find the time to check on it today? I don't trust this woman."

"Ms. Monday?" The deputy's smile spreads a little wider. "Well, I guess I can understand that. She can be a tough customer."

"You know her?"

"Oh yeah. We've all had our dealings with Leslie Monday."

"I see. Well, thanks." I start to leave, but something else occurs to me and I turn back. "By the way, do you happen to know anything about Leslie's parents, about how they were murdered?"

The young deputy has started toward his office. He stops and turns back to me. "Murdered?" He smirks again. "Well, I guess you could say murdered. That's probably how she'd describe it."

"What?"

"They died in an accident."

"A car accident?"

"Yeah. Drunk driver. Pretty sad."

Chapter Eighteen

Although our old nemesis, Pete Hurley, was found innocent of intentionally hitting Juan Estrada, his case has inspired changes that are important and timely. Life is unpredictable, my friends. You never know when someone who's a real prick is going to end up bringing good to the world.

Theyankeeyipper.com
Blog entry for November 25, 2005

What is wrong? This is the question that plagues me. It's two questions, really. Both important, both evasive, both perplexing.

The question of what's wrong with me matters less, probably. It's less urgent. How can I see it? How does anyone see their faults without finding some way around the truth? Isn't this the nature of humans? To fool ourselves, and then reflect and realize later that we were wrong? It's easier to look back—to ask "What *was* wrong?" Hindsight.

Here's what I really wonder. What is *the nature of* wrong? Is it what we do? Or is it how we respond? What is more painful to live with—killing a man, or avoiding responsibility for the crime? Is it more difficult to plan a robbery, or to cover your tracks? Are all things that are wrong equally wrong? Is it up to us to decide? How is it that some people skip through life with little regard for others, and still manage to be indifferent to what we've come to know as conscience? And others sit on the other side of the smallest mistake with no relief, no capacity to forgive themselves.

All I know is that I've never felt completely redeemed. I've known few moments of complete, unadulterated peace. And I have no idea how to attain that feeling.

FOR THREE DAYS I tried to get in touch with the Watsons. For three days, I tried to persuade the hospital staff to allow me to see Simone, or to explain what happened. I even lied about who I was, disguising my voice. I showed up at the hospital several times, hoping to find a sympathetic soul that would let me get close enough to corner one of the Watsons.

The hospital staff threatened to call the police if I didn't stop harassing them. They mentioned a restraining order.

On the evening of the third day, after leaving countless messages on Charlie's voicemail, begging him to at least tell me what happened, he finally called. I was sitting alone in the dark, just having cracked the seal on a bottle of whiskey.

When I realized it was Charlie, I kept quiet, waiting for him to set the tone.

"What are you up to?" he asked.

"Nothing." The moment this word left my mouth, I felt the need to impress upon Charlie that I wasn't brooding. "I was just about to head out for dinner."

"Mind if I join you?"

"Not at all."

We agreed on a restaurant, and I told him I'd be there in a few minutes. But hanging up, I realized that I hadn't bathed or changed my clothes in three days. I jumped in the shower, shaving after I scrubbed, cutting my chin, and for good measure, slipping when I stepped onto the tile. I fell on my ass, and bounced an elbow off the bathroom counter, scraping a couple of inches of hide.

Dave, still four-legged, followed my manic preparations, excited by this sudden burst of energy after three days of darkness and lethargy. She got rambunctious, anticipating her first walk in days.

"Sorry, girl. Got other stuff to take care of."

I let her into the back yard, bandaged the cut on my elbow, put on a long-sleeved shirt, crawled into my pants, and rushed out. Charlie was waiting, his glass of coke almost gone. I read his expression, and it was unyielding. But he did stand and offer his hand, which warmed my heart.

"Sorry I'm late. Got another call."

He took one look at my face, at the fresh wounds, the damp hair. And he dropped his eyes, acknowledging and accepting the lie.

We sat.

"How is she, Charlie?" I almost burst into tears.

Charlie shook his head. "Not good, Pete. She doesn't have any feeling below her waist."

I closed my eyes, and then I did cry. "Jesus."

"I guess you want to know what happened."

"Of course I do."

"Did they tell you anything?"

"Only that she fell. Charlie, nobody's told me a thing." The waitress approached. I was desperately trying to wipe away my tears. "We need a few minutes," I said.

She was apparently prepared to give a speech as she responded to my abrupt statement with a frown and an impatient turn on her heel. Charlie took a deep breath, pinched his lips, and let the air escape slowly. He lifted his eyes to the ceiling.

"What do you remember, Pete?"

"Well, I dropped Simone off at the house, then I went to a bar. I don't remember leaving."

"Well, you came back." He leveled a narrow eye on me. "You bastard. You son of a bitch."

I dropped my eyes.

"I'm sorry," Charlie said. "I just had to get that out of my system."

I nodded. "It's okay."

Charlie took a long, deep sigh. "So…everyone was in bed when you showed up—it was three in the morning. And when nobody answered the door, you started pounding on it, yelling."

Charlie had to stop again. He dipped his chin deep into his chest, and closed his eyes for a moment. Then he continued. "It was obvious you were drunk, so Dad tried convincing you to leave and come back in the morning. But you demanded to see her. Dad offered to let you spend the night and sleep it off. But you were out of your head, Pete. You started making threats."

"I did?"

He lowered his eyes, not bothering to answer a question that was rhetorical.

"Were you there?"

"No."

"So this is what your dad told you?"

Charlie nodded, then measured me. "Are you questioning..."

"No no no. I just want to know everything. I just want to know."

The waitress circled our table, looking for an opening.

"Maybe we should order...get her out of our hair," Charlie suggested.

"Fine. I just want a burger."

Charlie motioned her over, and she took our order, still showing her irritation, chewing hard on her gum.

"Something to drink?"

"A beer," I answered.

"Two," Charlie added.

"What kind?"

"Doesn't matter. Whatever you have on tap."

She frowned and walked away.

"So Simone came down?"

"Eventually. She heard the argument, of course."

"And?"

"Well..." Charlie started to speak, but suddenly he couldn't. He lowered his head, and shook it slowly, and his face clenched. A tear dribbled from the corner of his eye. "Pete, I don't know how you're going to live with this. I hate to even tell you, because I don't know how you can possibly live with what you've done."

"What, goddamit?"

He inhaled deeply. "You must have been so drunk, Pete. You started yelling at her...you weren't making any sense. They kept trying to get you to leave, or go to bed...anything. And at some point you stopped talking, looked at both of them and your eyes rolled up in your head, and you started to fall. You fell, and Simone rushed over to try and catch you. When you guys came down, she hit her head on the side table." Charlie took a breath, through his nose. He wasn't crying audibly, but the moisture continued to slide down his cheeks. But his face suddenly squeezed together, lips upward, eyes clenched, like a perverted smile. He tried to hold back his anguish, but the tears burst free.

"We both fell?"

"Yeah."

"How could hitting her head causes that much damage?"

Charlie sighed. "I don't know. I don't get it. It must have snapped her neck to the side somehow."

We sat quietly for several minutes. Our eyes didn't meet. Our food came, and I could see the waitress trying to ignore Charlie's tears. I couldn't eat. I wanted to cry myself, but something held me back. As horrifying as the facts were, and as sick as I felt, my mind was working hard to hold onto one immeasurably small tidbit of relief, an end to the days of wondering, and imagining.

"What can I do, Pete? What do you want me to do? I'll do anything."

"Honestly, Pete, the best thing you can do is stay away. My mother would kill you if she saw you right now. I'm not exaggerating."

"Jesus. Yeah, okay." I ran my hands through my hair. "I'm so sorry, Charlie. I can't even think of how to express it. There's no possible way of saying anything that…"

"I know." Charlie pressed his palm against my chest, as if he was trying to stop my heart from beating, or somehow contain the words that were bubbling up out of me. "I know."

Later, when I walked into my house, I collapsed.

Chapter Nineteen

*If the bedroom serves as the heart of your house, then
the soul resides squarely in the middle of your living
room. This is where the most meaningful moments
of your life should take place. Entertainment,
discussions, private moments, and hard choices.
This should be the room where life happens.*

Your House, Your Self
Chapter 8
"Heart and Soul"

Every day is the same. Every day I try not to think about a frosty
bottle of beer, or the warm burn of whisky in my throat, down
into my gut, up to my head. And every day, the harder I try not to
think of these things, the more I crave them.

And every day I tell myself how ridiculous it is that I'm thinking
about all this. Every day I tell myself that it was everyone else's
notion in the first place—this notion that I need to quit drinking.
It was never my notion. And the more I repeat this, over and over,
the more it becomes a lie. Because the notion has become my
notion. It may not have started as my notion, but I have adopted it.
Somewhere in the muddle of dissonant voices in my head, the atonal
symphony of discontent and guilt and resentment and suspicion, a
tone sounds clear and pure.

It cuts through the voices, and it rings repeatedly—not in a
clanging way, like a dinner bell or the starting bell at the local race
track. It's more somber, like those in a bell choir, with a long, slowly
diminishing resonance. That's why it can't be ignored. Because it
resonates in such a beautiful way. It is seductive, and truthful. It is
undeniably truthful.

THE DEPUTY HAS informed me that Leslie doesn't have Dave. She's managed to convince him that she had nothing to do with Dave's disappearance. So the deputy filed a missing pet report. The pound hasn't seen her, either.

I'm alternately convinced of Leslie's innocence and of her guilt. After several hours of mulling it over, I decide to call her.

"I had a visit from the authorities," she tells me.

"And according to them, you don't have Dave."

"I really don't, Pete. I wish you'd believe me. It's a horrible thing, what's happened. I know what she means to you."

Again, if this woman does have Dave, she has a future in community theater.

"Well, let me just ask you something—hypothetically."

"Pete, please."

"If you did have her, hypothetically..."

"Pete, I know you're upset, but..."

"What would the terms be? What would you hypothetically want?"

"Pete, stop. Stop it now. I will not have this discussion with you."

"So you won't tell me the terms?"

"I don't have her, Pete. If I knew you'd broken our agreement—which I don't, by the way—I would never just take her from you. I just wanted to get your attention. Do you really believe I'm that cruel?"

"I don't know."

"Pete, I'm sure it's awful for you. I'm so sorry she's gone."

"I did," I say.

"What?"

"I did break our agreement."

"Of course you did."

"Why do you say that?"

"Well, why else would you suspect me?"

"So you knew?"

"Not until now. But I suspected it when you showed up at my house that morning."

I hear my own breathing.

"Pete, if there's anything we can possibly do to help find her, let us know. We'll put up flyers—whatever. We both feel horrible about this."

"Thank you, Leslie. Really. And I'm sorry. I just don't know what to do."

FOR ALL OF MY adult life, I've been busy. My baseball career and business interests have demanded enough time that I can't remember two days in a row with nothing to do. Even during the off-seasons, or vacations, which were rare, I inherited my father's need to fill his days.

It's now been five days since Dave disappeared. For the first two days, I was frantic. I searched the woods around my property. I even considered extending my search to the mountains beyond, but I soon realized the futility of that. I took a photo of Dave and had two hundred flyers printed up. I stapled them to telephone poles, taped them to windows, and tacked them on bulletin boards all over Bozeman. I didn't get a single call.

I visited the pound twice a day. On the third day, I couldn't think of anything else to do, so I repeated the same things over, searching the woods, visiting the pound, putting up more flyers. But the silence started getting to me. I glanced at the clock each morning and, instead of looking forward to a full day ahead of me, I wondered how I would possibly fill the hours.

So I picked up *Your House, Your Self*, read the chapter on fixtures, and spent many hours at the local home furnishing store, wandering the aisles. And I fell in love every five minutes, with a faucet, or a light fixture, even baseboards. I never knew there were so many variations. I can't buy anything because I have nowhere to store it, but I start making lists of what I want, and they change every time I go in there. The folding closet door that I decided was perfect on Wednesday looks too cheap on Thursday. I decide instead on the sliding, slatted style. And that handle-style doorknob that I loved on Friday just wouldn't look right on Saturday. The glass one would match the Plexiglas table I've chosen for the living room.

But while my house changes in my head, the actual scene remains the same. Outside, the frame for my foundation sits waiting, ready to be filled. Behind it, the mountains remind me constantly of what I miss. Like those mountains, Dave and Charlie and Simone and the Watsons are far away, but so incredibly present during these long, empty hours.

IT'S LATE IN THE afternoon of the fifth day. The sky is half-filled with clouds, and the air is cool. I emerge ~~from the woods~~ after scouring the area one more time, looking for any trace of Dave. Parked in the middle of my driveway is the big black pickup belonging to Mr. Burt Mackie. I groan. The driver's door swings open, and Mackie steps down.

"What a pleasant surprise," I say.

"Good to see you too, Hurley." A smirk curls his lip.

"You came by with a housewarming gift, no doubt."

"Well, you have to understand, Mr. Hurley, that there are laws for this type of thing. You can't just make up your own rules."

"And these laws—they're the same for everyone, right?"

"Of course." Mackie is holding a sheaf of papers, and part of me wants to snatch them and tear the whole stack in half.

"You guys must be pretty damn busy driving around town inspecting all these properties, writing up all these forms."

Mackie looks at me sideways, and he reaches up and takes off his straw cowboy hat, revealing a forehead that is stunning. It looks like a balloon with too much air. He places a palm against that bulb, as if he has a splitting headache. "You trying to say something, Hurley?"

"No. Hell no. I'm just worried about you guys."

Mackie grins, pulling his hat down over his eyes again. I visualize the explosion of his forehead, splattering straw everywhere. "Well, you're right about that." He hands the forms over. "But you might want to think about something, Hurley. There was a guy moved here a few years ago. Young fella—probably twenty-seven, twenty-eight—moved out from California. So this fella was going to build a big old house, just outside of town. It was very impressive. Swimming pool. Tennis courts. Marble everywhere. Eight-car garage or something."

"What was he, a movie star or something?"

"Can't remember—might of been, now that you mention it—anyway, he must have figured we were just a bunch of backwoods cousins who didn't have two ideas to rub together."

"So let me guess; he came in and thought he could tell everyone what to do."

"Something like that."

"And you guys felt obligated to teach him some manners..."

"Damn, you're a smartass."

"Actually, I just don't like being talked to like a kid. And I don't have much respect for a man who can't fight his own battles."

Mackie points at the papers in my hand. "Everything in there is legitimate. If you're smart, you'll pay close attention to what it says in there. If you decide to be stupid and fight—well, you might not like the way things turn out."

"Can I quote you on that?"

Mackie smiles, shaking his head. "You like it here?"

I decide not to answer this question. I look at the papers in my hand.

"This is a nice town, Hurley. It's a great place to live. You might keep that in mind."

"WHAT NEXT?" I ask Dave, wishing she's there to hear me. I sink into my chair, and I crack a beer, without thinking. I ignore the bell.

I JUST REMEMBERED something I haven't thought about for a long time.

My father used to tell people that he quit drinking. He'd cite the year: 1969; the date: January 28; the place: some Irish bar in Boston. He told this story all the time, whenever anyone offered him a drink, or when the barmaid came to our table in a restaurant. It became embarrassing.

Occasionally, if he caught a captive ear, he'd even relate the incident that finally got his attention. A night when he'd come out of a blackout, and found himself about to hit his wife—my mother—who was cowering in the corner of their bathroom.

I remember this now because I just realized he was lying. He never did quit drinking. The reason it was easy to buy into this lie, and the reason he believed it himself, was that he never got drunk again. To my knowledge, anyway. In fact, I don't remember seeing him drink in public. But he didn't quit. Instead, he practiced a regimen of controlled maintenance that amazes me now.

Every Sunday, at seven o'clock in the evening, after we'd finished Sunday dinner, Dad opened the cabinet above our kitchen sink and pulled down his one and only shot glass. It was a thick, crystal glass, with an elaborate Danish coat of arms ground into its side. A beautiful piece of work.

Danielle and I learned early in our lives that on Sunday afternoon, Dad was not to be disturbed. He was like a starting pitcher preparing for the big game. Any interruption sent him into a simmering rage. If anyone called, we knew to tell them he was out. His girlfriends always disappeared on Sundays.

Taking his shot glass, my father would retire to his study and close the door, and we wouldn't see him for the rest of the evening. For years, I didn't know what happened behind that door. But my curiosity got the best of me one evening, and I crept outside to his window, my heart beating through my ribs.

I watched my father open the bottom drawer of his desk and pull out a bottle. I later found out that his drink of choice was Chivas Regal. After unscrewing the cap, he filled the shot glass as full as he possibly could. Then he leaned back in his thick leather captain's chair, propped his feet up, and closed his eyes. He lifted the glass to his lips, and held it there for five seconds. Then he tipped his head slowly backwards, draining the glass. When it was empty, he held his head back for another ten seconds, the glass still at his mouth, tapping the base with his pointer finger.

Then when he lowered his head, he studied the inside of the glass. He poked the same finger into the glass, rubbing it around the edge. Then he sucked that finger dry, and let his head fall back again. He held this pose for a very long time. I thought he might be asleep. But his lips were moving.

I expected him to pour himself another drink, but he didn't. When it became clear that nothing else was going to happen, I tried to sneak away, but he must have caught the motion. Moments later, he was outside, holding me by the collar. And to my surprise, he hit me, right in the face, with his fist.

For years, I tried like hell to understand why my father would do this. Now I do.

Chapter Twenty

Pete Hurley is no longer the Robert Downey, Jr. of major league baseball. He has now become the Lindsay Lohan of major league baseball.

Bill Simmons
The B.S. Report
November 12, 2007

I can't find Dave. I've looked everywhere. I sneaked onto the Monday property at two in the morning, just to assure myself once and for all. I found nothing suspicious or incriminating. No dog piles. No chewed items.

So I turn my focus toward the next most likely suspect—Clint Weaver. I find out where he lives, and set my alarm for three o'clock in the morning, taking Barb's working hours into account. And I do exactly as I did at the Monday ranch, creeping around Clint's property, searching for evidence. The quest proves disappointing. Nothing.

I post another round of flyers, this time adding a modest reward, and offering anonymity to whoever provides information, or returns my dog. I finally get a call. A man tells me he's seen a three-legged dog with a brindle coat. My heart starts to beat harder.

"Where?"

"It was a dream," he says. "I saw the dog running. It was a baseball field. The dog was running across the baseball field."

"And this was a dream," I state.

"Yes. It was very powerful. The most powerful I've ever had."

"Well, thank you very much."

"That's it? Don't you want more information? My number or anything?"

"Yes. Give me your number. I'll call you if I think of any more questions."

He gave me his number, but I didn't write it down. And after he hung up, I chuckled for a moment before I surprised myself by bursting into tears.

The only good news—the weather has finally cleared. For two days, the sun has filled the sky. It's now unseasonably warm—in the high seventies. A warm cotton blanket falls around my shoulders when I step outside.

I call Barry and arrange for him to come on Saturday to discuss Burt Mackie's code violations.

"I'm gonna bring some mud," he says.

"Mud?"

"Yeah. Cement. Let's get this thing poured."

"But what about these code violations?"

"We'll take a look at those, too. But if we pour the cement, what are they gonna do? Make you break it up and haul it away?"

"You never know."

"Ah hell, Pete. I'll look at the papers just to make sure I don't get you into any more trouble, but I think we'll be all right."

So Barry arrives early Saturday morning, driving the cement truck, his round face beaming from the cab. A greasy baseball cap, advertising some auto parts store, looks like it's painted on top of his head. Or as a teammate once said of another teammate's hat: like flypaper stuck to an elephant's ass. The truck's heavy barrel rolls slowly, preventing the cement from setting. Barry jumps down, slamming the door. He pounds the truck with his palm.

"God, I love these old trucks," he shouts. "It's like driving a goddam tank out there. People practically drive off the road when they see you coming, like you might start firing at 'em." He laughs. "So you ready?" He swings his fist around in a sideways arch, smacking me on the upper arm. "Shall we get some mud in that hole?"

"I'm ready." I rub my hands together. "Where do we start? What the hell are we doing?"

Barry holds his palms up. "You tell me, house boy. This was your cockamamie idea." He surveys the hole, walking around it. But he stops, looks around for a moment, then turns to me. "Where's Dave?"

"Gone." This simple word gets caught in my throat.

"Gone? What do you mean gone?"

"She's gone."

"What happened?"

"Don't know. She disappeared about a week and a half ago."

Barry drops his eyes to the ground. "Damn." He shakes his head. "You've tried the pound, I s'pose."

I nod.

"Well hell, that really sucks, Pete." He thinks for a moment. "What about your neighbor there?"

"She doesn't have her."

He shakes his head. "That really sucks."

Then, in a mutually silent decision, we end the conversation and start toward the truck. I pull the violations from my back pocket.

"We should probably go over these."

I hand the papers to Barry, who unfolds them, smoothing the wrinkled sheets against the truck's black fender. "So what do we got here?" He plucks a worn leather glasses case from his shirt pocket and dons a pair of black plastic-rimmed glasses. From the minute he starts reading, a smile comes to his face. He shakes his head. "Damn, they really went to some trouble here, digging this shit up. They must have brought out the manual, looking for the most obscure regulations they could find."

He flips through the pages.

"Look at this...the valve on your water line is too small. Jesus H. Christ. To think some poor son-of-a-bitch probably spent months writing up a proposal for that, then had to go through the board to get it approved." Barry chuckles. "Waste of time. At least they didn't figure out some way to tell you your hole was in the wrong place. That's what I was afraid of."

"I'm sure they would have if they'd been able to find a reason."

Barry whacks the top page with the back of his hand. "Well, you know what, Pete? We really need to get this cement poured first. These are all things we can do after we're done with that. Okay by you?"

"Yes sir. Absolutely. You're the boss."

"I'm the boss? I thought you were the boss."

"Hell no. I'm not the boss."

WE WASTE LITTLE time. Barry claims that he hasn't worked on a foundation since the Trojan War, but he takes us through the steps with authority. He backs the truck up to one corner, and works a hydraulic lever in the cab, raising the front of the barrel. Then he mounts a chute at the mouth, hands me a shovel, grabs one for himself, and opens the gate. A nice even flow of cement rolls down the chute, filling the space between the sheets of plywood. We guide the blue-gray mishmash with our shovels, keeping most of it within its intended target. I watch Barry, who tilts his head to show where to direct the flow. He drops to his knees and pushes the cement further along.

Then he jumps up and closes the gate. He adjusts the chute, so that it will send its cargo ninety degrees to the west, along the other side, starting at that same corner. And we begin again.

Barry moves the truck along each wall, and we repeat the process until two of the four sides have been poured. After we smooth out the cement, Barry studies the plat, and we set bolts. I worry about how quickly we are doing this task, as I've determined that it's a very precise part of the process.

Barry catches my worried look. "Hey, dumb ass, we drill the holes to fit the bolts, not the other way around."

I wink. "You think I didn't know that?"

By the time noon rolls around, just as we're completing the third side, Danielle arrives with the boys.

"Hey, look who's here," I say.

"Yeah," Barry says, his voice flat.

The boys pile from the car and rush toward us. Danielle opens the back hatch, and pulls out a huge picnic basket. The boys cradle liter bottles of soda. Pop.

I stand to greet them, and realize that my body is one big ache. I love this feeling.

Danielle wordlessly spreads a blanket on the ground while the boys race around my property. Barry goes straight for the basket, opening the lid and burying his face inside.

"Oh boy. We got sammiches. We got every kind of sammich you can think of. We got peanut butter. We got tuna. We got egg salad." He holds up each example as he calls them out. "We got more sammiches than we got stomachs to hold 'em."

At the sight of food, I realize just how hungry I am. I approach the keeper of the basket. "I'll take one of those tuna."

"There you go, Mr. Hurley. And for you, Ms. Danielle?"

Danielle ignores him, leaving Barry holding a limp sandwich. "Okee dokee, then. I guess I'll take a couple of these peanut butter and…" Barry studies the sandwich, prying the bread apart. "Looks like honey. My favorite."

"Boys!" Danielle shouts, and I jump.

The boys continue their chase between the sparse stalks of brown grass.

"*Boys!!*" Danielle bellows. "Get over here."

I look at Barry, who catches my eye and shakes his head. I can't tell if he means he has no idea what's wrong, or if I shouldn't ask.

"We're coming," Gus answers, but he suddenly stops mid-run. "Hey…where's Dave?"

"Dave's missing," I answer.

Danielle looks at me for the first time since they arrived. "She is?"

I nod.

"I'm sorry." Danielle's eyes drop. "I had no idea. Since when?"

I tell her, and this information seems to trigger a re-evaluation of her mood. She stares thoughtfully at the basket. But in the next instant, she snaps out of this trance. She advances toward the basket, and Barry retreats. Her hands dive into its depths, pulling plates, forks, and napkins from within. She distributes the paraphernalia across the blanket, her motions quick, as if we are working against the clock. And once the boys settle in, her attention is on them.

"Don't bother your brother, Gus."

"I'm not."

"Yes you were. Just finish your lunch."

"What happened to Dave?" Gus asks, his brown eyes wide.

"I don't know," I answer.

"Just eat," Danielle says.

Barry and I eat quickly, as if she's talking to us.

"Stop dawdling, Stevie," Danielle barks.

"I'm not even hungry." Stevie's eyes become slightly moist.

The meal lasts less than fifteen minutes, but it feels as if it will never end.

"This potato salad is really good." Barry doesn't direct the comment at Danielle, but it's clear what he's hoping to accomplish. She doesn't bite.

Barry leans toward her, his voice louder. "Boy, this potato salad sure is good."

Danielle turns a sour look toward him. "Thanks."

"Why did you even come?" Barry asks.

The question is rhetorical, and as a couple they both know this. Danielle doesn't even acknowledge it. As soon as she's finished, she packs everything as quickly as she unpacked it, although the boys are only half-finished with their sandwiches. She refuses Barry's offer to help lug the big basket to the car. She threatens the boys with dismemberment to get them into the car. And they're off.

The car kicks up dust as she whisks down the dirt driveway. Barry and I watch the cloud form, and I turn to him.

"What the hell?"

Chapter Twenty-One

A major league fastball can travel at speeds as high as 100 miles per hour. This means that the batter, standing sixty feet six inches away, has just more than a second to react to a pitch coming at his head. A baseball is hard enough to kill a man if it hits him at just the right angle, in just the right spot. So technically, if a man throws a baseball at another man's head, it's attempted murder. The Hurley rule is necessary because it's a crime not to pass it.

George Will
Washington Post
October 23, 2006

Danielle left for Montana when she was nineteen. And she never visited Amherst again. Dad never came to Bozeman, either. So they didn't see each other for the last year and a half of his life.

Before they left, I'm sure it was Barry's idea to talk to my father instead of simply eloping. Dad and Danielle had fought incessantly about her relationship with Barry. Not because Dad didn't like him, but because Dad knew there was a good chance they'd move to Bozeman. But Danielle and Barry showed up at the house one night after dinner, and even in my teenage oblivion, I could see that this visit was important. When I said hello, neither of them responded.

I planted myself close to Dad's study, but the discussion was neither long nor loud. Barry and Danielle emerged after only fifteen minutes, both wearing expressions of serious contemplation. Barry said hello but he was clearly not interested in talking. After they left, I waited in the living room for Dad, curled up on the couch, eyes glued to network TV. But his door remained shut for the rest of the evening. Maybe he interrupted his routine and broke out the

Chivas Regal. I don't know. I fell asleep.

Danielle and Barry left Massachusetts two days later, and I don't think my father ever forgave her. It was a tragedy for all three of them, especially because my father never found out that he had a terrific son-in-law.

NOW I SIT ALONE with this man, the husband of my sister, and I see a rare look of despair. He kept up a good front while Danielle was here. But he apparently held it for as long as he could, because his whole face and body have collapsed into a slump, a pile of flesh and bone.

After a long silence, I ask, "What's happening?"

Barry stares off at the mountains. "I'm not sure. It's a mystery."

We don't speak for a moment. The only sound is the rolling of the cement barrel, around and around, the soft shuffle of the contents shifting.

"Lately we haven't been able to talk about the weather without it turning into a rassling match," Barry confesses. "I don't know what's going on. It's especially bad on weekends. She'll cook up the most amazing meal every Sunday night, but while she's doing that, she also spends the whole day doing laundry, and she approaches it like she's preparing for war. She piles up these baskets of laundry around the bed like a fort, so I can barely get to the bed." He plucks at the grass.

"You know what…she used to do that same thing when we were kids."

"Which part?"

"With the laundry."

"Weird." Barry shakes his head. "We've been through rough patches, but this one's bad."

"Really?"

He looks at me, one side of his mouth stretching into a grin. "What?"

"You've been through rough patches?"

"That surprises you?"

"Hell yes. I thought you guys were some kind of aliens. I've never heard you fight."

"Well, we do try to spare everyone else from our little spats… usually."

I shake my head. "So what do you think is wrong?"

"Everything. Nothing. Who knows? Danielle's angry about something. She's probably not even sure herself what it is. She usually gets these things out of her system when she does know." He continues to pluck at the grass. "Until she figures it out, we'll all have to suffer a bit. I haven't been much help, either."

"How's that?"

"I've been too damn tired to talk about anything. When she starts talking, no matter how hard I try, I can't seem to concentrate. My mind just goes..." He raises a hand and lets it flutter in the air, watching it. "Or I fall asleep. She really hates that."

"I bet."

We sit for another silent moment, until Barry jumps up, brushing his hands together. "We better finish up here before this stuff sets."

We immerse ourselves into the more predictable, satisfying world of work. We're nearly done with the fourth side when the rumble of a vehicle echoes across my land. I groan. A black pickup.

"Is that Mackie?" Barry asks.

"Sure is."

"Pesky son-of-a-bitch."

Mackie's immaculately polished pickup slows to a stop. His dome is apparently already hurting him as he climbs from the cab. His straw hat is in his left hand, and he cradles his forehead like he's testing a cantaloupe for ripeness.

"Howdy, boys. How's it goin' out here?"

"Good, Burt. Real good," Barry answers, propping his arms on the handle of his shovel.

"How you doin', Pete?" Mackie asks.

"I'm great. Watching Barry here do all the work."

Mackie smiles, easing his hat onto his skull.

"What can we do for you?" I ask.

"You looked over those violations yet?"

"Sure did. We're gonna get to those as soon as we're done pouring here."

This is more than Mackie's poor forehead can bear, as he plucks the hat from his head and grabs the front again. "Well, that's good to hear. The only thing is—well, I guess you didn't read those very close, because it's pretty clear in there—you really needed to get those taken care of before you got going on this foundation."

"You gotta be kidding me," Barry says. "Burt, come on. We're gonna get those fixed up today. You can see we're almost done with the mud here."

"Well, like I said...you know, the law is the law, Barry. I'm gonna have to write up a citation for that."

I bite my tongue, tasting blood.

"Burt, goddamit, get the hell out of here," Barry says. "You know damn well this is bullshit."

"Excuse me?"

"They paying you for overtime today, are they?" Barry starts toward him. "Double time for Saturdays? They tell you to go ahead and clock in for a full day, even though this is the only thing you're gonna do all day?"

"Easy, Barry." I grab his elbow.

Mackie ignores him, pulling a pad from his back pocket. He flips it open and writes.

"Jesus Christ, I hate guys like you," Barry says. "You ever heard the word 'ethics,' Burt, or did you drop out of school before they got to the E's?"

Mackie's head jerks up from his writing. "You're not helping here."

"Helping? I'm not worried about helping. I'm just trying to get it through that bowling ball of yours that this ain't right." Barry points at his own head, and I almost bust out laughing.

But Mackie is not the least bit amused. He doesn't respond, finishing the citation with a flourish. He rips the slip from the pad, and tosses it, letting it flutter to the ground.

"You need to pay that within thirty days." And he turns and leaves, but not without removing his hat one last time. As he climbs into the truck, he holds his head as if he's about to lose it.

As soon as Mackie's door closes, Barry says, "I'm sorry, man."

But just as he says this, I explode in laughter.

"What's so damn funny?"

"Bowling ball?"

EVENING. LATE. IT's still warm outside, although I need a jacket. I lounge in my lawn chair, down in the hole, nursing my third beer. Barry left a couple of hours ago, after we corrected all the little code violations. He had a beer before he left, and watching him nurse that Budweiser, I couldn't wait for him to leave so I could drink one of my own.

I'm unsettled by the news of Barry and Danielle's difficulties. I know that even good marriages have low periods, bad patches, ugly moments. But a part of me wanted to believe that the fantasy relationship is possible.

But there is a crack in my heart. It's a small crack, but this is a tender area, my heart.

The sky is in transition, from blue to black. There is just enough blue left that the silhouette of the mountains is visible, and magnificent. The moon has little to offer, a thin sliver off to one side, an afterthought. This gives the stars their moment to shine, and they do so in brilliant spots of white. I study the plywood walls around me, imagining the cement behind them, trying to picture what the foundation will look like.

My body is exhausted. I know I'll sleep without moving tonight. But not for a while. I know that if I lay down now, my mind won't allow sleep to come. My mind is alert, sharp, and working as hard as my body did earlier. Too hard. Too hard.

Chapter Twenty-Two

During the course of building your house, you should celebrate certain milestones along the way. You'll find that this makes the process seem much less daunting, like a series of accomplishments rather than one big job. And if you plan something for each of these celebrations, even something small, it will remind you that you are making progress, rather than thinking about all that is left to do.

Your House, Your Self
Chapter 9
"Building Blocks"

Today I unveiled my foundation in a private ceremony. I tore down the plywood, freeing the concrete from its bondage. I now have a gray cubicle, and I haven't felt this proud for a long time. It's a cool day, cloudy, and I stand in the center of the empty space, surrounded by cement, wondering how I could possibly be so happy in the middle of so much gray. I pop a Budweiser.

But as happy as I am, I'm also nervous. Because I'm going to visit the Mondays tonight. I called Leslie to ask if she knew any lawyers who might be able to advise me about the citation, and how to avoid any further problems with Mr. Weaver or Mr. Mackie.

"Why don't you come over?" Leslie suggested, to my surprise. "We can talk about it. Arlene and I will make some dinner."

"You don't have to do that."

"Come by around seven."

I've cut myself shaving, and I haven't been able to stop the bleeding. I resort to the old-fashioned remedy—a tiny piece of toilet paper. It seems to have stopped the flow, but I suspect that the instant I pull it off, the red will trickle down my jaw again. I choose a maroon shirt, just in case.

I decide to walk, and after donning a wool-lined denim jacket, I tromp through the woods, climb the barbed wire fence, and pass the spot where Leslie confronted me with a rifle. I remember Dave trotting unevenly through these trees, a thought that makes me sad. The darkness has settled. The air is nice. Cool. So fresh. I breathe it deep into my lungs. I arrive at their door and knock. And just as I hear the echo of footsteps, I remember the piece of toilet paper, and pluck it from my chin.

The door opens a crack, and Leslie's face appears. She smiles, and I bow.

I follow Leslie down the hall. It's a tunnel of aromas, stimulating my appetite. We enter the kitchen, where there are two places set. A large pot simmers on the stove. Blue flames dance under a second large pot. I'm engulfed by the rich smell of fresh bread. A hum involuntarily tickles my throat.

"Where's Arlene?"

"Got called into work. Someone was sick."

"Ah." My reaction to this information surprises me. I'm happy that this leaves Leslie and me alone.

"And in answer to your next question, we're having lentil soup, and steamed artichokes."

"And homemade bread," I add, inhaling that smell.

Leslie lifts the lid of one pot, inserts a wooden spoon, and stirs. "And homemade bread."

"I love lentil soup. *And* artichokes."

Leslie tilts her head. "Good." She goes back to stirring, then checks the bread through the oven door window.

"Is there anything I can do to help?"

"No. Please sit down. There's nothing left to do but stir."

"I'm horrible at stirring, so that's a relief."

Leslie's movements are swift. She nearly burns herself lifting the lid off one pot. She drops the lid. But she doesn't panic, or make an audible sound. The lid clatters on the stovetop. She picks it up with her oven mitt, and replaces it.

"No word on Dave?" she asks.

"Unfortunately."

"Sorry to hear that."

"Yeah. It's been pretty tough."

"Losing someone is always tough, isn't it? No way around that.".

"Speaking of which, I found out—sort of accidentally—what happened to your parents."

Leslie's stirring seems to become more vigorous. Her lips get thin. "And?"

"Well, I guess you could call it murder. But I thought it was odd—a bit misleading, don't you think?"

"No."

"No?"

"No. Not at all. What's misleading about it?"

"It just conjures up very different possibilities from what happened. It's not any less horrible or anything. I'm just saying—considering how direct you usually are—I was kind of surprised."

"Why does it matter?"

"I'm curious, that's why. It's a big part of who you are, right? It just made me wonder."

"So that's why you're bringing it up?"

"Well, yeah. As a matter of fact. Because it seemed like we were becoming friends. And then things kind of soured. And I'm not sure why. But that felt like one more indicator."

Leslie pulls the bread from the oven, setting it on the stove. She turns, planting her oven mitts on her hips. "I don't talk about that with anyone. It has nothing to do with you."

I keep my eye steady on hers. "Why not?"

She doesn't move for a moment. Then she turns quickly, shutting down the burners. "I just don't."

Neither of us speaks. Leslie carries our plates to the stove and uses tongs to pluck the artichokes from the pot. She ladles soup into two bowls. Then she slices the bread, setting thick, uneven wedges on each plate. And she ducks into the refrigerator, where she retrieves another small bowl, which she pops in the microwave. She pulls it out after a few seconds, and sets it in the middle of the table. I lean forward, and smell lemon. It's melted butter.

"What do you want to drink?" Leslie asks.

"What do you have?"

"Seltzer, coke, juice, beer, milk."

"Seltzer, please."

Leslie fills two glasses with ice, then seltzer. After dropping a lemon wedge in each, she sets the glasses on the table. And finally she sits, taking a deep breath. "Okay then." She picks up her spoon.

"Let's feast."

The soup is superb, spiced heavier than I'm used to, but not too much. And the artichokes are cooked perfectly. The leaves pile up on our plates. The bread is soft, rich with flavor. We don't speak for most of the meal. And finally, between bites, leaning back for a moment, and just having taken a big drink from her seltzer, Leslie looks at me. Her eyes hold mine, and they tell me that she has considered something, and come to a conclusion.

"Arlene was driving," she says quietly. Then she looks away.

"Arlene?"

Leslie nods. She still looks away. "Yes...she was driving."

"Was she drunk?"

Now her look turns sour, baffled. "Drunk? No. Why would you ask that?"

"Well, I know that the accident..."

"The other guy was drunk," she says. "We got broadsided by a guy who was pig-drunk."

The conversation doesn't follow this track any further. We finish eating, and the instant I put down my fork, Leslie stands, and begins clearing the table. I help. And she transitions right into washing the dishes—wordless, both of us keeping our bodies in motion. We finish them all—pots and everything.

Finally, she breaks the silence. "Coffee?"

"Love some."

She fills the coffeemaker, then grinds beans and dumps grounds into the filter. The smell fills the kitchen.

"What are you going to do about Dave?" she asks.

"Same thing I've been doing, I guess. Keep checking the pound."

"I saw your flyers. They look good."

"Thanks."

"Have you considered getting a new dog?"

This question catches me off-guard, and for the first time since the day at Barry and Danielle's house, I don't appreciate Leslie's directness. I haven't even considered the possibility of not seeing Dave again. "No."

"I guess I can see why you'd want to wait."

The suggestion bothers me. Thankfully, Leslie doesn't prolong this conversation, either.

"I have some dessert." She moves to the refrigerator, where she retrieves two cellophane-covered ramekins.

"Do I have to?"

"Yes." She sets the ramekins on the counter, removes the cellophane, and places one in front of me. It's some kind of custard, or pudding, lemon yellow with blueberries sprinkled all over the top.

"Wow."

"It's lemon. I remembered that you like lemon."

"Yes, I noticed it was a theme tonight."

I spoon a small bite into my mouth, and it's delicious—creamy and citrus-tangy. The blueberries balance the lemon with perfect sweetness, the juices mingling. I have to remind myself to eat slowly.

"So I guess we should talk about this legal stuff," Leslie says.

"Yes." I adopt a businesslike manner. "We wouldn't want to neglect the purpose of this summit."

But Leslie is in full lawyer mode now. Her body language has shifted. She sits up straighter, her brow lowers, her voice drops. She reads the violations, and begins explaining the possible avenues I should consider, people that she'd recommend for advice, and so on.

She talks for several minutes, and I hear every word, but I'm not listening. I'm lost in the mystery of this woman—whether she has any interest in relationships, or whether she might even be a lesbian. I've never heard either Monday sister mention anything about Leslie's boyfriends, past or present. In all the time I've spent with her, Leslie has shown a complete lack of consciousness about her sexuality. She doesn't flirt. She doesn't respond to flirting. This is probably a big reason I'm so attracted to her. Trying to figure out what will get a response. I berate myself for not paying closer attention to what she says, but it doesn't do any good.

"What are you doing?" Leslie asks.

"What?" I sit up. "What do you mean?"

"You were moving your lips, like you were talking to yourself."

"Oh. I do that sometimes when I'm thinking."

She looks skeptical.

"I'm sorry," I say. "I'm a bit distracted. But I really appreciate this."

Leslie nods absently, then studies me for a moment, her eyes on my mouth. Her hand starts toward me, one finger slightly extended, bent just a little, as if she's about to slide it into the handle of a teacup. She's about to touch me. She's going to place her finger against my mouth. I'm amazed that this is about to happen—that I'm about to see a side of Leslie that I didn't believe existed. I wonder whether I'm ready for this. I reassess my need for time alone. I revisit the breakup with Simone, and the tragic consequences of that. And I tell myself that I don't want to experience any of that again. I decide this is absolutely wrong. But it makes no difference. As her hand moves toward me, I anticipate her touch with the rising excitement of a thirteen-year-old boy.

Her finger brushes my chin, then stops. "What is that?"

"What?"

"There's something on your chin."

Her finger twitches, and I feel a tiny prick, and I remember the razor cut. "Ow." I reach for my chin. "It's nothing—a cut. Shaving."

Leslie chuckles, embarrassed. "I'm sorry. I thought it was a piece of blueberry." She stands, obviously flustered. "Well, maybe we should call it a night," she says. "I know most people can only take so much of this legal-speak before their eyes glaze over."

I stand. "Well, it's not you. My eyes tend to glaze easily. A menu usually does the trick."

She laughs. I don't think I've ever heard her laugh before. A shame, too. It's a beautiful laugh, escaping in a flurry, as if it's been restrained for so long that it's out of her control. Leslie covers her mouth, stifling it.

But the secret's out.

IT'S THREE O'CLOCK in the morning. I turn my clock radio to the wall, punishing it for reminding me how long I've been trying to sleep. My legs itch, as they have every night. Itching like crazy, as if I've contracted fleas. I've tried lotions, creams, ointments, baths. Not surprisingly, only one thing stops it. Whiskey. And not on my legs.

Tonight I try to tough it out. But in these restless hours, I've been thinking about Leslie. The night crawls onward. Silent, still, lonely hours. I itch. I jerk off. I listen to Bill Evans, hoping his soothing melodies will lull me to sleep. I stretch my legs time and again.

It's three in the morning before I finally surrender to the only remedy that works. Several shots and the itch is gone. And a few more just to make sure. Two more as a reward for solving the problem. And then a full swig from the bottle to quell the guilt. But just as I'm drifting off, the silence is interrupted by a rustling outside.

I hear footsteps. They sound clumsy, lumbering. I decide it's an animal, maybe even a bear, although I haven't heard about any bear sightings nearby.

But the footsteps come closer and then a knock sounds. A human. The knock is muffled but it is rhythmic—definitely a knock. It's not just accidental bumping against the door. My face burns, and my heart pushes blood in great gushes through my veins. I curse myself for being drunk, for trying to decipher what's happening without a clear head. I approach the window at one side of the door, and pull the curtain to one side.

On the next knock, the figure speaks.

"Pete!" it calls out. The voice is feminine.

"Pete, are you home?"

"Who is it?"

"Arlene."

I open the door. "What's wrong?"

"God, I feel stupid." Arlene starts laughing. "What time is it?"

"Late. Really late; what are you doing here?"

Arlene laughs again, looking down at herself. She shakes her head. "Oh, I had this crazy idea that you probably miss Dave, so I'd…" She can't continue, she's laughing so hard.

"Are you drunk?" I ask.

Arlene crumples into herself, laughing and nodding.

There was a time when I would have welcomed the opportunity to share my state of inebriation. But my drinking is now a private matter. I say nothing.

Arlene's head falls against my chest, and she laughs silently.

"Did you want some coffee or something?"

She chuckles. "Coffee?"

"Beer?"

"Don't you have anything stronger?"

"Are you sure that's a good idea?" I ask.

Arlene tilts her head to one side, smiling. "Pro'ly not."

"Why don't you have a seat? I'll make some coffee." I lead Arlene by the elbow to the sofa. I try to maintain the illusion of control, slowing down my actions, paying close attention to each detail.

"So how are you doing, Pete?" Arlene asks.

"Real good," I answer. "Life is pretty good."

"That's great, Pete...I'm glad to hear it." Arlene falls back onto the sofa, a big smile on her face. She looks at the ceiling, as if there's something there that she finds amusing.

As the coffee brews, I sit across from her, in my recliner. "So what brings you here, Arlene, in the middle of the damn night?"

Her head rolls lazily to one side, so that she's looking at me that way, sideways. "I was lonely, Pete. Do you mind?"

"I guess not."

"Do you ever get lonely?"

"I s'pose. I try not to think about it."

"Why? Too painful?"

"Maybe. I don't know."

Arlene studies me, her gaze kind of dreamy. "Do you believe in God, Pete?"

"Do I believe in God? Why in the world would you ask me that?"

"Do you?"

"Jeez...I guess so. I just don't think he believes in me very much."

"Oh," Arlene says. "You shouldn't say that."

"Yeah, you're probably right." I get up to pour some coffee.

"Pete, do you have any friends? Who do you talk to when things get hard?"

I take a large swig of coffee. "My god, Arlene. You really are drunk, aren't you? These questions."

"I'm sorry, Pete. It's none of my business. I just wonder, you know. Everyone needs someone to talk to sometimes."

"Of course," I say, clearing my throat. "Yes, well, since you asked. I do have a good friend—my best friend Charlie, back home."

"Yeah?"

I nod, feeling like a bit of a fraud. I haven't talked to Charlie for months.

"Well tell me about him; tell me about Charlie. Was he a baseball player, too?"

I shake my head, chuckling. "No, not even close. Charlie had no interest in baseball. But we've been friends since we were ten."

Arlene looks at me with that goofy expression drunk people get, halfway between an orgasm and a coma.

"You miss him?" she asks.

I tuck my chin into my chest. "Yeah, I s'pose."

"It's probably like me and Leslie; sometimes she drives me completely nuts." Arlene closes her eyes and takes a deep breath. "But I can't imagine life without her."

"You two are really close."

Arlene hums. "We've been through a lot together." A tear trickles down her cheek.

If I wasn't drunk, I probably wouldn't do this, but the words are out there before I've given it much thought. "Do you ever talk about your parents?"

Arlene looks at me. Her eyes are still droopy, but the smile disappears. "Oh, Pete. That's...that's a hard question. Of course I want to talk about them, but do I really want to talk about them?"

"I'm sorry. You don't have to, of course."

Arlene studies me, long enough that it becomes uncomfortable. Finally, she sits up straight on the sofa, and props her elbows on her knees. "You know how people sometimes turn the ones they've lost into saints? Make them out to be the best people they ever knew? All that shit?"

"Yeah."

"Well I think that's disrespectful. It doesn't give people the true picture. It's a lie."

I look at my hands, wondering whether I really want to hear where she's going with this.

"My parents were not saints; they were hard people. I never saw either of them cry, never saw either of them break down and ask someone for something, for help." Now she herself is crying. "But you know, it was just the way they grew up...emotions scared the hell out of 'em."

I think of my own father, who had no patience for tears, no tolerance for anyone who showed weakness. I also think of Leslie, who seems to have come by her hardness honestly. "So how did you get to be so emotional?"

Arlene laughs. "It was hard work, I'm tellin' ya. My parents didn't know what to do with me." She pauses. "You know, Montana is a lot different than people think it is; have you noticed this?"

I frown. "What do you mean?"

"Well, think about it. Have the locals welcomed you with open arms?"

I scoff, and Arlene nods. "See, it's a very different experience for everyone. My mom was part Indian."

"She was?"

Arlene holds out her arm. "That's where I got this coloring. Anyway, growing up here was a completely different experience for her than it was for my dad."

"His family was here for a long time?"

"Uh huh. This place is hard on people. You couldn't have picked a much harder place. But..." She holds up a finger. "Once you establish yourself, it's worth it."

"And how long will that take?"

She smiles. "That's up to you." She turns her face toward me. "Speaking of establishing yourself, I hear you were at our house for dinner. How was it?"

"The food was great."

"And the company?"

"That was fine, too."

She studies me, the light green of her eyes showing even in the dark. A slight smile curls her lip.

"Does Leslie know you're here?" I ask.

She nods, her expression now increasingly bleary. "Are you falling in love with my sister?"

The silence is a long one, and the lack of sound in the trailer, and outside, and in our little world, begins to press down on me as I ponder this question. Whether I am, whether I should admit it, whether Arlene would tell her sister, and whether any of that should affect my answer. I wish I wasn't drunk.

"I'm not exactly sure what that feels like any more."

"Mm." Arlene turns her head to the side. "Yes."

"You know what I mean then."

"Unfortunately."

"And Leslie? Do you think she knows?"

"She hasn't allowed herself to think about that for a very long time."

"Why is that?"

Arlene turns toward me again. She looks at me with a kindness that warms my drunken heart. "I think she ought to tell you that herself. But let me say this, Mr. Pete Hurley. You better not fuck over my sister if she gives you a chance." She speaks with a gentle conviction, and it impresses me. She points at me. "Got it?"

I feel my face redden.

Arlene's look becomes more solemn, but her eyes don't leave me. "Can I ask you one last thing before I go, Pete?"

"Okay."

Her eyes tear up. "Why not me?"

Chapter Twenty-Three

I'm so sick of hearing about Pete Hurley, I'm about to scream. Just shut up everyone.

Michael Wilbon
Pardon the Interruption
October 1, 2007

I approach Danielle and Barry's door with some apprehension; I haven't seen them since the day Danielle was in such a horrible mood. My knock is answered by a breathless, ruddy-cheeked Gus, his chocolate eyes wide as plates. In one hand, he holds a bright green plastic weapon. The gun sports an equally bright orange Nerf dart.

I cover my face, assuming I'm about to be assassinated. But Gus wheels and shoots at his father, who has just popped up from behind the couch, wielding his own bright green weapon. The dart smacks Barry's forehead and miraculously sticks. Gus squeals, racing from the room. Barry nails him right in the butt.

"Damn, you guys are good," I say.

"Got you, you dirty Etruscan," Barry shouts.

"Etruscan? What's an Etruscan?"

Barry shrugs. "I have no idea. I asked him what he wants to be, and he said 'an Etruscan.'"

"What are you?"

"An engineer."

"I know that. I mean..."

"That's what I am. I asked him what I should be, and he said 'an engineer.' The Etruscans versus the Engineers—the battle the world has feared for centuries. Will it end in mass destruction?" Barry crouches, doing his best John Belushi, clenching his teeth. "Now I must discontinue this idle chatter and pursue my enemy." He waddles toward the stairs with the stealth of a league bowler. The pounding of his feet up the stairs destroys any chance of a surprise attack. Gus begins to squeal before Barry even reaches the top of the stairs.

I make my way to the kitchen, where Danielle stands at the stove. Her weapon—a wooden spoon. A pan of onions and mushrooms sizzles in butter.

"God, I love that smell," I say.

"Hello." She sets down her spoon and rises to her toes, kissing my cheek. I wrap an arm around her.

"Thanks," I say to this subtle gesture of reconciliation.

Back at her post, Danielle says, "I'd do the same for a friend."

I smile. It seems we will never be comfortable with these little moments of warmth. "Smartass."

"I'm sorry you haven't had any luck finding Dave."

"Yeah. It sucks."

"I really can't believe she'd run off."

"I don't either."

"What else could have happened?"

"I wish I knew. I've tried to get the sheriff's department to investigate. They look at me like I'm asking them to declare war on Wyoming. Especially when Clint's name comes up."

"Ah yes. What's going on with that?"

"Another pleasant topic."

"Sorry, but it's the bed you made."

"...and other clichés."

Danielle sticks out her tongue at me.

"Leslie referred me to a couple of lawyers. I called them, but they weren't very encouraging. They both said pretty much the same thing—that if these violations fall within the law, he can do whatever he wants."

"So?"

"So what?"

"What are you going to do?"

I take a deep breath. "How about if I set the table?"

"Pe-te."

"I don't know, Danielle. For now, all I know is I'm gonna go look for my dog. That's all I know."

She nods as she scoops the onions from the pan into a bowl. "Well, if I think of anything while you're gone, I'll let you know."

"I appreciate that."

BARRY IS IN rare form at dinner. His jokes center around my house, his stomach, and the dreaded Etruscans. Just before we dig in, he lifts his glass. "Here's to the great builder. The man whose vision was met with scoffs, taunts, and rotten cabbage. The man who dug a hole..." Dramatic pause. "...and filled it."

He drinks, and we all try to drink without laughing.

"And to Dave," Danielle adds.

We raise our glasses again.

But Barry's joviality is only momentarily subdued. As we eat, the discussion turns to what I'll need for my trip to the mountains. My flyers finally led to a tangible result. I got a call from a man who spotted a three-legged dog near a camp site just outside of Bozeman. He tried to coax the dog into going with him, but he couldn't get close enough. It's a long shot at best, I know. But I would never forgive myself for not trying.

The conversation starts simply enough, with the basics—tent, mummy bag, propane stove, a knife, food. Barry encourages the boys to come up with other things I'll need, and their experience as campers shows.

"First aid kit," Stevie says.

"Extra batteries," Gus adds.

"Plastic bags to keep your matches and other stuff dry."

"Gus, why don't you write this stuff down?" Barry suggests, and Gus is thrilled to take on this responsibility. He digs a pencil and paper from a drawer and starts recording.

"Don't forget the cement," Barry says. "For the foundation for your tent."

"Yes," I agree, and Gus dutifully spells it out, his grin spreading.

"And your workout videos," Barry adds. "So you can stay in shape."

"Barry, stop," Danielle says, but she's smiling.

"Let's see—you'll need Gus here to clean your boots at night."

Gus writes down his own name, giggling.

"A dryer, for your clothes, in case it rains, or you fall in the lake."

"What about me?" Stevie asks.

"No no no." Barry shakes his finger. "No, you need to stay here so Mommy and Daddy have someone left to boss around."

Stevie nods, adopting a serious expression, as if he recognizes the importance of this responsibility.

Barry continues the list, moving on to famous actresses, and while the boys are doubled over in laughter, Danielle is beside herself. She finally waves, unable to even voice her request for a reprieve.

Barry holds up his palms, as if he has absolutely no idea what he's done.

After supper, Barry and I wander out to the garage to retrieve the propane stove I'm going to borrow for the trip.

"Things seem better," I say.

"Oh, I suppose they are. You know how these things go, Pete. Up and down." He tilts his head back and forth. "Up and down."

"Well, Barry—if you ever need to blow off some steam."

"Yeah, okay. Thanks." But Barry heads out toward my truck as if I've just asked him for a kiss on the lips.

"Pete!" Danielle shouts from inside.

"Yeah?"

"I almost forgot. There's a letter for you."

"Okay."

"You want me to bring it out?"

"No, I'm coming back in. I'll get it."

When we finish loading the camping gear, I head back inside, and Danielle hands me the letter. The handwriting is completely unfamiliar, as is the name. But the address is not. It's from the Watson house.

"Weird, huh?" Danielle says.

"I'll say. Can you read the name?"

"I couldn't make it out."

I tuck it in my back pocket. "Well, thanks for dinner. It was delicious."

Barry comes inside, and for the final goodbye, they present the image of solidarity, standing with their arms around each other.

"Be careful," Danielle says. "Make sure you take enough clothes. That's the mistake I always make."

"Okay, Mom."

She punches my arm. "Somebody has to worry about you."

I shake Barry's hand.

"Bring home a bear for us. We need the meat for winter," Barry says.

"You got it."

I WAIT UNTIL I'M HOME to open the letter, but not from lack of curiosity. The letter is in the same unfamiliar hand:

> *Mr. Hurley,*
>
> *My name is Brenda Walters. I am a home nurse, and I'm writing this for Simone. I've been tending to her since she moved back into her parents' house. She has asked me several times to do this, but I've refused because I don't think it's a very good idea. But I'm tired of listening to her, so here it is. Simone wants very much to see you. To tell you the truth, I think she's just going through a phase, feeling guilty about how this all turned out. So she's got big ideas that seeing you will help her forgive you, and herself. But I think she's in for a big surprise. I've seen it too many times, working with people who are going through this. I've been at it for twenty years, so I do know a thing or two. She wouldn't be any happier than she is now. She obviously didn't tell me to write this part. She told me to let her read the letter before I sent it, but I didn't show her this copy. I fooled her. Anyway, as you probably figured out by now, she wants to see you. Here's what she said to tell you:*

> If there's any hope of forgiving each other, please come and see me, even if it's just for a few hours.

> *I don't know, Mr. Hurley. To me, I can't imagine*

that seeing her is going to do either one of you any good until you've both had some time to heal, but that's what she wanted me to say. I suppose if there's any chance that seeing you would make her feel any better, then it might be worth a shot. But you should know that she's actually doing pretty well—better than a lot of people I've worked with. She lives with her parents, and it would be best if you didn't tell them you were coming. They are still pretty pissed off at you.

Sincerely,
Brenda Walters

P. S. Go Sox!!

Chapter Twenty-Four

Rumor has it that with so many of their relief pitchers injured, the Yankees have talked to Pete Hurley's agent about his availability. This might be the only thing that would ever convince me to move out of New York City.

Theyankeeyipper.com
Blog entry for April 30, 2008

The early morning, pre-dawn light on an autumn day in Montana, a day with no clouds, is as purely black, with the same sheen as a satin nightgown. The air is brisk, and dry, cool. I rake it in, filling my lungs. A thermos half-filled with coffee sits on the seat next to me.

In the twelve hours since I read it, I have been able to think of little else but the letter from the mysterious Brenda Walters. I came very close to canceling my trip to the mountains. The remote possibility of redemption versus the remote possibility of discovery was a tough call, although I'm drawn to something—that the hope of redemption with Simone seems more significant, more important in the long term. There is also the idea of taking on the challenge Simone has presented. As angry as she may be, I know that at the heart of her letter is a plea—a desire to find some peace for both of us. But the trip to Amherst is also something that can be delayed. I keep coming back to Dave—to the last bit of hope of finding her.

A map lies on the seat next to my thermos. I've outlined the route to the campground where the caller spotted Dave, and I turn onto a gravel road that twists its way through the thick pine forest. The road will barely accommodate two vehicles, and I realize that turning back is virtually impossible now.

The sun makes its appearance, first throwing a visual warning skyward with a splattering of silvery orange. And finally, its crown shines through the trees. The black sky slowly gives way to its gentler sister blue.

As I wind my way along this narrow road, I'm amazed how far I've gone without coming to a turnoff. If I do come to a branch in the road, I have another decision to make. Should I search for Dave along the side roads? The deeper I go into these woods, the thicker they become, and I can't help but notice that there is a lot of rough unexplored land where Dave could get lost. I try not to think about this. There's a lake near the campground, and I cling to my theory that she would head for the water if she was lost.

The issue of turning off the road becomes moot when I arrive at the campground. I'm surprised to see only two tents among the trees. But when I step down from my cab, I understand why. It's freezing. My breath suspends in midair. I feel as if my ears have been slapped. I thrust my hands in my pockets, and my body emits a low, audible shudder. I choose the site furthest off, in one corner, and I quickly gather some firewood and get a blaze going. The warmth inspires me, and I take advantage of the inspiration to organize my camp.

I pitch my tent, unroll my sleeping bag inside, and set up the propane stove near the picnic table. I fill the wooden locker with food and apply the padlock that Stevie suggested I bring for this purpose.

Finally, I unfold a canvas sling chair I borrowed from Barry. I pour the last coffee from my thermos and settle in front of the fire. And I promptly fall asleep.

WHEN I WAKE, I'M sweating like a racehorse. The fire has nearly died, but the sun fills the gap between the trees above me, as if it has just sprayed me with a hose and is making a half-hearted attempt to hide behind the branches. I peel off my jacket and survey the scene. There's no sign of life. The other two campsites are still intact, but the inhabitants are apparently off to other things.

I've slept for almost three hours, and it's just after noon. Amazed at how much warmer it is, I pack several energy bars, eating two.

I add a baggy full of trail mix and a Nalgene bottle full of water. I consult the map.

There are two trails to the lake, and with the day half-gone, it's clear that I only have time for the shorter loop, which is about seven miles. I can tackle the long one tomorrow.

For the first mile, although I check for signs of dog life, my attention is captured by the incredible scenery. The trail is narrow, barely wide enough for a person. It's rocky, but not steep. The branches of spruce and pine brush my arms and legs. I see several deer and smaller animals—squirrels, mostly. And each time I see movement, my heart quickens.

The walk is as invigorating as it is beautiful. Then I round another bend, and everything shifts. I'm suddenly standing in a field. To my right, the woods are still thick and fragrant. But spreading out to my left is a wide expanse of dry, waist-high grass. A herd of deer raises their ears, spots me, and scampers into the trees, led by an impressive buck, his rack sporting five points per side. Barry will drool when I tell him. Hunting season begins in a couple of weeks.

I cross the field at a slower pace, breathing it in, and when the trail plunges into the trees again, the proximity seems to pull my thoughts in tight. I stare at the ground, striding forward with a purposeful, steady determination. The sun becomes more intense. I force my eyes up from my shoes, to the landscape around me. The last leg of the trail is an upward climb—a fairly steep one. I begin the ascent with optimism, lengthening my stride. My breath comes in a steady rhythm, deep into my lungs.

I look for dog signs—paw prints or piles. On each lunge forward, I feel the muscles pull in the back of my legs. The climb continues for a hundred yards, then another fifty, getting slightly steeper. I push onward, striding, arms pumping, my breath loud in my head. I don't see any indication of dog life. Sweat gathers on my forehead, and inside my shirt.

I push myself, but suddenly I don't feel right. The heat presses against my forehead like a hot water bottle. My hands start trembling. I develop an ache in my side—not like a cramp. It's different. More frightening. A piercing pain. I stumble onward, but my head feels light. Light, then airy, then swirling. I consider turning back.

In the distance, I see a couple coming down the trail toward me.

The heat on my forehead turns to liquid, running down my face, first in trickles, then sheets, coating my cheeks.

I come to a flat, wide stretch. The tremble moves from my hands, up my arms. The couple is still a good hundred yards away. Suddenly, a dark blur passes in front of me, across the trail. I stop for a moment, then stumble forward. The figure crosses the path again.

"Dave," I yell.

The figure reappears, standing in the middle of the trail. It *is* Dave. I try running, but my legs are weak. My pack feels like a car on my back. I fall to my knees. Dave starts toward me. I tumble to my side.

And the tremble moves like a current through the rest of me. It takes over. The heat. The sweat. The shakes. I call Dave's name again. I try taking deep breaths, but I have no strength. The tremor is everything. I vomit.

My mind is here. Then it's not. My body moves around me, then it's as if I'm not inside it any more. I see swirling trees. The sky. The grass pressed against my nose. I hear birds. And my own voice—guttural, grunting, tongue-impaired efforts to say Dave's name. I wonder whether I'm dying.

And finally, as my mind tries desperately to hang on to some sense of what's happening, my body says, "No, that's enough. You can stop now." And everything goes black.

I WAKE TO THE face of a man. He rubs a damp cloth against my forehead. The pain in my side is so intense that I can barely think. I don't recognize this man. But I don't even wonder who he is. I only wonder about two things—the pain, and Dave. A stab hits me. I shout, doubling up, wrapping my arms around my midsection.

"Hold still," the man says, pressing a firm hand against my forehead. "You need to lie still. Sheila went to get help."

"Sheila?"

"Yes."

"Where's Dave?"

"Dave?"

"My dog. Where is she? She was right there." I try to turn and point, but the pain makes me shout.

"She was?"

"She was right there."

"I didn't see her. I'm sorry."

"I saw her." And I burst into tears.

I surrender, lying back. The pain digs toward my heart, and I can't help myself. I have to disobey this man's command to lie still. I fold myself into a ball and cry. And my sight fades. And the sky turns a strange shade of gray, then purples, oranges, and greens, and finally—again—black.

Chapter Twenty-Five

Whether the decision is a conscious one or not, your personality is bound to be reflected in the house you build. A lot of people will make these decisions with others in mind, thinking of their reputation, and the image they're projecting. But you are the one who will spend every day in your house. You will be surrounded each day by these choices, and the reminders of what led to these decisions.

Your House, Your Self
Chapter 10
"House Envy"

The doctor didn't even have to consult the tests to figure out what happened. That first morning, after I'd choked down a couple of pieces of toast, she stood over my bed, looking over the top of half-lens glasses.

"You suffered a seizure," she said, her look slightly disapproving.

"A seizure? I've never had any kind of seizure before. What kind of seizure?"

"Withdrawals...alcohol withdrawals."

"But I've hardly had anything to drink for days."

She studied me as if she wasn't sure I was worthy of this discussion. "That would fit very nicely into the definition of withdrawals, wouldn't it? How much do you normally drink, Mr. Hurley?"

"Not that much."

She closed her eyes.

"Not lately, anyway," I qualified.

"Okay, now we're getting somewhere. How about before?"

I don't know why I answered her honestly. I'd never done it before. With anyone. And I'm still shocked at what came out of my mouth. It was surprising not just because I admitted it to someone I barely know. But it was as if I had been keeping the information a secret from myself. As if I'd been drinking behind my own back, hiding bottles from myself.

I told her that I drink every day. I told her that on the days I don't drink, I want to drink so bad that it's sometimes the only thing I can think about. I told her that before I moved to Bozeman, I sometimes lost track of time. I would lose a few hours here and there. I told her that I once forgot where I was or what I'd been doing for three straight days.

"Three days?"

I verified this with my silent shame, staring at my feet, which were the only exposed part of my body. They seemed far away, like another set of feet—a spare set. "Mr. Hurley, I'm going to give it to you straight, because in my experience, it's the best way with people like you. Your liver is in bad shape. You might be able to drink for another twenty years, and still not feel the effects. On the other hand..." She tilted her head. She had metallic hair—light copper with streaks of silver. "It's impossible to guess, but in some cases, the alcohol works very fast. But think about this—things like this don't happen to people who drink socially, Mr. Hurley."

I took this in. "Are you saying I'm an alcoholic?"

"I'm not going to say that. But for a man your age, and an athlete, your liver is way too big. That indicates something."

"Do you know Leslie Monday?" I asked her.

"Who?"

"Never mind."

A TINNY KNOCK on my trailer door interrupts the earnest performance of a soap opera star who is threatening to kill his ex-wife's new boyfriend. I shake my head at how upset I am about this interference. In the seven days that I've had a television, I'm embarrassed at how quickly I've become addicted to daytime TV. Being laid up is not all it's cracked up to be.

It's Danielle.

"Well, this is a surprise." I look past her, out into the yard. I can't remember the last time she came to visit me alone, but it's been a long time, probably since before she met Barry.

"Hello." She walks right in, but she moves slowly, heavily. She wears a denim jacket, which she hugs around her torso.

"Why aren't you at work?" I return to my chair, trying to sneak a peek at the television.

Danielle also sits, across from me. "I left early." She looks around, but it's clear she's not really looking at anything. "How's it going?"

"Good. Fine," I answer, noticing that the two men on *General Hospital* are engaged in a wrestling match.

Danielle scans the room, and her eyes stop on a box of Snickers bars on the table next to my chair. "A new diet?"

"They're good for the craving." I form quotation marks with my fingers.

"Ah." Danielle nods once, then stands, walking around the trailer, studying. She picks up *Your House, Your Self* and leafs through it. But her eyes don't focus on the book. After a brief tour of the room, Danielle sits again. I keep one eye on the television, but watch Danielle look down at her knees. She sits frozen like this for a good minute, hands folded on her thighs.

"What's wrong?" I ask.

"I don't know, Pete. I've been so...so angry lately." The words come deliberately, her voice deep but quiet. "I've been yelling at the kids, for the stupidest things—shoes in the living room, spilled food. I scream at them like they set the house on fire." She finally looks up, her eyes showing a helpless fear. "And I've been hitting Barry. I hit him hard the other day, with my fist." She makes a fist and stares at it.

I freeze up.

"Hello." Danielle waves. "Did you hear anything I said?"

"Yes."

"And?"

"Well, I'm really sorry. I guess I'm not sure what to say, sis."

Danielle's face turns downward again. She hasn't done anything with her hair, which falls loosely around her shoulders. She stands. "I don't know what to do, Pete."

"Well, I'm not exactly the best person to ask, am I?"

"No." Her answer jumps from her mouth. "But believe it or not, you're not the only one in this family who has problems."

"I never said I was."

"Well, if you realize the rest of us might need a kind word now and then, you certainly don't seem too concerned about it."

Danielle paces, and I can hardly breathe from the nervous air that blocks my throat. Her statement is undeniable, and it only makes my helplessness more powerful. There's something I've been meaning to ask her, but this doesn't seem like the right time. "Do you think you could turn off that television long enough to have a conversation?"

"I'm sorry." I'm embarrassed that this didn't even occur to me. I punch the remote.

Danielle starts talking again, but she doesn't stop pacing. "I know you've got a lot on your mind, but I thought you might like to know that you're not alone. I thought you might like to know that someone still needs you." She stops, facing me, and beats her chest with her palm. "I fucking need you, Pete. Can you step outside that little circle of yours long enough to think about that?"

I look at her, and I wish like hell I could. I wish like hell I could get up and wrap my arms around her. That I could say something useful. "I'm sorry."

"You bastard. You selfish bastard," she says with a quiet reservation. "Do you think you're the first person to lose someone you love?" She points at my chest. "You can't stop loving people just to avoid getting hurt again...it doesn't work that way."

"But I don't feel anything...I can't feel anything."

"It's not about feeling anything, you idiot; it's about imagining what other people feel. It's about empathy."

"And how do you feel empathy? What if it's just not there?"

And before I even see her move toward me, I feel the sting of her palm against my cheek. The tears spring from my eyes, but Danielle doesn't see that something has broken inside, because she flees, slamming the door with a hollow aluminum thud.

I tilt my head back, wanting more than I can ever remember to drown this pain.

I HAVE DIFFICULTY seeing as I drive. The tears won't stop, blurring the road, the signs, the cars around me. I keep the speed down, despite my desperation to get where I'm going.

The intended path, the journey that I want to take, is toward downtown Bozeman, to The Sportsman. But as my vision becomes more obscured, I can't tell whether I'm going in the right direction.

I can make out the truck stop, at the end of Main just before the turnoff to the highway. I know I'm on track. But when I'm several blocks from The Sportsman, my pickup seems to veer off on its own. Without any conscious effort from me, we turn left on Elm. I wipe my eyes. The cries sing in my throat. I have to wipe my nose.

Six blocks down Elm, the pickup takes a sharp right. And halfway down that block, the vehicle swings a wide arch into the driveway of a white clapboard house, two stories high, with a Jeep Cherokee parked out front.

And before I have a chance to think about it, I jump out and dash for the door. I knock, not waiting for an answer. I enter, moving as swiftly as my aching body allows. Through the living room, which is empty, and into the kitchen, where my sister has just risen from her chair to answer the door. She sits again, also crying, and I fall to my knees, and bury my head in the crook of her neck. I grip the back of her chair and pull her spry little body tightly against me. And we cry together.

Chapter Twenty-Six

Food and emotion have a relationship that most people don't understand, or even recognize. The kitchen may be the most important room in your house.

Your House, Your Self
Chapter 12
"The Way to a Man's Heart"

It's the first time Danielle and I have shared a good cry since before my father died. She cried at his funeral, but I held firm to the memory of my father and his brothers at *their* father's funeral. My father had five brothers, and these six men stood in a row on one side of my grandfather's coffin—six men in black suits, with thin black ties, shedding not a single tear. They were like Secret Service agents without the sunglasses. I didn't like my grandfather much, and as far as I could tell, nobody else in the family did either. So I was baffled by the wailing among my relatives. I felt much more like my father and his brothers looked. And for years, I felt a sense of pride about not crying at the funeral. As if it said something about my masculinity.

Now this afternoon with Danielle reminds me of something else. That a good cry in our house always ended with a good laugh. After we hold each other for a long time, Danielle and I look up and, without speaking, start laughing. We laugh until we're crying again. Then there's an awkward silence as I let go of her and settle into the chair across from her.

"Do you remember Sunday nights when we were growing up?" I ask.

Danielle frowns. "You mean the way you used to go out and

throw that horrible rubber ball against the house?"

"On Sundays?"

"Oh yeah. You don't remember? Every Sunday night? For hours."

"I thought I did that every night."

Danielle laughs. "Well, that's true; you did. But Sundays you were out there until well after dark."

"Hm."

"What made you think of that?"

"Oh nothing. I was thinking of something else, I guess."

"No, really. What made you think of it?"

"You don't remember Dad disappearing into his study?"

Danielle shakes her head.

"Nothing else?"

"No. What are you talking about?"

"Never mind."

"God, I'm suddenly really hungry."

LATER THAT NIGHT, I choked down a sense of nerves and punched out the numbers of the Monday house. Arlene answered, and I nearly hung up.

"Hello…"

I didn't respond.

"Hello?" Arlene repeated.

"Hey Arlene. It's Pete. How are you?"

"Good. You?"

"I'm doing well."

"Good." Pause. "What's up?"

"Um…is Leslie around?"

Now there was a healthy pause. "Yeah. Just a sec."

It seemed to take Leslie forever to come to the phone. And once she did say hello, she was on a second line. Arlene didn't hang up right away.

"How are you?" I asked.

"Fine. Busy. But that's nothing new."

I cleared my throat, waiting for a click, but it didn't come. "What are you up to this evening?" I asked.

"Working on a case. Not a very interesting one, I'm afraid. I get about five of these for every one that's interesting."

Finally, I heard a click.

I wiped a bead of sweat from my forehead. "I was wondering whether you might want to do something one of these evenings... maybe have some dinner, or take in a movie..." A pause. "Bowling?"

"Bowling?"

"That was a joke."

There was a slight chuckle, then another pause, and I was sure I'd made a big mistake.

"Pete, are you asking me out?"

I thought of backpedaling, trying to cover my tracks. But I knew that if anyone would want a straight answer, it would be Leslie Monday. "Yes I am."

"All right. I have a suggestion. What if we just spend an evening together? Not a date."

"And the difference?"

"You know the difference. No threat of sex."

"Threat?"

She laughed. "Well, I didn't mean it that way."

"All right. I can live with that."

So I'm on my way to the Monday house. My first date (I'm not convinced) in many months. Since the accident.

My knock brings Leslie to the door. Her hair is pulled back, with a wide barrette holding a flowing blonde wave that cascades down her back. Her boyish cheeks are slightly flushed. She wears an olive green silk blouse, and a darker green blazer. It looks as if she's also forgotten that this isn't a date.

I've noticed since I met her that Leslie's beauty has a quality I can't quite identify—something different, something that draws me to her in a way most beauty doesn't. Tonight, as she pulls an overcoat over her blazer, I realize what it is. It's a guarded quality. A discomfort with the fact that she's beautiful. Not in the sense that she tries to hide it. But more in the sense that it's not important to her, and that she wishes it wasn't important to others.

"You look very nice," I tell her.

"Thank you. It appears you've made something of an effort yourself."

I hold my arms out. "I wore my best jeans."

I made a reservation at the best restaurant I've been to in Bozeman—a place on Main that serves excellent steaks. They also manage to find decent seafood, considering Bozeman is hundreds of miles from the scent of salt water.

The talk on the way to the restaurant is stiff, minimal. We've never been particularly comfortable in conversation to begin with. But this evening, it's worse.

"What are you going to do about your house over the winter?" Leslie asks.

"Study, so I know what to do when spring rolls around."

She looks out the window. It's snowing, and by the time we reach Main, the flakes shine in the streetlights, sending tiny flashes into the black sky.

"That snow looks amazing," I say.

"Hm." Leslie looks again. "I guess I don't even notice any more. I've never lived anywhere else."

"Well, it snows in Massachusetts, too."

"Not five months out of the year."

"True. But everything looks different here. Bigger somehow."

I park a block from the restaurant, and we hunch our shoulders against the cold. Minutes later, our coats hang specked with moisture in the corner, and we rub the cold from our hands as we sit.

We both order steaks. Leslie orders a glass of wine, then watches me closely as I refuse the same. Or so I imagine.

"How's the boring case coming?"

"Very well, actually."

"So you manage to find pleasure even in the boring cases?"

"Not always. But when I do the best I can on a case, it usually gives me a sense of satisfaction."

"That sounds like something my father would say."

"Does it?"

"Yep. Most of his happiness came in the form of work."

Leslie smiles. "I wouldn't go that far."

The waiter delivers her wine, and my seltzer water. We toast.

"To boring cases."

Leslie chuckles, and we drink.

"So what have you been doing since you got out of the hospital?"

I relate the activities of the past couple of weeks, and as Leslie's genuine interest melts away my defenses, I become more comfortable.

"Have you been seeing anyone?" she asks.

"Very funny."

"Why?"

"Do you think I would've called if I was seeing someone?"

"It wouldn't be all that revolutionary. People do date more than one person these days."

"Some do. I've never been able to do that, for some reason. Besides, this isn't a date, remember?"

"No it isn't." She looks down, and one side of her mouth curls.

"What about you?" I ask. "You don't seem to mention anyone, past or present."

She drinks, thinking. "You're right...particularly present." Leslie sips more wine, then sets her glass carefully back on the table. "I don't have time for men."

"You are busy."

She nods. "You've been single for a long time too, haven't you?"

"Sort of." I wonder how she knows this.

"Was the last one the woman who's injured?"

I pull my head back. "How do you know about that?" I try to ask casually, but my voice is strained.

"Danielle told me, that day we all talked to you." She shares this easily, as if it is the most natural thing in the world, telling very tenuous friends your darkest secrets.

"She did?"

"Does that bother you?" Her look challenges me.

"A little, yeah. But maybe that explains why you were so hard on me that day."

"I was, wasn't I?"

"I think your intentions were good, though. Now."

"Do you really?" Her eyes grab mine.

"I do."

"I'm not very objective when it comes to booze."

"You have good reason."

"Maybe." She drops her eyes again, studying her wine glass. I sense it's time to change the subject.

"You were never married?"

Leslie's eyes remain fixed on her glass, which she raises again, sipping. After swallowing, she takes a deep breath. "I never was." She places two fingers on the base of the glass, and she begins rotating it slowly, pushing with one finger, pulling with the other, so that the glass twirls clockwise. The wine rocks slightly, coating the sides. "Engaged once. A long time ago." She sits forward, suddenly. "So how have you been feeling? Have you recovered?"

"I've been feeling pretty good."

"It must be hard."

"What?"

"You know." She tips her head toward her wine glass.

I clear my throat. "It is hard," I admit, to my surprise. "But I'm doing okay."

"Yeah?"

I study her, looking for signs of the judgment I saw at Barry and Danielle's house. It's not there. Her expression is steady but concerned. Not quite soft, but definitely not hard.

"I haven't had a drink since."

"Really?"

I nod, almost taking offense that she's surprised.

"That's great. It really is."

"Yeah, well it doesn't feel so great. It feels like..."

"Like being tied to the front of a car going through a carwash?"

I laugh. "Maybe. Where the hell did you come up with that?"

"That's how a friend of mine described it once."

"It's probably different for everybody. The hardest part is the time alone." The minute this thought leaves my mouth, I regret it. I don't want to admit this, especially to Leslie. I don't want her to think I'm suggesting anything, or looking for sympathy.

"That's hard for everyone," she finally says.

"I suppose that's true. But for most people, the stakes aren't as high."

Her expression takes on a very subtle softness, even revelation, as if this aspect has never occurred to her. "Very true."

"And speaking of changing the subject..." I say as the food arrives.

Leslie frowns as the waiter sets our plates in front of us. He asks whether we need anything else. And as he walks away, Leslie asks, "What do you mean?"

"*You* did. You changed the subject, and not very gracefully, I might add."

She drops her eyes with a slight grin, but it's shaded with

something a little darker. "Ah, well—right now, this steak needs my attention."

"Very smooth. The lawyer in her comes in handy at times."

As we eat, the conversation becomes decidedly lighter, which seems to be a relief to Leslie. But I want to talk more freely, about things that matter.

So as we near the end of the meal, I prop my arms up by my elbows, lacing my fingers at chin level. I rest my jaw on my knuckles.

"So..." I say. "What happened?"

Leslie wipes her mouth. "He was killed."

"Oh." I sigh. "I'm so sorry. I seem to do this to you a lot."

"It's all right." Her voice doesn't waver, nor do her eyes. "Like I said, it was a long time ago."

"Still..."

"Yeah. Still." She nods, but maintains her gaze, as well as her firm tone of voice. She leans toward me, and lowers her head, pointing at her forehead, near the hairline. "See this?"

I study her forehead. Running nearly parallel to her hairline is a scar, about three inches long. I'm surprised I've never noticed it before, although it's very pale.

"There were five people in the car," Leslie says.

I have to think. The car? Then I realize. "Five?" I pause to think again—Arlene, Mrs. Monday, Mr. Monday, Leslie, and...

"The same accident?"

Leslie lowers her head, and her inability to even answer this question tells me more about her than anything she's ever said.

A HALF HOUR LATER, we step out into the cold, dry air of Montana winter. It's so cold that I take the chance of wrapping an arm around Leslie's shoulders. She doesn't flinch. And we hunker down, making ourselves as small as possible as the wind whips our faces for the one block journey to my truck.

"Well well well...what have we here?"

The voice is familiar, but when I look up, the wind blurs my vision.

"Hello, Clint," Leslie says.

"I had no idea," Clint says.

"You still don't." Leslie's voice is teasing. We stop, facing Clint.

"No? Well, it seems pretty clear from this angle." Clint's smile is wide, and he raises his eyebrows in an exaggerated gesture.

"How you feeling, Clint?" My vision has cleared. Clint's eyes are bleary. I think back to what Arlene told me about Clint's struggle with booze, and his unfocused gaze reveals a hint of hopeless desperation behind the swagger. For a moment, I actually sympathize with the guy.

"Oh, I don't know. Maybe I'm a bit thick-headed, but I have a hard time believing that you actually give a shit, Hurley."

"You're right, actually. I don't care at all. But I guess I'm not very good at holding grudges. Some people aren't worth the effort."

"Now, boys." Leslie maneuvers her body forward, at an angle, so that she's between us. "I've just had a good meal, and I'm too full to wrestle both of you. So why don't we just move along." She grabs my arm, tugging.

But I hold my position, staring at Clint. "Before we go here, Clint, maybe you can answer some questions about my dog."

"What?" He grins, and I notice that his lower lip is swollen, with a slight smear of blood, as if he's just been punched.

"What did you do with my dog?"

Clint takes a step, and Leslie reacts, pulling at my arm, harder this time.

"I don't know what the hell you're talking about, but if I knew where your dog was, I'd be more than happy to lose it for you."

Leslie wraps an arm tightly around my waist. But my anger is too strong. I break away. Clint steps forward, and I meet him. We stand face to face, and I feel and smell Clint's breath, which reeks of alcohol. My own breath races. I study his eyes, the bloodshot whites, the swollen rims. His expression is dead, so fraught with unhappiness and contempt that it's hard to imagine him feeling anything about anything. And despite my anger, I'm struck by the sad absurdity of the situation. At this moment I find it impossible to imagine him coming up with even the simplest scheme to steal my dog. I'm overcome with a desire to laugh, and in order to avoid laughing, I do something completely spontaneous. I lean forward, and plant a quick kiss on Clint's forehead.

His first blow is immediate—a reflex. The punch deflects off my chin, and my teeth clash. I hit him back, my fist glancing off his cheekbone. I feel a crack of pain in my knuckles. And then the action comes in a flurry. We collide, arms wrapping around each other, fists emerging, then plunging, mostly missing. We groan. We swear. Our heads butt. I draw one fist back and try to thrust a punch into his stomach, but Clint's arm shifts, and my fist meets his elbow. A shout escapes my throat. It occurs to me that we must look hilariously inept.

Then something pounds against my ribs, and I feel a pressure against my midsection. I'm being pushed away from Clint, and I realize that Leslie has wedged her body between us, trying to pry us apart. Her silky hair feels soft against my jaw. Suddenly she flies out from between us, falling with an ugly thud. Clint has thrown her down.

A roar rises up from inside me, a roar that is fueled not just by this single act, but as if every injustice I've ever experienced or witnessed has converged. My legs pump. I drive Clint backwards. He stumbles for a few strides, then cannot keep up with the pace. He falls, and I tumble onto him, my shoulder piling into his chest with the force of ten of my best punches. And all the pain bursts from his throat in a violent groan, followed by the desperate sigh of a man trying to catch his breath. I pummel him, landing four hearty blows into his chest and head before a torso lands on my back and falls to one side, taking me with it. I land on my stomach, and Leslie growls in my ear, "You dumbass, do you want a lawsuit on top of everything else?" She lies on top of me, her limbs wrapped around me. "Take a deep breath," she says quietly. "Breathe."

"Let me go," I utter through my teeth. I try twisting my head to see what Clint is doing, whether he's conscious or not. But Leslie has me pinned so that my head is pointed in the opposite direction.

"No," she says. "You can't afford more trouble."

"I don't care about that." I'm amazed at Leslie's strength, as I cannot move.

"Think about it, Pete."

"God dammit, Leslie, stop lecturing me and let go."

And then a frightening smack sounds from behind me. Leslie's torso lands on the back of my head. Clint has hit her. Her arms go limp, so I roll over, preparing to take her in my arms. But a fist catches the side of my head. I stumble, and the bright white of violence blinds me for a moment. I have just enough consciousness to raise my arms, covering my face. A second blow glances off my forearm.

I shake my head, clearing the fuzz. Clint comes into focus, advancing toward me. His teeth are clenched, and the intent of more violence shows in his eyes. From the corner, I notice that Leslie is motionless, and this jars me from the semi-consciousness.

But my intentions are hampered by the damage from Clint's blows. I swing, but my fist follows a wild arch, like an untrained golf swing. And whether Clint possesses more fighting skill than I do or whether he's just more awake, he manages to throw his next punch just as mine misses, in the direction of my left ear. His fist lands hard, sending the sound of a church bell bounding inside my skull. I fall, and have just enough awareness to look to my right, where Leslie is not moving. I see blood next to her head, and I try to reach for her, to put an arm around her, to pull her toward me. But before my hand gets that far, another blow lands. Or so I'm told.

Chapter Twenty-Seven

Today, in a nice bit of irony, the first pitcher to be suspended under the Peter Hurley Rule was none other than Roger Clemens, for throwing at Kevin Youkilis in the sixth inning of a game at Fenway Park. Are you guys buying that Clemens threw at him on purpose?

Tony Reali
Around the Horn
June 25, 2008

Coming out of the trees, back onto my property, I am greeted by the unpleasant form of a black pickup, hovering like a rain cloud in my driveway. It's been three days since I got out of the hospital again, and I've just come from the Monday house, where Leslie and I began discussions about a legal suit against Clint Weaver. My head throbs, and a bandage covers my right ear, which is swollen like...well, like a cauliflower. Leslie has a broken wrist, and two cracked ribs.

Burt Mackie climbs from his pickup, grinding a cigarette into the dirt with the heel of his boot. He carries a sheaf of papers in one hand.

"How you doin', Pete?" This is by far the friendliest greeting I've ever received from Mr. Mackie.

"Well, aside from this big ol' bell clanging in my head, I'm not doing too bad. How about you?"

Burt reaches to shake, and I comply without enthusiasm. "I'm good too."

"Let me guess—you brought me an invitation to your daughter's wedding?"

Mackie looks at the papers, a slight smile curling one side of his mouth. "Not exactly."

He hands me the papers, and I leaf through them. It's all the work permits, signed off.

"Well now, that's a nice present."

"You better look at the last page," he suggests.

I pull a sheet of cream-colored stationary from the bottom of the stack. It is a letter agreeing not to press charges against Clint if he pays all medical expenses.

"I'll need to think about this," I say.

"Well, I'll have to take these with me then." He reaches for the papers.

"I don't think so."

I think Burt's head very nearly explodes at this point. He takes off his hat, and it appears that just the act of touching the shining red skin on his forehead is painful. "I was afraid you'd say that."

"And?"

"Well, there's not much I can do about it, but I hope you sign that agreement. I'm getting a lot of pressure."

"Oh?" It's so tempting to tell him how little I care. "Like I said, I'll think about it. I need to talk to a lawyer."

Burt nods, then turns and starts to put his hat on. But I think he knows that the pressure would be too much. So he swings it at his side as he strolls back to his pickup, then drives away.

I decide to go directly back to Leslie's house to share the news.

"OH, THIS IS beautiful, Pete." Leslie reads the letter again, a pair of rectangular reading glasses nearly toppling from the tip of her nose. "He's scared. We don't have to do a thing. We can just wait, and eventually he'll panic."

"You don't want to sue?"

Leslie tips her head to one side. "What the hell for? Neither one of us really needs the money, right? It's not worth the aggravation." She pauses, then turns, looking at me over her glasses. "Unless you want to."

I hesitate, thinking fond thoughts of putting Clint through his own hell.

"Another thing." She takes off her glasses. "As much as Clint would like people to believe otherwise, he doesn't have a dime. We'd probably never see the money. With court costs, it would probably end up costing *us*."

"Okay. That's good enough for me."

Leslie smiles, which is rare enough that I notice it. And sad, because her smile is so lovely. She puts her glasses back on, and reads the letter one more time. The look of joy on her face is infectious.

"You really love this stuff, don't you?"

She raises her brow. "I told you I did."

"I wish you'd been my lawyer," I say.

"For what?"

"Oh, the Yankees...they sued for what happened to that guy I hit."

"Why?"

"They're the Yankees, I guess. Steinbrenner wasn't happy with the offer from the Sox."

"And you lost?"

"Yeah. I don't know where they found this guy, but he was a joke."

"How much did that set you back?"

"Fortunately, the Sox covered it. It was more the humiliation of having the whole thing dragged out for months. Being in the public eye isn't all it's cracked up to be sometimes."

Leslie studies me for a long time, until I want to hide my face. "You know, you have no reason to feel ashamed of what happened... it was an accident, right? You didn't try to hit that guy."

I meet her gaze, and the sincerity of her expression makes me wish it was that easy. "Believe me, I've thought that same thing every day since it happened. There are plenty of things I'd love to be able to let go of."

"Yeah? What else? The accident with that girl?"

"Mm hm."

"That was an accident, too, wasn't it?"

I think about Leslie's take on her parents' death, and wonder whether she'd see it as an accident if she knew the whole story. "That's open to interpretation."

Leslie drops her chin, thinking. "You were drunk?"

"Yeah...I was in a blackout. I don't remember it."

"So what happened?"

I hesitate, but only briefly, before telling her the story.

Leslie takes it all in, then sits deep in thought for a long time.

"I hope you don't take this wrong, Pete, but I think it's going to take years to get over that." She shakes her head. "I mean, I just don't see any other way around it."

"I thought you said I have nothing to be ashamed about."

"I'm not talking about shame. I'm talking about remorse."

"So you think I deserve to punish myself for awhile, is that it?"

Leslie gets a look of profound impatience, her mouth pinching tighter. "Hell no," she says. "The only way to get through some things is to go through them—that's all I'm saying. You can't just pray or work out or take a pill to make this stuff go away."

"I agree with you there."

"How many years has it been since you hit that guy?"

I look at her. "I thought you didn't know anything about baseball."

She tilts her head. "I did a little research."

"Ah." This pleases me more than I'd like to admit. "That was about four years ago."

"Have you seen anyone about all this stuff, Pete?"

I shake my head. "Well, the Red Sox sent me to see a shrink, but that was just to try and get me pitching again."

"Pete." Leslie grabs my eyes with an uncompromising gaze. "You need to get some help; you can't expect to get through this on your own."

I study Leslie. "Aren't you the same person who told me you never talk about what happened to your parents—to anyone?"

Leslie smiles. "You must have me mistaken with someone else."

"How are your ribs?" I ask.

"Oh, they're fine." She touches her side, just below her breast. "You know, sore."

"Sure."

"Pete, can I just tell you something?"

"Of course."

She pushes her lips forward, frowning, thinking. And then she bobs her head once, indicating she's got the wording down. "It's important that you know—there is no way, Pete, that I would ever get involved with someone who has a drinking problem unless they'd been sober for at least a year."

"Oh?"

"That's right."

I'm stunned into silence for a moment. "I'll make a note of it," I finally say.

"Thank you."

OVER THE NEXT week, before my trip to Amherst, I push away all thoughts of fear and rejection and call Leslie every single evening, asking if she'd like some company. And to my delight, she keeps saying yes. So just as the sun sinks below the horizon, I take the short walk over to her place, and we talk. It's frightening, but comfortably so. I tell her more about myself than I've told anyone. And she never once runs screaming from the room.

The night before my trip to Amherst, as I'm leaving, she takes my hand. "Pete, I don't think it would be a good idea for you to call me while you're there."

"Okay. Why?"

"I don't know. It's just a feeling."

"Are you jealous?"

She looks down.

"You *are* jealous."

"I will neither confirm nor deny these allegations," she says.

"Well, I'll honor your request," I say, "but I don't like it much."

Leslie chews the inside of her lip. "Well, there's one exception."

"And what's that?"

"If you think you're going to drink, call me. Or call somebody."

"I'm not going to drink," I say.

"Just promise me."

I hold up three fingers, Boy Scout fashion.

Leslie smiles. A moment later, she reaches into her pocket, and pulls something out. She grabs my hand, and presses a cool, hard object into my palm. "Take this so you'll think of me."

I look down. It's a pocket watch. A gold pocket watch with ornate etchings on the cover. I touch a knob, and the lid flips open.

"It was my father's," she says. "He carried a pocket watch and a knife. Arlene got the knife, and I got that."

"You're kidding. I can't take this." I hold it out to her.

"Pete...just take it."

"Well I'm sure as hell not going to keep it."

"We can talk about that when you get back."

Chapter Twenty-Eight

Bud Selig denied an appeal from Roger Clemens into his suspension for intentionally hitting Kevin Youkilis in the head with a pitch on June 24. Clemens has been suspended for twenty games in accordance with the new Pete Hurley Rule. Baseball is finally doing something right!

Michael Wilbon
Pardon the Interruption
June 30, 2007

I follow the dark tunnel, my feet thumping against the thin floor of the passage leading from flight 1085 to the terminal of Bradley Airport in Hartford, Connecticut. I haven't told anyone in Amherst that I'm coming, to make sure the word didn't get back to the Watsons.

I drive my rental car from Hartford to Amherst, toward my old home, doing much the same as I did on the flight out. I review the plan for my arrival at the Watson house. I imagine different scenarios, and script my response to each.

Traveling down the familiar route to the Watson house, for once in my life, I have a specific plan. I am going to offer my services to the Watsons. If they'll have me, I'm willing to do whatever I can do to help. I will propose that I move back to Amherst if they think I can be useful. Even if it's only for a few months.

The drive is interminable. As if I'm driving through my lifetime. I pass my grade school, and the steak house where I had my first job. I pass the mall where Charlie and I used to glue our sweaty palms to video games for hours at a time, or wander the cavernous halls in search of the mythical loose girls.

I approach the Watson's, passing the park where Simone and I had our last big fight, and the corner where we were nearly flattened the first time we rode my bike. Although I'm wearing a t-shirt, the collar is choking me.

The house looks the same. The house has never changed. It's the same light green it was when I met Charlie. The trim is also still green, a few shades darker. The shrubs around the front are thicker, but still impeccably shaped. One of Mr. Watson's obsessions, his shrubs.

I survey the front yard, where Charlie and I fired ten-year-old fastballs to each other the first time we met. My mind works hard, reviewing my opening speech, and my rebuttal to each argument. I pull my shoulders back, prepared to defend my plan.

I knock, and footsteps echo from inside. I wonder who it will be—Mr. or Mrs. Watson, or perhaps the mysterious, frank Brenda Walters. The weeks of practiced dialogue echo through my head. Mr. Watson would be the easiest, I know. He's the least likely to display his anger in an obvious way. A handshake will probably break the tension. With Mrs. Watson, it will be more complicated. Much of her identity was wrapped up in Simone and her accomplishments. And our relationship was strained even before the accident, with her silent disapproval. I've imagined Mrs. Watson's cool but cordial greeting, and my plan is to apologize profusely, letting my sincere grief show as raw and unpracticed as possible. Brenda, of course, is the unknown quantity, the one I hope will answer the door. Besides knowing nothing about Brenda, her letter showed little chance of sympathy. So I intend to focus on humility with her—humble, hat-in-hand earnestness.

And because my mind is locked in on these three possibilities, and no others, when the door opens, and it's Charlie's face that greets me, I'm thrown completely off-balance. I haven't prepared for this, assuming Charlie would be at work, or at his own home. So what comes out of my mouth is spontaneous, the first thing that enters my head.

"What are you doing here?"

Charlie's eyes get wide. "I think that's my line." He frowns. "Wow, this is a big surprise."

"I'm sorry I didn't call. I was worried someone would tell me not to come."

Charlie nods. "Listen, as it turns out, this is a really bad time.

Maybe you could come back tomorrow morning. Simone just had some tests done and she's out of it. Plus I have to be somewhere in a half hour or I'd invite you in."

"Okay...yeah. Sure. I'll come back in the morning."

Charlie reaches out and shakes my hand, and then pulls me to him and wraps his arms around me. I fight back tears. We part.

"Good to see you, Pete."

"Thank you, Charlie. It's really good to see you too."

Chapter Twenty-Nine

*The trouble with being labeled as troubled is that it
ends up being the only thing that interests anybody.
So you start to believe it.*

Pete Hurley
Interviewed by Bryant Gumbel
January 24, 2007

Driving away from the Watsons, past my old house, I'm surprised
how emotional I am. At the moment, what I think of is a dark,
isolated bar. In an unfamiliar section of town. I could avert this
temptation. I could call Leslie, as she asked. Or Danielle or Barry.
Even Arlene.

I drive through the town where I grew up. Away from all the
places I know. I avoid all landmarks. I avoid the house where my
mother died. All buildings where I ever worked or lived. I avoid
every baseball field I ever played on. I avoid all reminders of Simone,
of all the Watsons. Anything that will make me think of Dave.

I check into my hotel room, and the clerk says, "Hey, you're
him!"

I don't respond, but he is compelled to add, "Man, that was
really fucked up what happened to that girl."

I don't make it to my room. Instead, I find a nondescript brown
tavern with cheap siding and a hand-painted sign: "Vin's." An
uneven string of Christmas lights circles the name. When I walk
inside, I know I've found just what I'm looking for. The floor is
stained linoleum. The pool table lists to one side, with one leg
completely broken off. Most of the plastic seat covers are split.
I slink inconspicuously into a corner where I'm approached by a

bleached, blue eye-shadowed barmaid.

"Can you sell me a bottle?"

"Why not?"

"I was hoping you'd say that."

"What do you want?"

"Whiskey."

She brings me a fifth of rot gut, and a water glass. They don't fuck around at Vin's. I fill it, and drain half the glass in my first drink. I close my eyes, and as the burn passes down my throat into my belly, I wait for warm euphoria to travel into my head. But it doesn't. I don't feel anything. I open my eyes. I hold up my glass, toward the single bulb that dangles from the ceiling. The liquid looks to be the right color, the right consistency for whiskey. I see the alcoholic swirl snaking through. I drink again, emptying the glass. And I wait again, knowing that tolerance can vary. Surely ten ounces is enough to get some kind of kick. But no. I feel nothing.

I motion for the barmaid.

"Yeah?"

"You guys don't happen to water down your booze, do you?"

She looks as if she's going to slap me. "Did you break the seal on that bottle or not?" she asks.

"I'm sorry. I just...well, I'm sorry."

She turns, expressing her disapproval with the swivel of her hips.

After downing two more tumblers, I still feel nothing, and I leave, bottle tucked under my arm. The barmaid doesn't acknowledge my "Thanks...seeya." In the parking lot, I drink straight from the bottle, until it's almost half gone. And when I still feel nothing aside from the acidic fire in my throat, I begin to panic. I've read somewhere that this can happen—that it's possible for a person's tolerance to reach a level where the alcohol simply doesn't work. I thought this was a myth—just one more theory cooked up by alcohol counselors to scare the shit out of people like me. But this isn't right. I drain several more fingers from the bottle. This time, I begin to feel ill, but there's still nothing happening upstairs. I glare at the bottle, as if I can somehow scare the whiskey into doing its job. "Please," I say quietly, talking to the bottle like an old lover. I drink again, and when this mouthful comes right back up, I throw the door open just before my stomach empties onto the asphalt.

The surge throws me to the ground, and there, on my knees, in the parking lot of an anonymous bar in Amherst, Massachusetts, I am overcome with a feeling of panic, a fear I've never experienced before. I've always known what to expect. Alcohol has been reliable that way. I'm terrified by the thought that it might not work anymore. I sink to my elbows, resting my head against my forearm, and I cry like a damn baby.

THE NEXT MORNING, I stand at the Watson's front door, hoping it's not too obvious that I've spent a good portion of the past twelve hours crying. I checked into a hotel and tried to sleep, with no success. I drank the entire fifth of whiskey, and never did get drunk. This morning, I ate a piece of dry toast, showered, and put on clean clothes, although I was too shaky to wrestle with a razor. I hope it doesn't show that I'm completely defeated. At least I know that the Watsons won't be able to tell that, just twelve hours ago, I was on my knees, praying my ass off. No one will ever know that.

I realize immediately who answers the door, although I've never seen her before. Brenda Walters looks very much as I pictured her. She's whippet thin, with the leathery complexion of someone who's smoked way too much for way too long. Her hair is wispy and dyed an unnatural reddish brown. She appears to be close to sixty.

"Well well well...you're back." She seems amused.

I duck my head, a smile of complete chagrin. "Charlie told you, huh?"

She nods, and although she smiles, it's a wary smile. Not skeptical, though. Not mistrusting. Just wary. There's a gentleness to it that is immediately likable. I am also charmed by the fact that she makes no move to introduce herself. She knows that I know.

"Any chance of seeing her?"

"Who?" And now her smile tells me that she's also a smartass.

I hold my hands out, presenting myself.

"You look horrible, you know."

I act shocked, and she chuckles, showing her appreciation for a fellow smartass. "Are you drunk?"

This doesn't even offend me. Her manner shows no judgment. It occurs to me that my blood alcohol level is probably off the charts. But still, I can answer honestly, "I'm not."

Brenda Walters steps outside. "Let's walk."

"Okay." This woman is foreboding, I realize. Despite her lack of physical presence, I'll get away with nothing here. But it's a relief to not feel the need to hide anything. For the moment, I feel oddly comfortable.

"Come on." She grabs my elbow. I follow, and her lead is assertive, with a strong grip. "What exactly do you hope to accomplish here?"

"I have no idea," I admit. "I thought I did when I showed up. But now, I just want to see her."

"But why?" Brenda looks straight up at me as we walk, her body pivoting so she turns toward me. She still has a solid grip on my elbow. "You want to apologize?"

"Of course. That's part of it."

"But you've already done that. You've apologized over and over, right?"

"Not really."

"Yes you have. You left a bunch of messages. You wrote letters to her parents, e-mails to Charlie. You've apologized many times." She emphasizes "many."

"Well, I feel awful about what happened."

"Sure you do. Who wouldn't? You feel so bad, in fact, that you keep doing the same damn thing, drinking yourself into a stupor, creating more havoc."

"What are you talking about?"

Brenda stops. She faces me, finally releasing my elbow. "Pete, don't bullshit me. We hear things. You don't think the Watsons are interested in what's going on with you out there?"

I stand motionless.

"Listen, Pete. You're useless to anyone this way." She points right at my chest. "Believe me, I know. I've been there."

I question her with a look.

"That's right. That's why I know you." Her expression is like one big wink.

My face turns hot.

"And if you're anything like me…" she continues. "You came out here with some grand idea of saving Simone." She makes quotation marks with her fingers. "But instead you got drunk. You got emotional about being back home, and it was more than you could handle. So you got drunk."

Although I could make a technical argument about the drunk

part, the accuracy of her assessment leaves me speechless. There's no point in denying any of it, nor is there any reason to confirm it. She's speaking for me, and about me, and she knows it.

"But you have nothing to offer these people in your condition." She grabs my upper arms. "You know that, right?"

"I think so."

She smiles broadly. "I think so," she echoes, mocking me. "You know," she states. "You know as well as I do." Now Brenda grabs my elbow again, pulling. We resume our military march. I feel like a dog. I feel like stopping to lift my leg at the next tree.

"I still want to see her."

"Yes. 'Course you do."

We walk silently for a few strides, and I realize we're across the street from the Watson house. In front of my old house.

"I may be tough, but you don't really think I'm that cruel, do you?"

"I have no idea what to expect from you."

She laughs. "I scare the hell out of you, don't I?"

"You could say that."

She laughs again, and her laugh is really quite delightful, despite the smoker's rasp. It's a joyful laugh. In fact, there is something undeniably joyful about Brenda Walters.

"You wanna hear something interesting, Pete Hurley?"

"What?"

She looks sideways, up at me. "I knew your mother."

I stop, causing Brenda to lose her grip on my elbow. She spins a quarter turn.

"How?" I ask.

"Well, Pete, this isn't exactly New York City now, is it? I knew her pretty well, actually."

"Wow." It's all I can say. I've always wondered why I haven't heard more about my mother. It was almost as if nobody around us knew her. My questions about her were always met with mute stares.

I gather myself, and start walking again, although my pace is decidedly slower. "So was she nice?"

"She...could be."

This catch in Brenda's delivery says so much. And not just about my mother. But about Brenda being incapable of telling even a small lie—even one that might soothe a bruised soul.

"She had an interesting sense of humor," she says, and I feel the desperation in this attempt to give me something to hold onto.

And this tiny fact does bring a smile to my face. But this is all I want to know. Brenda has confirmed what I always suspected, that perhaps my mother was not a pleasant person. It reminds me of Arlene's assessment that it's disrespectful to recall people as anything other than what they were. Knowing the details might be a little too much at the moment.

"Thank you for telling me that."

We're now standing at the front door of the Watson house. "You're in luck," Brenda whispers. "Nobody else is home."

"Good." I don't remember being so nervous.

Brenda leads me through the living room, then down the hall. She holds up her palm. "Wait here for a second."

She ducks into Simone's room, closing the door. And I feel violently ill. I make it to the bathroom just in time. I empty my stomach, although there's not much left. Then I sit for a few minutes, holding my forehead. I feel those pinpricks of sweat all over my face. A gentle knock sounds.

"You okay in there?"

"I just need a sec."

I douse my face with cold water, then stumble into the hall. Brenda wraps an arm around my waist. "You sure you're okay?"

"Fine." I nod. "So does she want to see me?"

"'Course she does."

I run both hands through my hair, realizing that it's been months since I got a haircut. My hair's like a goddam feather duster. "I'm ready."

Brenda stops me, placing a hand firmly against my chest. Her manner shifts, becoming very business-like. "Keep it short. I don't know how long they'll be gone." She tilts her head, indicating the Watsons. "And if you so much as bring a tear to this girl's eye, I swear I'll wring that big ol' neck of yours." She stops, studying me, her brown eyes snapping.

"You made your point."

"All right. Sorry; I'm a bit protective."

"It's okay."

I'm trembling as I enter the room. Brenda's warning gives me the impression that I'm about to be confronted by a frail, withering shell of a human being. But Simone looks terrific. Although she's slightly pale, her face is full, with much more color than I expected. Her arms come together on her lap, where her hands look almost normal, and it makes me unbearably sad thinking that they are no longer able to hold a violin.

Simone and I lock eyes, and the connection paralyzes both of us for a moment.

"You look great," I manage to mutter.

"Right."

"You really do."

"You're serious." She turns her head to the side, still looking at me. Her hair is shorter, cut in a fashionable style. And she's obviously put on some makeup.

"I am."

She shakes her head, smiling skeptically.

"Simone, I'm so sorry."

"I know," she says.

"How are you doing?" I ask.

"I feel a little better."

"What about your dad?"

"He's not good. They don't expect him to live much longer."

This hurts. "I'm so sorry." There's a long pause, during which we simply look at each other. "I don't know what else to say."

"Well, what did you come for? Why don't you start there?"

"I thought you wanted me to come."

She breathes in, closing her eyes. She nods, very slightly, and her eyes open in a slow reveal. "This is harder than I thought it would be."

"Well, let me just come out with it. I came here to offer to move back here. To help out."

Simone looks at me with her mouth half open, a smile of incomprehension curling one side of her mouth. "Are you kidding?"

I look down.

"You think having you here would help? Pete, I was so glad you left."

"Why did you want to see me then?"

Simone turns away, her jaw locked. "I thought it would help—maybe help us both put all this behind us." Her eyes get moist.

"Plus I missed you."

"But you broke up with me," I protest.

"You don't think I can miss you just because I broke up with you?"

I take a deep breath. "There must be things you want to say to me."

"I thought so, too. But now that you're here..."

I hold out my arms. "Well...go ahead."

She looks at me sideways. "What possible good would that do?"

"It might help."

"I don't think so."

I'm surprised to find myself thinking that we really don't have anything else to say to each other. "Well maybe I should leave."

She ponders this, chewing on the inside of her cheek.

"Simone, sweetheart...remember what we talked about." Brenda's gentle reminder comes from behind me, and it startles me. I had forgotten she was in the room.

Simone glares past me, still thinking. Then she turns away, closing her eyes, breathing deep. She drops her jaw, as if she's about to say something. But instead, she shakes her head slowly. "Listen, Pete. We both know what happened was an accident, but I wasn't able to tell you the truth about why I broke up with you."

"So there was someone else?" I ask.

She shakes her head. "No."

Simone opens her eyes and looks past me at Brenda, as if she's looking for help.

"*I'm* not gonna tell him," Brenda says.

Simone sighs. "I was really worried about your drinking, Pete. You scared me sometimes."

This shouldn't surprise me, should it? But it does. And it hurts.

A car door slams outside.

"Oh oh," Brenda says.

"Are they here?" Simone asks.

"Yep," Brenda answers.

"You should leave," Simone says.

But it's too late to make an effort to escape without some kind of ridiculous scramble out the back door. Besides, part of me wants to stay.

The front door opens.

"Pete," Simone says.

I ignore her. The floorboards moan from footsteps, which move through the hallway. The door swings open. Mr. Watson's face goes slack.

"Pete," he says flatly. He looks horrible. Emaciated.

Mrs. Watson elbows her way past her husband, right up to me. "Pete Hurley, what are you doing in this house?"

Charlie follows her into the room, also pushing past his father. "I asked him to come," he offers, to my relief.

"You should not be here," Mrs. Watson repeats. "Are you okay, Simone?"

"I'm fine," Simone says. "I asked Pete to come, too."

Mrs. Watson looks surprised. "You asked him?"

"How are you doing, Pete?" Mr. Watson reaches to shake my hand.

I start to respond, but a weak slap knocks my hand away. "Bernie!" his wife scolds. "He should not be in this house. What on earth are you doing?"

"I'll leave," I say.

"Yes," Mrs. Watson says.

"Would you all please just relax?" Simone suddenly shouts.

The demand brings a complete, still silence to the room. Nobody moves.

My face is burning. I feel their eyes on me like swift jabs. I have never in my life felt so unwelcome. I find my voice. "I'm sorry. I shouldn't have come. I wanted to offer my help, but it's clearly not the right time."

"The right time?" Mrs. Watson asks.

"I'll go."

"The right time? Do you honestly think there's ever going to be a time that's right?"

I turn to leave, dipping a shoulder between Charlie and Mr. Watson. I put a hand on Mr. Watson's shoulder, feeling the bone. "I'm sorry."

"Thanks for coming, Pete." Simone's voice sounds calm, peaceful.

Outside, my head feels light. It spins. My walk is unsteady. When I get to my car, I lean against it for a moment, letting my forehead rest against the roof. Sweat prickles my hairline.

"Pete?"

I turn my head sideways, still resting my skull against the car. Brenda comes toward me.

"I'm sorry, Pete. I should have trusted my instincts. I should never have sent that letter."

I can't really think. "It's okay," I finally say. "Charlie wrote to me too, so it wasn't just you."

"Are you going to be okay?"

"I think so."

"No you're not," Brenda said.

"Yeah, well. I think your patient there is a bigger priority."

Brenda looks at me with what can only be described as a tough softness. "My patient..." she says, making quotes with her fingers, "...is indeed my priority, because I am a nurse...however, I am also human, and a drunk."

I chuckle. "That's not a very nice thing to say about yourself."

"What, that I'm human?"

"Exactly."

The front door opens. Mrs. Watson appears on the doorstep. "Brenda, Simone needs your help."

I sing softly to Brenda. "You're going to get a spanking."

"Pete..." Brenda lowers her chin, looking stern. "Don't drink over this."

I look down.

"I mean it," she says. "The Watsons will be fine. They're strong people. You know it as well as I do. Worry about yourself."

"Oh man, Brenda. You don't know me very well if you don't think I worry about myself."

She steps toward me. "You just think you do."

"Brenda!" Mrs. Watson commands.

"Promise me, Pete."

"Okay. Thank you."

"Don't mention it." We share a look that says we would probably hug, or at least shake hands, under different circumstances. "Goodbye."

RETURNING TO MY HOTEL, I lay for an hour staring at the television, sprawled on my bed. I click through the channels, but all I experience is the sting of Mrs. Watson slapping my hand away.

An itch has started to tickle my legs. I picked this hotel because I noticed a liquor store a block away, and I get up several times to take a little walk. But each time I get to the door, I turn around and flop back onto the bed.

I flip the channel to SportsCenter, and I'll be damned if they're not showing the infamous pitch. Why, I wonder? But then the announcer explains that it was four years ago today that Pete Hurley hit Juan Estrada with an inside fastball that broke the socket around his eye, and that neither man ever played baseball again. And they talk about the new rule that came about because of the incident. They explain that Juan Estrada is now a contractor in Connecticut, and that Pete Hurley's whereabouts are currently unknown. "Isn't that the truth?" I turn off the television.

It occurs to me that so much of life is a matter of angles. I think about how a few increments one way or another could have resulted in very different circumstances. Two inches higher, and my pitch would have bound off Juan Estrada's helmet instead of his eye. Two seconds later, and Dave would have just missed running in front of that Volkswagen. If Simone had fallen at a slightly different position, she wouldn't have hit the table and broken a bone in her neck. So many things could have been different, but the vectors all converged at angles that changed my life in dramatic ways. Is that fate? Bad luck? I really don't know what to make of it.

I decide to go to bed. Taking off my pants, something falls from my pocket. The watch falls to the floor, and when I decide to call someone and tell them that I'm thinking about a drink, there is only one person that comes to mind.

Chapter Thirty

Rule 59.25 of Major League Baseball (aka the Pete Hurley Rule): *If a pitcher is deemed to have thrown a pitch deliberately at a batter's head, said pitcher will be immediately ejected from the game, and will also face a suspension of twenty games to be served immediately. All appeals will go directly to the commissioner's office.*

I stretch my legs after parking my rental car in front of a nondescript white house in New Haven, Connecticut. And after a deep breath, I approach the front door and knock.

When Juan Estrada answers, I'm surprised to see little physical evidence of the incident that ended his baseball career. His left eye looks very much like the right, as does the bone structure around it.

"Come in, Pete!" he says pleasantly. I have called ahead this time, learning my lesson from my experience at the Watson house. "It's very good to see you." He reaches out to shake my hand, and his sincerity is just as baffling now as it was over the phone.

"Have a seat." He extends a palm toward a nice leather sofa, and I sink into it. "What can I get you...beer, soda, coffee?"

"If you have some coffee made, that would be perfect," I say.

"So you drove down from Amherst?" he asks over his shoulder.

"Yeah. Nice drive. It's the best time of year up here, with the leaves changing."

"Yes," he agrees, returning with two mugs of hot coffee. He hands me one and I set it carefully on a cork coaster on the table next to the sofa. I turn down an offer of cream or sugar. "So what's the occasion?" Juan asks. His accent is still there, but barely.

"Honestly, I'm not sure," I admit. "Something compelled me to look you up."

"Well I always think about you this time of year, when they run those damn replays over and over again." Juan laughs, gesturing toward the TV.

"Yeah, me too..."

"Well, it's good to see you."

"Seriously?"

"Sure, why not?" I didn't remember Juan Estrada being such a handsome man. He has one of those thin, neatly trimmed mustaches that seem to look better on Latin men, and his dark eyes reflect a subtle joy that indicates an eternal optimism.

"I guess I just assumed I wasn't one of your favorite people, Juan. I mean..."

But before I can finish, Juan leans forward in his recliner and holds a palm toward me. "Hold on a sec, here, Pete. No. You've gotta be kidding me." And then it seems he simply can't help himself. He stands up and comes over to where I'm sitting, and for a minute, I panic. But he spreads his arms out wide. "Look at this house, Pete. It's a nice place. I have this house because of you, my friend."

"Oh no. That's just wrong—you were on your way up, Juan. You would have made a hell of a lot of money playing ball if your career hadn't been cut short."

Juan laughs, throwing his head back. "How the hell do you know that? You don't know that. Nobody knows. Jesus, sometimes you Americans amaze me."

"What do you mean?"

Juan walks in a small circle before making his way back to his recliner. He sinks back into it, taking a sip from his coffee. "You always think you need to fix everything, like the rest of us can't take care of ourselves. It's a funny kind of arrogance, really. I don't mean you, Pete. I don't think anything bad about you at all. It's just—well, did you expect to come here and find someone who's suffering?"

I shrug. Of course, that's exactly what I expected.

"I have a good life, Pete. I have my own company. I didn't feel *entitled* to anything."

"Construction, right?"

"Yep. You saw that on ESPN." Again, Juan laughs heartily. "I have a nice family, good friends. Life is good, my friend."

I smile to myself, thinking that I planned to offer to hire Juan to work on my house. I can just imagine his response to this suggestion. "You have no idea how happy this makes me," I say.

"Well hell, Pete. You should have come years ago, then."

WHEN THE PHONE rings on the day I arrive home, I secretly hope it's Leslie.

"You're home!" Her voice is like a song.

"Yep."

"So are you okay?"

"Better."

"Oh good."

"I'm okay. I really am."

"You want some company?"

"I'd like that."

Fifteen minutes later, she sits next to me, sideways on my bed, holding my eyes as I relate what happened. I tell her everything, about meeting with the Watsons, and Brenda Walters, and the conversation with Charlie, and meeting with Juan Estrada. And this time I include the part about my effort to get drunk.

"Goddam it, Pete," she says quietly.

I hang my head.

Leslie stands, and paces the small bedroom.

"I don't see how you can do that to yourself."

"I don't expect you would."

"Does it matter to you that people care what happens to you?"

I think about it, and for an instant I consider telling her what she wants to hear. But I realize that I owe her the truth. "In that moment, no." I shake my head. "The truth is, all I'm thinking about at that moment is getting drunk."

Leslie shakes her head.

"But that's why I called the next night," I explain hopefully, and behind the explanation I feel a definite freedom. "Something shifted out there," I add. "Something happened."

Leslie sits down, looking at me with a sad but hopeful smile. "That's great, Pete."

And as much as she means it, I can see the skepticism in her eyes. I realize at that moment that this battle is going to be mine alone. It doesn't matter whether anyone else understands.

"So what happened when you visited Juan?" Leslie asks.

And when I tell her, she sits thoughtfully for a moment, a slight smile on her face.

"What are you thinking?" I finally ask.

"Well, I was thinking about how different your experience with Juan was from what happened with Simone."

I nod.

"And you know what's interesting about that?"

"What?"

"They each arrived at these very different places without any input from you."

I frown. "I think you're trying to tell me something."

THE NEXT DAY, Barry greets me with a big bear hug, squeezing me so hard that it hurts. Danielle's hug is also enthusiastic, if not quite as painful.

"So?" Barry asks. "How was it? Was it good to see everyone again?"

"Barry!" Danielle scolds.

"What?" Barry's shoulders rise up.

"It's all right. It wasn't what I hoped. But I'm glad I went. It was important."

"Oh." Barry sits. "So are the Watsons talking to you again?"

"Barry!" Danielle plants her fists on her hips. "Is it possible for you to show a moment of restraint just once?"

"It's okay," I say. "He's just asking."

Danielle glares at me briefly, and Barry looks embarrassed. But after pondering, she backs up and sits on the sofa.

"So how are things around here?" I ask.

Barry throws his hands in the air. "Oh, you know...same ol' same ol'. Kids are a pain, job's a pain."

"Did you see anyone else?" Danielle asks.

I describe my visit with Juan Estrada.

"Wow," Danielle says. "That's pretty cool."

"It was," I admit. "It surprised me."

Suddenly, from upstairs, a squeal echoes through the house. It's followed by a sustained wail. Barry and Danielle exchange a weary look.

"I'll go," Barry says.

"Thanks, honey."

Barry rises without hurrying and clomps up the stairs.

Danielle and I share a smile, listening to her children, our lineage. And in the moments that follow, a calm comes over the room. In the world of siblings, there are lines that are seldom crossed, questions that are never asked, subjects that everyone understands will never be addressed. But in this moment, for one of the few times that I can remember, I feel as if these rules might not apply.

"Did we ever fight like that?" I ask.

"I don't think so."

"That's what I was thinking. Doesn't that seem odd?"

"It does."

There's a long pause, during which we avoid each others' eyes.

"You know what's really strange, Pete?" she says. "For all these years, I had this picture of you out there—the successful athlete, with a good, stable life. I thought you had it all together. I thought you were the strong one. Because I knew I wasn't. And because you're the only family I have, I've been hoping that if you can develop some sense of peace, maybe I will too someday." A tear leaks from the corner of one eye, and she swipes at it with the back of one hand. "You have no idea how hard it is to see that you are just as fucked up as I am."

"Nothing like reality."

Upstairs, we hear the animated world of children again, this time joyful, with occasional outbursts from Barry.

"He's so great," I say.

She looks down. "Did Dad ever talk about me not coming back?"

I raise an eyebrow.

"Yeah, right. That wouldn't be like him, would it?"

I shake my head. "Nope, it certainly wouldn't."

"God, he was stubborn."

"Unlike us."

"Yeah. Thank god we didn't inherit that."

We sit in a mutual silence that isn't quite silent with the sounds of the kids.

"So why didn't you?" I finally ask.

Danielle dips her head. Her eyes close, and she reaches up and pushes a thumb and forefinger against the lids, pinching the bridge of her nose. When she speaks, her voice breaks. "God, why do we do such stupid things when we're young?"

"You mean there's an end to it?"

She smiles behind her wrist. "I knew, Pete. I just knew that we'd come out there and that Dad would fall in love with Barry. I knew everything would be fine once they spent some time together. Because he didn't hold grudges."

"That's true."

"I just couldn't believe it when he died, Pete." She lays her head against my chest. And she rests a hand on my shoulder. I hold her, squeezing the back of her neck. "That wasn't how it was supposed to end. We were supposed to see him, and have that storybook ending."

"It's really sad."

"That's just it, isn't it? That's the worst part."

After another silent moment, I ask, "Do you remember when I asked you about Sunday nights?"

She has to think. "Yeah, I'm still not sure why."

"Think about it, Danielle...Dad used to go to his study."

"Well I vaguely remember something about that."

"And then, after that, I would listen to him go to the next room over, and close the door."

She frowns.

"That's why I went outside and threw that fucking ball for hours."

"My room?"

"Your room, D...he went to your room."

Danielle looks me square in the eyes, her face showing no emotion for a long minute. "Why are you telling me this?"

I take her cheeks in my hands. I hold her face. "Because it's the truth, Danielle."

Her hands drop, and she looks at me. "But why are you telling me?"

"I just figured it out myself, sis...I've had a lot of time to think."

She pushes against me, but it's a weak effort. "Goddammit, Pete...why would you want to put shit like that in my head?"

"I just thought it might be the cause of all this, D. I thought it might explain things."

"The only thing I remember is the night you broke my window. I remember wondering how Dad got there so fast."

"That was it, D. That was the last night."

"It was?"

"Yeah, I threw the ball through the window. That was the night he hit me."

Danielle sits quietly for a long minute, her eyes blank. Staring. And at last she turns to me. "No," she says. "I don't think that's what happened at all. I think you're imagining things."

I sit open-mouthed. And for a moment, I think about trying to convince her. But that blank look, the eyes narrow and unyielding, convinces me that I would be wasting my breath. I suspect this is the same look I had on my face when people tried to talk to me about my drinking. I suspect this is how I have looked most of my life.

Chapter Thirty-One

When you hear the word Tara, the image that comes to mind is a southern plantation, with lavish furnishings, a wide staircase, and melodrama to spare. Giving your house a name can help establish the personality you want for your home. It can also make your house feel more personal to you. You don't need to share your name with anyone. It can be a secret between your house and yourself.

Your House, Your Self
Chapter 13
"Something in a Name"

The story of Dave's name is one of my favorites. It comes from my own birth, and it is one of the few windows I have into the relationship between my parents.

Apparently, Dad and Mom were so convinced I was a girl that they didn't bother to discuss boy names. Dad said that this conviction was based on nothing but a mutual hunch. They weren't interested in having the doctor tell them the truth.

Oddly enough, their prediction was verified when I first emerged. The doctor took a quick look at my crotch, where my parts were tucked behind my pudgy thighs. "It's a girl!" he announced. "It's Adriana!"

The nurse discovered the truth moments later, and my organs threw my parents into a quandary. For two weeks, I had no name. And for two weeks, my parents fought. Dad wanted to name me after his grandfather, a kindly old man who treated him better than his own father did. The problem was that my great grandfather's name was Hiram. Although my mother also adored the old man, she was (thankfully) adamant. But she couldn't come up with an alternative.

Because my mother had hemorrhaged badly during delivery, she and I spent another week in the hospital as a precaution. Over the course of that week, one of the nurses got tired of calling me "baby Hurley." She dubbed me Dave, a name that stuck with the entire staff. The name caught on with my parents, and for the week after we left the hospital, I was Dave.

But they didn't like it enough to keep it. Once my father relented on Hiram, they settled on Pete.

When I heard this story, I decided I would name my first son Dave. But by the time I got the dog, it was beginning to look as if I would never become a father.

I HAVE A VAGUE memory about a house. Building one. Was that a dream? It must have been. I couldn't have possibly thought I'd have the know-how and the perseverance to come to this faraway land and build my own house.

I've been home from Amherst for two weeks, and this dream is not the only thing that has become a memory.

For the time being, I'll also have to settle for the memories of some of my favorite people. The Watsons I prefer to think of now are the Watsons of my past. I'll remember the round face of Charlie when he came to the door with his baseball mitt tucked under one arm. I'll remember the Mr. and Mrs. Watson who welcomed an orphaned and angry young man into their home, and treated him like one of their own. I'll remember the Simone who swayed gracefully to the rhythm of her violin. The one who tickled my wrist with her fingertips, and lowered herself onto me in a public park one warm summer night. I'll carry these important people forward on the backs of these images, and cling to the hope that the story of our friendship is only temporarily interrupted.

LESLIE AND I SIT in my favorite Bozeman restaurant, cleaning our desert plates of the last smears of chocolate.

She raises her coffee cup. "Here's to settling." We clink mugs.

"I can't believe he agreed to all the terms," I say.

She shrugs. "He finally backed himself into a corner."

"Speak of the devil," I say.

She turns her head. "You're kidding."

Clint sits slumped at the bar, propping his head up with one hand. But it keeps slipping out of the palm, as if he's just about to fall asleep.

"He's really drunk," Leslie says.

I think about the fact that this was me, just a few short weeks ago. And I'm hit by a growing unease. I zero in on a glass of draught beer at the next table. The foamy head. The moisture trickling down the glass. I can taste it. I start sweating.

"What's the matter?" Leslie asks.

"Nothing." I wipe my forehead.

The waitress approaches, asking whether we want more coffee. Leslie looks at me.

"I don't," I said. "But go ahead, if you want some."

"No no." She turns to the waitress. "Just the check, please."

As the waitress leaves, Leslie leans across the table. "Pete, what's wrong? And don't say nothing, because I can tell."

"I need to get out of here."

"Wait outside. I'll pay the bill," she offers, and I want to kiss her.

"All right." I give her some money, and outside, I stalk around, taking deep breaths, trying to exhale the craving.

Leslie comes out and I try to think of something witty, something to break the mood. But I just stand there.

"How about a walk?" Leslie asks.

"That sounds great."

She takes off, and I follow. She clearly has a destination in mind, and I'm in no state to question it. I simply trace her steps.

Leslie walks as if we have an appointed arrival time. I've always been a stroller, a hands-in-my-pocket, lumbering traveler. So it takes some effort to keep up.

"So what's the next step on the house?"

The question confuses me. My mind is so focused on other things. I chuckle.

"What's so funny?"

"Oh nothing...I'm just not sure what kind of future that house has any more."

"Come on, Pete. You need to get back on track. You were so excited about it in the beginning."

"I know. Of course. I'll get inspired again." I'm not sure I even believe this, but it sounds good.

Leslie looks up at me. "You know the first night we met, in the bar?"

"Yeah. Although I might remind you that we met before that."

She smiles. "Right. Anyway…that night in the bar, when you told me you were going to build a house…it made a big impression on me. It was the one thing you talked about that made your face light up."

"Well…that's nice to hear."

Leslie chuckles. "Try to tell me that your first impression of me was any better."

"Good point. I thought I'd stumbled onto some local branch of the Montana Militia."

Our pace doesn't slow, and as we round a corner, I realize we've come to the park where Barry and I used to bring Dave. The park is empty, quiet, and the grass has a frosty coat that sparks in the moonlight. We step off the sidewalk, and the grass crackles.

I think about the handicapped boy I used to watch in this park. I remember the day he tossed the ball forward, and his joyful cry when it landed in front of him. This thought eases the chill for a moment, as does the realization that the craving has passed. My nerves have steadied.

I feel Leslie's hand slip into the crook of my elbow. It happens so quickly that I think at first that it's accidental. I wait for her hand to jerk away just as suddenly. But she clutches my arm, and I feel her nestle closer.

The contact strikes us mute. We don't speak for a long time. Three times around the park we walk, wordless. My breath quickens. I can hear it getting louder in my head. Clouds of air float from our lips. And the cold, still night increases the silence. Only our feet, crunching through the frosted grass.

"I'm cold," I say after the third round.

"Yeah, I'm about ready to go."

So we head back to my truck, still wordless. Leslie's hand remains in the crook of my arm. We're almost to my truck when I see Clint again, walking toward us. Well, walking might not be the right word. I'm not sure I've ever seen anyone so drunk.

"Oh oh," Leslie says.

"Hello, Clint." I walk right up to him, and instead of offering a handshake, I put my arm around his shoulders, pinning his arms to his sides. "You need a hand?"

"Get away from me, you freak."

"I'm just trying to help, Clint, honestly."

"I don't need anyone's help, 'specially not yours." He tries to throw an elbow into my ribs, but he ends up flinging himself to the ground instead.

I reach down and grab his elbow to help him up. He jabs at me, but I easily dodge the punch. "Okay, Clint. You've made your point."

"You want me to call someone? Should I call a cab?" Leslie asks.

"Hell no," Clint slurs. "I'm fine."

We raise our brows, and she calls a cab anyway. We wait, watching Clint drift in and out of consciousness, lying cold on the sidewalk.

"How could you want to go there?" Leslie asks.

"Right now I don't," I say. "Right now, I really want to be right here."

HALFWAY HOME, LESLIE turns to me and says, "How would you like to come over to my place?"

I nearly choke. "I'm sorry?"

She gives me a sly smile. "Don't get any big ideas, buster. I have something to show you."

My face must show how I feel about this.

"I don't think you'll be disappointed," she says.

When we arrive at Leslie's house, Arlene is sitting in the kitchen, with a cup of hot cocoa. She doesn't seem surprised to see us. In fact, I detect a slight nod between them.

"How are you, Pete?" Arlene asks.

"I'm doing good. Happy about settling the case. How about you?"

"I'm fine. Yeah, that was good news."

At that moment, I hear something that sounds suspiciously like a bark, and both Leslie and Arlene look at me with the same frightened expression. Leslie moves quickly toward the door to their basement, where she stops and turns.

"Listen, Pete—we have something to tell you."

"Was that what I thought it was?" I ask.

"Yes," Arlene answers.

"Dave!" I shout. Another hearty bark echoes from the basement. I rush toward the door, and Leslie stands in front of it until she sees my expression, when she steps to one side.

"Pete, seriously—you need to let us explain. It's not what you think."

I fling the door open and rush down the stairs, and footsteps follow me. "She was choking, Pete. That night you got drunk, we heard her howling, and we rushed over and found her all wound up in her chain. You were passed out in bed."

I find Dave in a small room, with a comfortable bed. But that isn't all. "Puppies?" I ask, turning to Leslie and Arlene, who stand at the base of the stairs as if they're ready to rush back up.

"That's why we didn't tell you sooner, Pete. We were just going to keep her for a couple of days, but we realized she was pregnant. We were worried." The words flow from Leslie's mouth in a rush of fear and apology.

I wrap Dave up in my arms, and she cries and licks my face. "Oh God. I can't believe you're alive." She's so excited she can't stop whining, and she wriggles out of my arms and hops around the room, her tail wagging so ferociously that she keeps falling over. I can't stop laughing.

As the scene unfolds, Leslie and Arlene move closer. "Did you see how beautiful these babies are?" Arlene exclaims.

"Wait a second. You said she was choking?"

Leslie nods. "We got there just in time, Pete; she almost died."

"What night was this?" I grab Dave and hold her tight. Her whines grow to barks, which hurt my ears, and it's the best possible pain.

"It was the night before you showed up at my door."

"Of course—right. So you heard her and came to my house, and I was gone?"

"No, that's just it, Pete. You were there. You were passed out. Arlene got Dave untangled from the leash and I was trying to wake you up, but you didn't budge."

The more I hear, the harder it is to breathe. I stand. "Okay. I think I need some air. I'm going to take Dave."

"Well you have to take them, too." Leslie points to the puppies, who are squirming and grunting, poking around the floor.

"Can you guys watch 'em just for the night?"

Leslie shakes her head. "No, Pete. That ain't how it works. They're still nursing. They need to be with her."

"Okay." I take a deep breath. "Okay." And then something occurs to me. "Why did you decide to tell me now?"

Leslie looks at the floor. "I don't know."

"Because you need to grow up," Arlene says.

BACK AT MY TRAILER, I study the wriggling figures of two puppies as they search for food, prodding Dave's belly with their square snouts. Dave smiles at me from her prone position, and I struggle to believe that she's really there. I haven't seen her for more than two months.

It's hard to reconcile the wide gap between the way other people see me and the way I see myself. Of course I've made mistakes. And some of them have been costly. But does that mean I'm incompetent? I watch the puppies burrow deep into Dave's soft underbelly, sucking away.

I move my chair next to Dave's head, where I can reach down and stroke her neck as she feeds her babies. I study the nub that used to be her leg. I'm so happy to have her back that I decide for the moment not to worry about the events that brought her back. I feel her coat, lean down and inhale her scent, and feel her moist tongue on my cheek.

My phone rings, and when I answer, the voice at the other end is strained.

"Pete, he's gone," Simone says.

"I'm so sorry, Simone."

"Yeah."

"If there's anything I can do."

"Just take care of yourself, will you? Find some peace out there."

"I'll do what I can. You do the same, will you?"

"I'm going to be just fine."

After we hang up, I realize something important. I realize I don't miss her any more.

Chapter Thirty-Two

Other than the incident with Roger Clemens two years ago, baseball has not found it necessary to suspend any pitchers for throwing at a batter's head since the Pete Hurley Rule was enacted in 2007. Sometimes the rules actually work. Which means they'll probably find a reason to repeal it at some point.

Tony Kornheiser
Pardon the Interruption
October 1, 2009

The next morning, I stand at the Monday door and nervously push the doorbell. When Leslie answers, she seems to know who to expect. She steps to one side. "Come on in, Pete."

"Thank you." I wipe my feet, and she leads me to the kitchen, where we sit at the table.

"How are you doing?" she asks.

"I'm okay."

"Are you angry at me?"

"I'm not sure. I'm still trying to sort it all out."

Leslie's eyes tell me she's willing to help me get there. They're so kind. She almost looks like a different person.

"I don't know how you could lie to me for all those weeks."

She shakes her head. "I didn't like that. It was really hard."

"I thought she was dead," I say.

"I know." Leslie's eyes pool. "I'm really sorry."

"Did you really think I couldn't take care of her?"

Leslie pulls her mouth to one side. "It was so hard to know what to do. Like I told you, Pete, she nearly died. We thought about just telling you. We thought maybe it would help you realize how bad things had gotten."

"Why didn't you?"

"When we realized she was pregnant, we just thought the risk was too big. I still don't know if it was the right thing to do."

It's impossible to question the sincerity, either of her decision or of her torment about it. "Do you think I'm that unreliable?"

Leslie shakes her head. "I don't know, Pete. That's just it. It changed from week to week."

"So where was she all that time? I would have known if she was here."

"We had a friend take care of her."

I try to think of another question—something that will burrow to the core of this situation, something that will extract the answer to the question of how this could happen, but I can't come up with anything.

"I've lost too many people, Pete. I've lost too much. I suppose I should have just let it go. I should have told you." Now tears trickle from the very fronts of her eyelids, like a leak. "I just couldn't do it."

"It's all right." What else can I possibly say? "Thank you for saving her."

THERE HAS LONG been a misconception about athletes that we're not capable of thinking much further than such trite ideas as "stepping up" and "making a play." And of course, there are a lot of athletes that fit the stereotype. The truth is, most of us soon learned that if you're going to get through 162 games over the course of the year, it's best to avoid giving the press a good quote. The minute you get the reputation of being a good interview, you end up having to stay behind for another hour after each game.

So we all learned to string a bunch of catch phrases together to fill up a five-minute interview without causing any controversy or creating any expectations. After a while, you don't even remember what you've said five minutes later.

The thing I didn't realize was how these clichés became a part of me. Four years after I threw my last pitch, it was still hard for me to respond to people's questions without falling into a dull monotone and starting in about "overcoming adversity."

So for the first few days after Dave's return, the old default starts to kick in. Watching these little guys waddle around the house, piddling randomly and rutting about for food, I realize that I have no idea how to take care of puppies. I wonder how I got through it with Dave, and remember that I was too young to realize there was something to worry about. With each day that passes, I become more anxious about how I'm going to manage. I look to Dave, hoping for some guidance.

And when nothing comes to me—no answers, no ideas—I find myself thinking that it's time to step up, put the past behind me, take it one bowl of water at a time. None of this provides any relief, because none of it has a damn thing to do with the real world. So each day leads to more anxious moments, more questions, and more fear of another incident. Another of my loved ones hurt by my actions, or lack of action. And the more these thoughts invade my days, and especially my nights, the thirstier I get. One night I sit in my trailer with Dave and her babies, feeling the space get smaller around me, and when thoughts of driving into town for a beer start running through my head, I realize it's time to do something different. Arlene got it right. Time to grow up.

DANIELLE OPENS THE front door and squeals. "Dave!!" She starts to cry. "Oh my God…she's alive!" She falls to her knees and holds Dave close.

I lean down and drop the puppies at her feet.

"You're kidding! Oh my God, they're so adorable."

The boys hear the ruckus and come running. Their joy at seeing Dave miraculously eclipses their mother's. They are especially excited about the puppies.

"Why don't you boys take these guys in the back yard and play for awhile," Danielle suggests.

She doesn't have to ask twice.

"Where's Barry?" I ask.

"Oh, he had some stuff to do at the office."

We settle in at the kitchen table. "Coffee?" Danielle asks.

"Love some." And as she pours us each a cup, I ask, "How are you?"

Danielle's expression turns thoughtful as she places a mug at my elbow and sits. "I'm okay, Pete."

"Yeah?"

"Yeah." She nods, as if to convince herself. "I was not happy about what you told me the other day."

"No...I'm sure."

"But I think it explains a lot."

"That's what I've been thinking too."

"About you," she says.

"Me?"

"Yeah...I've been thinking a lot about that. If you thought that's what was happening, no wonder you were so protective of me. Then after I left, it was almost as if you were off the hook. You couldn't do it anymore."

This stings.

"So I think it contributed to your drinking."

"I think I would have drank either way."

"Why?"

"Because it made me feel invisible."

"Really? Invisible?"

"Yes."

"I guess that makes sense, too, when you think about it."

"Especially once I started getting all that attention for baseball."

Danielle hmms.

We sit quietly for a long time, and I try to ignore the one question that still lingers, one that I'm dying to know, but don't want to ask.

"He was a good man, Pete."

Her eyes have that same look they did the last time this subject came up, and I realize there's no point in trying to convince her otherwise.

We sit in a comfortable but sad silence. The boys' shouts mingle with barks and yaps and thumps of a ball against the house.

Chapter Thirty-Three

*The roof is perhaps the most spiritual element of
your house. It provides protection, and safety. It
symbolizes security. The options for materials that
can be used for a roof are impossible to list. There
is asphalt, wood, metal, tile, cement, fiberglass, and
stone, just to name a few. Remember, your choice
will be hanging over your head for as long as you
live in this house.*

Your House, Your Self
Chapter 13
"Overhead"

I step out of my trailer on a Montana winter day. The snow has
begun to fall with the slow flutter of a baby's eyelids just as it
drifts off to sleep. The silence, instead of feeling oppressive, is
awesome, filled with a soothing serenity.

I lift my face, and the soft flakes tickle my skin, melting down
to spots of cool moisture. This is the best I've felt since we won the
World Series, and I enter the outside world determined to prolong
the feeling for as long as possible. I surrender to the irrational belief
that this feeling just might last forever.

I don't think I ever put much thought into what would inspire
a person to embrace sobriety. If I had, I probably would have
assumed it would be something from the outside world. The love
of a woman. The death of a loved one. Maybe barreling drunk into
some innocent soul. And I suppose all of these things have brought
various drunks to their knees.

But today, I review the last three months of my life, and a
turnaround that isn't quite that simple.

It was three months ago today that Dave came home, and a
miracle has taken place. After talking to many of the people closest

to me, and looking back over my life, I realized that since my father died, almost every single thing I lost was somehow connected to booze. It scared the hell out of me. But it also offered a freedom I didn't expect. It told me that there's a chance that life might get better if I stop drinking. So I'm trying. For three months, no alcohol has passed my lips. And each day gets a little easier.

SEVERAL YEARS AGO, I sat next to a very friendly guy on an airplane. It was one of those rare instances where, in a short time, we made a strong connection, and talked about things I never discuss.

In the course of the conversation, once he realized who I was, he asked how I was dealing with what happened with Juan Estrada. I made a comment about wishing the issue would reach a resolution someday. I probably made some inane comment about closure.

He nodded gravely, thinking for a moment, then said, "You know, I've decided that things never resolve. They're always there. You can forget about them. And it feels as if they're gone. And then you believe that they're gone. But eventually, some little reminder comes along and bites you in the ass, and because you were sure the memory was gone, it hurts even worse. So I think it's better to assume that these things will reappear. There's no way around it. They're part of you."

I found out just before we landed that this guy was a monk, which surprised me. He was a young guy, dressed much the same way I was. No bowl haircut, no scratchy wool smock or anything.

His theory makes even more sense to me now. The more I think about it, the more it surprises me that this theory came from a monk—from a man most people would consider an expert on resolution. I probably wouldn't have taken what he said that seriously if I'd known he was a monk. Besides, how can you not appreciate a monk who uses the phrase "bites you in the ass"?

I WALK OUT INTO the middle of my land, the snow blanketing my shoulders. I've built a small pen near the house, where the puppies romp through the snow, wrestling with each other. I've named them Bill and Bob. I've let Dave loose to give her a break from her babies, and she races around the foundation of my house, sniffing for food.

I feel compelled to climb down into the foundation. I stride forward, and at the edge of the concrete wall, I crouch, resting my weight on one hand, and hop into the hole.

I look straight up, and then all around me. And a part of me feels as if my world has shrunk. My world has been reduced to this small square that surrounds me. At the same time, I see more options that ever. This box doesn't contain me. It only houses me.

For the next hour, I run my hand over this concrete. I explore the foundation with my fingers, touching it everywhere. I crouch down, on my knees, and feel the bottom, where the concrete meets the dirt. I run my finger along this rough edge, memorizing each ridge, each bump. And I rise to my toes and feel the top, determined not to miss a single patch of gray. Dave follows me, barking from the ground above, wanting to join me.

"Hey."

A voice startles me, and I look over to the edge of the hole. Leslie stands poised, her hands in her pockets, a slight smirk on her lips. "What the hell are you doing?"

"Um...I lost a contact."

She laughs. And I feel goofy standing there, facing her.

She remains at the edge of the hole and studies me for a time. I hold out my arms, presenting myself, on display, like a zoo animal. But she doesn't seem to expect anything. She's not waiting for me to come to her, nor does she make a move to join me. She crouches, then sits on the wall, her legs dangling. Her arms extend behind her, supporting her weight. I smile at her.

"Is there anything I can do for you?" I ask.

She shakes her head, smiling.

And I decide that, whether she's here or not, I want to finish what I was doing. So I continue, dropping to my knees, touching the concrete, rising slowly to my feet, then to my toes. I scoot down and repeat the pattern, until I've studied the entire wall. And then I go around one more time, closing my eyes, picturing what I feel, and trying to remember what it looked like the first time. Leslie says nothing. She sits quietly watching, and I can imagine her smiling. And by the time I'm done, I know every square inch of this wall.

Acknowledgments

THIS NOVEL WAS ALMOST twenty years in the making, so I'm going to forget a lot of people I should remember. But there were key players along the way. This started as a short story that C. Michael Curtis at *The Atlantic Monthly* suggested should be expanded into a novel. And many thanks to the three excellent agents, Howard Yoon, Simon Lipskar, and Bill Contardi, who believed in this book and made gallant efforts to sell it. Many friends read early drafts and gave me feedback, so thanks to all of you, who know who you are. Many thanks to Leif Enger, Rick Bass, and Peter Fish for reading *High and Inside* and providing feedback before it was accepted for publication, and to Kim Barnes and Alan Heathcock for their flattering words. But most importantly, I owe the publication of this book to Allen M. Jones at Bangtail Press, who wrote to me and said "I dig it." Allen, your insights and suggestions made this a better book.

Finally, I owe this book and everything I've ever written to my father, who had the courage to get help, inspiring me to do the same. I wish he was here to see it.